"CALL ME LOGAN."

"Say it the way you used to when I was your patient and you wanted me to believe you cared."

"Logan."

His lips grazed Julie's cheek and caressed her ear. She felt his words more than she heard them.

"You can't know how many times I've fantasized about holding you like this."

"You fantasized about me? Like this?"

"Like this." He lowered her onto her back and stretched out beside her. "And this." His fingers explored her face as his dark eyes made seductive promises. "In my fantasies, you stroke my tongue with yours and let me taste you for as long as I want."

She pulled his head down to hers and whispered against his lips, "Like this?"

His groan of pleasure assured her that she was living up to his fantasy. . . .

ANNOUNCING THE
TOPAZ FREQUENT READERS CLUB
COMMEMORATING TOPAZ'S 1 YEAR ANNIVERSARY!

THE MORE YOU BUY, THE MORE YOU GET

Redeem coupons found here and in the back of all new Topaz titles for FREE Topaz gifts:

Send in:

 2 coupons for a free TOPAZ novel (choose from the list below);
- ☐ THE KISSING BANDIT, Margaret Brownley
- ☐ BY LOVE UNVEILED, Deborah Martin
- ☐ TOUCH THE DAWN, Chelley Kitzmiller
- ☐ WILD EMBRACE, Cassie Edwards

 4 coupons for an "I Love the Topaz Man" on-board sign

 6 coupons for a TOPAZ compact mirror

 8 coupons for a Topaz Man T-shirt

Just fill out this certificate and send with original sales receipts to:

TOPAZ FREQUENT READERS CLUB-1ST ANNIVERSARY
Penguin USA • Mass Market Promotion; Dept. H.U.G.
375 Hudson St., NY, NY 10014

Name_____

Address_____

City_____State_____Zip_____

Offer expires 5/31/1995

This certificate must accompany your request. No duplicates accepted. Void where prohibited, taxed or restricted. Allow 4-6 weeks for receipt of merchandise. Offer good only in U.S., its territories, and Canada.

WORLDS
APART

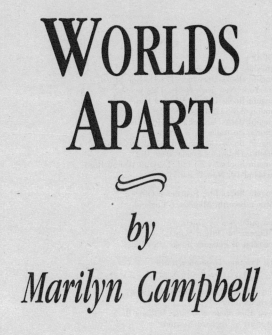

by

Marilyn Campbell

A TOPAZ BOOK

TOPAZ
Published by the Penguin Group
Penguin Books USA Inc., 375 Hudson Street,
New York, New York 10014, U.S.A.
Penguin Books Ltd, 27 Wrights Lane,
London W8 5TZ, England
Penguin Books Australia Ltd, Ringwood,
Victoria, Australia
Penguin Books Canada Ltd, 10 Alcorn Avenue,
Toronto, Ontario, Canada M4V 3B2
Penguin Books (N.Z.) Ltd, 182-190 Wairau Road,
Auckland 10, New Zealand

Penguin Books Ltd, Registered Offices:
Harmondsworth, Middlesex, England

First published by Topaz,
an imprint of Dutton Signet,
a division of Penguin Books USA Inc.

First Printing, December, 1994
10 9 8 7 6 5 4 3 2 1

Topaz is a trademark of Dutton Signet,
a division of Penguin Books USA Inc.

Printed in the United States of America

To my mother,
Josephine Bickart,
and her mother,
Maria Palmieri,
though you have both
crossed over to that other world,
you are still with me
in my heart

Chapter 1

Ex-Sergeant Logan McKay used the toe of his right combat boot to lift the weight of the iron shackle off his left ankle. A few minutes later he reversed the procedure. It was tedious, but effectively kept the blood circulating through his icy feet. Knowing that once the jet reached its assigned flying altitude the cabin temperature would be more comfortably regulated also helped. He only had to be patient, but after months of being half frozen on the Manchurian border, the anticipation of endless warmth seeping into his bones was more exciting than any woman had ever been.

Warmth was definitely the first thing he could appreciate about his current state. A sound sleep would come second—the kind of sleep that can't be had in a war zone, where bombs interrupt any moment of silence and the enemy could be ten feet away, just waiting for you to doze off so he can slit your throat.

After he was warm and rested, he might even give some thought to the shackles on his ankles, the handcuffs on his wrists, and the sentence he'd been given of life imprisonment at Leavenworth.

But at least for the next nine hours, while he was in the air over the Pacific Ocean, his dismal future was on hold.

Logan's eyes drifted shut in spite of his numb fingers and toes, but before he could enjoy the peace, a voice came over the loudspeaker:

"Good morning. This is your pilot, Lieutenant Boswell. We've been cleared for takeoff. Make sure all seat belts are fastened and loose items stowed away. There's an ugly storm hovering out there, so we're going to be taking the scenic route today. If there are any tourists on board who want to follow our progress, we'll be heading south off Hokkaido, past what used to be Tokyo, toward Iwo Jima, then east to San Francisco. At this time, we don't expect the detour to make more than an hour difference in our arrival time, but we'll keep you posted."

As the aircraft began taxiing down the runway, the military police officer sitting in the aisle seat next to Logan uttered an obscenity. Intent on sleeping, Logan pretended not to hear his armed escort, but the MP sitting in the opposite aisle seat couldn't ignore it as easily.

"What's the problem now, Higgs?" Corporal Gianni asked. "Forget to say goodbye to one of your sweetie-pies?"

"Didn't you hear what he just said?" Higgs asked in return, then went on before his superior officer made any comment. "A southern heading takes us right into the Dragon's Triangle. We'd be better off flying directly over China."

"For God's sake! You and your stupid superstitions again. Throw some salt over your shoulder or whatever you normally do and grab some sleep like McKay's doing."

Higgs's voice rose in pitch. "Sleep? I'd just as soon spend my last hour awake. And this is not superstition! I read a book about it. Hundreds of planes and ships and thousands of people have disappeared in the area between the Philippine Sea and the Pacific Ocean. There really is this triangle that runs from Yokohama to Guam to the Mariana Islands and back to Japan."

Gianni laughed. "You've got your triangles confused, kid. The *Bermuda* Triangle is where vessels supposedly disappear, and it's clear on the other side of the world."

"Oh, yeah? What would you say if I told you the Dragon's Triangle is on the *exact* other side of the world, and that there's a magnetic field that runs straight through the planet from one triangle to the other?"

"I'd say you spend too much time reading all that sci-fi garbage. Instead, why don't you find out if they put coffee on board?"

Logan heard Higgs huff, then unfasten his seat belt. He hoped the kid wasn't the kind that had to hear himself talk all the time, but he had a sinking feeling that he was. As the plane leveled out and he felt the first waft of heat, he decided he could even put up with a fruitcake like Higgs if his toes got thawed out in the meantime.

Suddenly he heard a woman's voice out of a dream, yet he knew he wasn't sleeping.

"Corporal Gianni? I'm Captain Evans. Private Higgs said you asked about coffee. There are meals and beverages on board, but no flight attendants. Since your prisoners aren't going anywhere and my nurses are busy with their patients, I would like to enlist the private's help."

"Sure. In fact, if you could keep him busy for about nine or ten hours, I'd appreciate it."

Logan raised one eyelid a fraction of an inch to see just how accurate his memory was. *Bull's-eye.* The voice did indeed belong to the Captain Evans that occasionally crept into his dreams despite his wish to forget she existed. She looked pretty much the way he remembered—not too short, not too tall, with a body that was female without being too obvious, and hair that was really neither blond nor brown pulled back in an unflattering roll at the base of her neck. There was almost nothing about her that could be called remarkable.

Except her angel voice, which was unlike any voice he had heard before or since. Somehow she made the most ordinary statement sound like a lover's whisper—husky and intimate, as if she were physically stroking him with her words.

And her angel eyes. It wasn't the blue-gray color that had affected his senses, but what he had seen in them.

Eight months ago he had been wounded during a shelling, and though it wasn't anything to be sent home over, he had spent four weeks in a mobile hospital unit. When he had first opened his eyes after surgery, he thought he'd died and someone had made a very funny mistake. Rather than being sent straight to hell, he'd apparently gone to heaven, for an angel was watching over him.

Her pretty eyes had been filled with compassion, tenderness, concern. They planted images in his mind of a loving wife, a home, and children. Since he knew none of those things were for the likes of him, he'd come to the conclusion that he hadn't died after all and that she was merely a post-anesthesia hallucination.

He told himself that her being on the same flight back to the States was pure coincidence; she would never remember him out of all the wounded men she'd cared for in the past months. All he had to do was ignore her existence for a few more hours. Then they'd be going their separate ways— her to some cozy little house in the suburbs, him to a men-only prison cell.

Julie Evans took one more glance at the sleeping prisoner, then led Private Higgs to the galley. She figured it was more efficient for one person to pass out cups of coffee than have everyone helping themselves. She had considered doing it herself just to keep occupied until she saw *him*. That convinced her to stay in the front of the plane with the patients and nurses. Not that he'd remember her, but she certainly remembered him and knew enough to steer clear.

How could she not remember Sergeant Logan McKay, the only patient she'd ever completely misjudged? Her ability to quickly analyze people was part of what made her a good nurse.

Her inability to turn down anyone who needed her help was what had prompted her to give up her nice, safe job in a pediatric office and enlist in the army when the desperate call went out for medical personnel. The horrible reality of war, however, had quickly clouded her altruistic enthusiasm. It was incredible that two years had passed since then.

Some people believed President Clinton could have done something to prevent the war, but after spending time in the Orient, Julie knew there was nothing anyone could have done. By the end of Clinton's term of office, the people of what was once the Soviet Union were in dire economic straits and ripe for a takeover by a hungry, overcrowded country. China made its move so fast and so secretly, it was weeks before the rest of the world realized that the sleeping dragon had truly awakened, and no country on the planet could feel safe from its voracious appetite.

Before the United States government could decide whether to reinstate the draft, China had attacked Japan and there was no longer a question of uninvolvement.

No one wanted another Vietnam, but for a while it appeared the United States had gotten just that. Now, three years into the Whitfield administration, the bloody war was at an end. After months of negotiating between China and the United Nations, they had found an acceptable compromise. China's border was to be extended westward to the edge of the Asian continent, and in turn, the dragon would keep its claws off Europe, Japan, and the American holdings in the Pacific.

As with Vietnam, there was no glory in this war.

The agreement allowed some enlisted men and women, like Julie, to head home finally. Though the manifest for this flight showed only names and ranks, she was aware of a little more than that. Of the hundred seventeen on board, three were crew, forty-five were critically wounded—mostly burn victims—with seven nurses to care for them, and thirty-one others were healthy male and female soldiers whose stints were up.

One of those was her closest friend, Robin Pascal, a tall, green-eyed redhead with a body that attracted every man within a mile, but a sharp wit that kept them at arm's length—unless *she* chose to let them come near. Though their careers differed drastically—Robin's specialty was airplane mechanics—she and Julie had enlisted together, and now they were headed home together.

In the back of the plane were two military police and their twenty-nine convicts.

When she'd heard the makeup of the passengers, she should have realized there was a possibility of Logan McKay being one of the prisoners. After all, everyone had been talking about his court-martial for weeks.

The sight of the shackles and armed escorts relieved her mind somewhat about spending a day in close proximity with that many criminals. From what she'd been able to learn, they were guilty of such charges as embezzling, assault and battery, rape, and smuggling.

Logan McKay had the dubious distinction of having single-handedly committed an entire list of crimes, including operating a drug ring, consorting with the enemy, and killing his captain.

How could she have been so wrong about him?

She recalled the first time she'd seen him being brought in on a stretcher. She had guessed his age at about thirty-five, which would have made him six years older than her, and seventeen years older than most of the wounded she had attended. Also, his straight black hair was trimmed short around the ears and neck and left longer on top instead of shaved off as most of the younger soldiers kept theirs.

The next thing she'd noticed were the scars—a wide one over his left brow that his hair probably covered most of the time, a straight, thin one on his jawbone which was almost hidden by the dark shadow of new beard growth, and several circular ones along his right shoulder and arm that she recognized as old wounds caused by an automatic weapon. Now he would have another, larger scar on the outside of his right thigh. Either he was a career soldier or had had one hell of a tough life.

Even unconscious, he had looked hard, not just the body, which was formidable, but the man himself.

She had been checking on him when he first came to, and what she'd seen in his eyes had totally belied his appearance. He had looked up at her with such open adoration and need, she'd been about to tell him she'd be there for him, when he laughed aloud. Grinning from ear to ear, his rugged face became quite handsome as he enjoyed some private joke, then dozed off again.

She thought she'd seen men like him before, all tough-guy on the outside but with a baby-soft center. Usually it took her only a day or two to peel the crust away. Logan McKay, however, wasn't like those men at all.

His initial reactions to her had been baby-soft, and he had seemed instantly enamored of her. Though other patients had developed temporary crushes while in her care, she had the feeling there was something different about Logan, something very special, and that there might be a chance for a true affection to develop between them.

Circumstances prevented him from wining and dining her, but it felt like a courtship nonetheless. Whenever he was awake during the first few days after surgery, she sat by his side and held his hand. They talked or she read to him, and by the end of the week they shared their first kiss. It was innocent and tender, but held a promise of passion in the future.

Then he said the three words that let her know what a mistake she'd made. "I love you," he told her, much too soon to really mean it. True, it sounded more sincere coming from him than the fifty other patients who had said the same words to her, but she reasoned that was only because he was older and more mature.

Unfortunately, she had already let him into her heart, desperately wanting to believe what he felt for her went deeper than the usual patient/nurse gratitude. So when she gave him her standard reply to professions of love from patients, she held on to the hope that his feelings for her would last beyond his release from the hospital.

Thus, it had hurt that much worse when his infatuation wore off so easily. Overnight he changed as drastically as Dr. Jekyll to Mr. Hyde. The more effort she made to comfort him, the nastier he acted, and the lewder his comments became. He never gave an inch throughout the remaining time he was in the hospital, nor did he give an explanation for his change of heart other than "he had finally sobered up."

Only recently, when she had heard about the crimes he'd committed, had she understood that the gentle man she had encountered had existed only because of the drugs that had temporarily altered his personality. Nor had he been the usual tough guy with a soft center for her to uncover.

The truth was, he was hard through and through—and she'd been a fool to believe otherwise.

Logan's toes were finally warm. Higgs was being kept occupied. His seat was a damn sight more comfortable than the ground or the cot in the brig. All conditions were perfect for him to catch some z's. Instead he was wrestling with old memories.

Why couldn't he let it go? Eight months had passed, most of which he'd spent in one nightmare after another, and still he was more haunted by images of Julie Evans than anything else that he'd run up against.

When he was being honest with himself, however, he admitted that he didn't always resent the memories. In the last few months, whenever things got too tense and he thought he couldn't take another minute of the insanity around him, she would slip into his mind, and he would welcome her. Eventually, fantasies about her became his mental lifeline, though he never completely forgot that they *were* only fantasies. In reality, he knew that he and Julie Evans had always been, and always would be, worlds apart.

As he had a thousand times before, he drifted back to the moment when he first realized that Julie was neither an angel nor a hallucination. . . .

He squinted his eyes in an attempt to focus on the woman looking down on him. Whatever drug they'd used on him for the surgery still had him feeling disoriented and drowsy, but the throbbing pain in his thigh assured him he was very much alive.

"Hi, Logan."

Her voice sent a shiver up his spine in spite of the numbing narcotic. The way she said his name suggested that they'd known each other forever. He looked into her angel eyes, and it seemed as though they really had.

Her fingers combed his hair back from his forehead. "I'm Julie. How do you feel?"

He wanted her to touch him again, but he didn't dare ask aloud.

"Hurts, doesn't it?" She lightly stroked one of the scars on his shoulder. "But it looks like you've been through this before."

"Kuwait."

Her fingertip traced the scar along his jaw, then his forehead.

"Detroit."

"Is that where you're from?" He nodded once.

"Too bad about the Tigers, huh? I thought they were a shoo-in for the pennant this year."

He wasn't that much of a baseball fan, but he was willing to discuss any topic that kept her by his side. The drug in his system prevented him from intelligently holding up his side of the conversation, but she seemed to understand and did most of the talking.

He remembered fading in and out for a day or two. Each time he awakened, she was there, smiling, telling him little bits of news and gossip. Once the amount of narcotic he'd been prescribed was reduced, he was able to get her talking about what he really wanted to know, which was anything and everything about her.

She was from Baltimore, Maryland, almost thirty, had a large number of relatives and friends, each of whom she could relate a humorous story about. She liked children, rescued stray animals, and had no husband, fiancé, or boyfriend waiting at home.

But more important than that, she acted as if she really liked him. For some reason she saw right past what everyone else saw when they looked at him. He even had the urge to tell her about his own life, thinking that she might be the one woman who wouldn't judge him by his past, but he needed more confidence for that.

With each encounter he grew more certain that she was feeling the same attraction to him that he was to her. And when he held her hand and she didn't pull it back, his hope rose.

His leg felt a little better by the end of the first

week, and her nearness was keeping him in a constant state of arousal. He could tell Julie wasn't the type of woman he usually associated with, and normally he wouldn't have even bothered talking to her, but everything about her had him believing his life could be different with her.

He wanted her, but he didn't want her to see him as an animal. He vowed to go slowly with her, but he couldn't stand another day of only holding her hand.

That night, after it was dark and quiet and she came by to say good night, he shifted to one side of the cot and asked her to sit next to him.

"I know it's only been a few days," he began, then stopped because her angel eyes were telling him he didn't have to explain. He reached up and, with his hand lightly stroking the back of her neck, he brought her head down to his. The moment her lips touched his, he knew she was the one he'd been looking for all his life—the sweet woman that would lift his dark soul from the depths of hell and stand at his side through good times and bad.

Knowing they had no assurance of continued privacy, he controlled the desire to pull her down onto the cot and bury himself in her softness. Instead he kept the kiss light and close-mouthed and his hands above her shoulders.

"I love you, Julie," he whispered, and waited for her to return the sentiment. For several heartbeats he was certain she wanted to do just that, then she sighed and slashed his exposed heart in two.

"Logan, I'm flattered. You're a wonderful man, and I'd be honored to have your love. But sometimes a man thinks he feels something for a woman who's taken care of him when really it's just gratitude. A few weeks from now, after you've gone from here, you might not feel like you do right this minute."

"That's not true," he protested, unable to keep the hurt out of his voice. "I'm not some kid fresh out of high school who can't tell the difference between love, lust, and gratitude."

She touched her fingers to his lips. "I know you're not. But I've been through this before with patients, and if I believed everyone who said he loved me truly did, I'd be perpetually heartbroken. Please don't misunderstand, I really care for you, but unless what you're feeling now lasts longer than your hospital stay, I can't afford to love you."

She dipped her head to kiss him again, but he turned his face from hers. It had been so long since he'd allowed himself to feel that to have it thrown back in his face hurt worse than any physical wound he'd ever received.

It made him remember the last time he'd been in love. He had been fourteen and his raging hormones had clouded his mind enough to make him forget who he was and where he'd come from. He'd gone ballistic over the prettiest girl in school. It had taken him weeks to get up the nerve to talk to her, and when she was nice to him, he'd bragged that she was his girlfriend.

As it turned out, she had only been treating him politely, as she had been taught by her upper-middle-class parents. Behind his back she told her friends what she really thought—that she'd rather kiss her dog than Dirty Logan McKay.

After that he improved his personal grooming habits, but remembered to keep his hormonal sights on girls who didn't mind being kissed by white trash.

The morning after Julie's rejection, he wised up and started paying attention to what was going on around him. The pain in his leg was tolerable now without any narcotics, so his mind was no longer clouded by that either.

The first thing he noticed was that there were a lot of other patients in better and worse shape than he was, and Julie was sweet to every last one of them. He told himself that was her job, that it was stupid to be jealous. But when he saw her lean over one young soldier and brush his hair back from his forehead, he pounded the last nail into the lid of the coffin that usually housed his heart.

He had been a fool again.

At least she hadn't lied the night before. She just called it like she saw it—and she was probably right. He wasn't in love. He was grateful. His mind, temporarily confused by drugs and pain, had mistaken her simple kindness for what she was rather than what she did for a living. He knew from personal experience how vastly different those two things could be.

By the time she came to visit him, he thought he had it all straightened out in his head, but he was still wrong. Just hearing her voice caused an ache inside him that no drug could fully numb. From that moment on, he did the only thing he knew to protect himself. He pushed her away. When ignoring her didn't work, he resorted to crudity to stop her from being so nice. Yet she kept coming back just as sweet and solid as hard candy, until he thought he'd go crazy before being sent back to his battalion.

And when that day finally came, he thought he'd be able to forget her, but he had needed the fantasy too much.

The plane took a sudden dip that almost made Julie lose her balance. Private Higgs wasn't so surefooted. He and two cups of coffee landed in one poor soldier's lap.

"Sorry about that," the pilot said over the loudspeaker. "We've found the edge of that storm we heard about, so I'd recommend you stay belted in until we can get clear of it."

As Julie and Higgs returned to their seats, the powerful air turbulence had the big jet vibrating like a washing machine with a lopsided load. Julie frowned at the dark clouds churning outside the window next to her and prayed that the "edge" the pilot had mentioned would be behind them soon.

She'd never liked storms, even in the safety of her parents' home. Being in the midst of one when the ground was miles below was as frightening as the first time she had heard bombs exploding outside the field hospital.

A moan of pain distracted her from her fears, and she quickly sought the source. The sound had come from one of the young men who'd suffered severe chemical burns over most of his body. He would have massive scarring, but it was a miracle he had survived at all. He was heavily drugged and special padded straps had been used to hold him immobile on the stretcher, which was bolted to the floor, but the turbulence was so strong, his body was still being shifted just enough to cause him pain.

Julie unbuckled her belt and staggered to the injured soldier. Sitting on the floor next to him, she held onto the side of the stretcher and leaned close to his ear. "Willie? It's Julie. I know it hurts, hon, but it will only be for a few minutes, and I'm going to stay right here with you the whole time. Okay?" She paused to softly touch his bandaged hand, and his body seemed to relax ever so slightly.

"Did I ever tell you about the time my friend Connie—you remember my talking about her, don't you; she was the one who always got me in trouble—well, anyway, she accepted a dare from these other girls for us to spend a whole night in a cemetery."

A streak of lightning flashed outside, instantly followed by an explosion of thunder that rocked the plane for several seconds. Julie pressed her hand against her chest as if that might slow the racing beat of her heart.

It took no more than a slight head nod at one of her nurses to remind them of their duty. If there was one thing they had all learned on the battlefield, the comfort of the patients came before their own needs or fears.

Julie took a deep breath and forced herself to keep talking to Willie. She wasn't sure which one of them needed her silly story more, but it didn't matter.

A second explosion of light and sound seemed greater than the first, and this time the plane made another sudden drop in altitude as well. Voices rose throughout the cabin, some with worry, others in anger over the crew's ineptitude. She heard one man question why the pilot wasn't taking them above the storm if he couldn't get around it, and she began wondering the same thing.

"I have to go check on something, Willie. I'll be right back, so don't you go wandering off anywhere."

Struggling against the vibrating and pitching of the craft, she made her way to the cockpit and yanked open the door. The frantic dialogue of the crew and the way the pilot was straining at the control wheel increased her nervousness. Pulling the door closed and bracing herself against its frame, she tried to guess what was going on without disturbing anyone.

The sky before them appeared to be an ocean of rolling, pewter-colored clouds, sporadically illuminated by jagged streaks of light. The continuous rumble of thunder no longer seemed to have a beginning or end.

"Can't you take us above this?" Julie shouted.

Without turning around to her, the pilot sarcastically yelled back, "What the hell do you think we're trying to do? Just get back there and buckle yourself in! Damn!" He pounded his fist against the altimeter.

Julie's gaze fell to the control panel, and she saw what the pilot was swearing at. Some of the indicator hands were spinning madly while other controls seemed to have stopped functioning completely. What in God's name was happening?

She was about to obey the pilot's order when the thunderous rumble around them rose to a deafening roar, and the vibration became so violent, she was positive the plane would be pulled apart any moment. Sheer terror now kept her standing there, clinging to the edges of the doorway.

All of a sudden the clouds began to part and roll to the sides as if an unseen hand were opening a pathway for the plane. There was light beyond the clouds, and the wider the gap grew, the brighter the light became, until there was a hole in the sky big enough for the jet to fly through, but the light was nearly blinding in intensity.

As if someone had flicked a switch, the vibrating abruptly stopped and the plane picked up speed with a tremendous jerk.

"Full flaps!" The pilot shouted. "Reduce power! We've got to slow this mother down."

Nothing the crew did seemed to make any difference. Julie found herself pinned against the cockpit door and comprehended that the increased gravitational pull meant they were going faster and faster toward the light.

She watched the navigator fight the g-force to bring his hand up to his forehead, then make the sign of the cross. A hundred different thoughts tried to form at once in her mind, but only one was coherent.

After surviving the third world war, they were all going to die anyway.

Chapter 2

Julie tried to block out the voices buzzing in her ears. She wasn't ready to wake up yet. Rather than fading away, however, the voices kept getting louder. After several more minutes of attempting to stay submerged in murky sleep, she reluctantly swam to the surface.

Even after opening her eyes, though, she wasn't certain she was awake. There were vaguely familiar faces around her, but the structure they were in was totally unfamiliar. It was obviously an enormous wooden barn, complete with horses, cows, stalls, and straw covering the ground; she just couldn't remember why she and the others were there.

A second scan of the building brought another oddity to Julie's foggy mind. Light was being provided by lanterns with burning candles in them, secured along the walls and on wooden posts. There wasn't a window or door in sight.

She forced aside the question of where she was and focused on the people. Some seemed very excited as they carried on conversations, but she couldn't distinguish the words. Others, like herself, were just rousing from sleep. Regardless of how conscious they were, however, everyone seemed to bear an expression of confusion.

Julie's eyes touched on a young man about twenty feet away, who was fretting more than most. *Private Higgs.* The name popped into her head along with an image of him losing his balance and spilling coffee from two styrofoam cups in his hands.

But in that picture he had been wearing a soldier's uniform, and now he was dressed in light blue cotton pajamas—at least that's what his outfit appeared to be. Glancing at the others and checking her own attire, she noted that they were all dressed similarly, in loose-fitting pants and short-sleeve, V-necked shirts, similar to hospital scrubs. Although the colors differed, they were generally soft pastel shades. Hers was peach.

She sat up and rubbed her temples as she concentrated on the image of Private Higgs that had come to her. That image blurred into others. Patients, swathed in bandages like mummies. Rows of cots. Logan McKay lying on one of those cots with blatant need. Logan, asleep in a seat with metal cuffs on his wrists. An airplane. Instruments going crazy. *The storm!*

As the pieces of her memory joined together, she rose unsteadily to her feet. Surely the plane they were on had crashed into the ocean. Hadn't they been hit by a series of lightning bolts? How had they all survived? How had they gotten into this barn? How—

The bewildered gaze of her friend Robin met her

own from across the shelter, and the two women rushed toward each other. The tight hug they shared said more of their fears and relief to see each other than words ever could.

"This is very weird," Robin said as they stepped apart. "Am I in your nightmare, or are you in mine?"

Julie shook her head. "Actually, I'm toying with the theory that everyone on the plane died, and this is some sort of transfer station before we're sent off to an afterlife."

Robin expressed her disbelief by cocking one finely arched auburn eyebrow.

"I just woke up," Julie responded to her unspoken criticism. "My brain's still only at half speed." She nodded at the large group around Private Higgs. "Let's see what they think." A man's voice stopped them before they took a step.

"Julie? Captain Evans?"

Julie turned around to see a slightly built young man with dark brown skin and a shaved head. His eyes begged her for help in the same way a thousand wounded soldiers had in the past two years, but he didn't appear to be in physical pain.

"You are Julie Evans, aren't you?" he asked, a bit less certainly.

"Yes, I'm Julie." She wondered why he didn't look at all familiar to her.

He gave her a shaky smile, then reached out and shook her hand. "I recognized your voice. It would be pretty hard not to, since it was the only thing that kept me from going crazy the last few weeks. I guess everyone tells you what a beautiful voice you have, but I just had to let you know how important it was to me."

Julie gave a slight frown as she tried to remember him.

His grin broadened to reveal one crooked incisor. "I'm Willy."

She took a step back and scrutinized him from head to toe. "That's impossible." Looking at Robin, she explained, "Willy was one of the patients on the plane. He suffered severe chemical burns. He was barely alive, let alone able to walk and talk."

"That's right," Willy said excitedly. "I don't understand it, but I'm healed. And so are the others. At first I thought maybe I'd just been unconscious for a long time, but that doesn't explain why there aren't any scars. Then I thought, maybe there was no war and I was never burned. You know, like it was all a bad dream. But everyone else remembers the same things I do."

"Did I say very weird?" Robin murmured to Julie. "Let me change that to incredibly spooky."

With a wave of her hand, Julie led Robin and Willy over to the group that now included most of the survivors. When she spotted three of her nurses, she moved next to them. Giving each a light pat on the shoulder, she tried to offer some reassurance.

Separated from the group, on the opposite side of the barn, four men were huddled together. They appeared to be having an intense conversation while keeping an eye out for any eavesdroppers. Julie was fairly sure all four were convicts.

Also standing apart, but quite alone, was Logan

McKay. He looked bored, leaning negligently against the post of a horse stall, yet Julie had the distinct feeling that he was absorbing everything and simply waiting for the dust to settle before getting involved. She looked away for fear he might catch her staring, but then her gaze darted back to him as another realization came to her. He wasn't wearing cuffs or shackles! A glance back at the four convicts confirmed what she feared; the prisoners were just as free as she was.

Her concern escalated as she noted that the two military police officers were now unarmed.

"It doesn't matter where we are or how we got here!" Corporal Gianni shouted to be heard over the multitude of speculations being thrown back and forth. "Everyone just break off and try to find a way out."

"Hold it!" yelled a man from behind Julie.

She turned to see that the small group of convicts had approached. Their spokesperson was a tall, muscular blond man who had a very threatening demeanor. He instantly commanded everyone's attention. The crowd parted as he pushed forward, followed by his three companions. Corporal Gianni stood his ground and tried to appear taller than his medium height.

"What do you want, Wilkes?" Gianni asked defensively.

"Nothin' much, 'cept I was wonderin' who the hell put you in charge?"

Julie swore she could actually feel the tension gripping the people around her as everyone began inching away from the two men. No words were spoken for several seconds, during which time the crowd seemed to divide into two distinct sides.

"The way I figger it," Wilkes said, "I outrank you."

"Like hell," Gianni countered. "You were stripped of your rank at the court-martial, and everyone here knows it."

He looked from side to side at the people he referred to as if hoping for a show of support.

When he didn't get it, Julie guessed that the corporal wasn't much more popular than Wilkes. Accustomed to being in a military environment, however, the soldiers were prepared to obey the orders of a superior officer whether they admired that person or not. They simply needed to know who was in charge.

It looked as though Wilkes and Gianni were about to resort to physical violence to answer the question of command when another man spoke up.

"Excuse me, gentlemen."

The words were spoken with a British inflection and came from a nice-looking man with short ash blond hair. As he strode into the center of the ring of people, Julie could see that he was about the same height as Wilkes but considerably leaner. She recalled seeing him on the plane mainly because Robin had made some comment about personally inducting him into the "mile-high" club before they reached the States.

"I believe this matter can be settled without fist-icuffs," the Britisher stated politely but with supreme authority. "I am *Major* Geoffrey Cookson, and I outrank you both."

Wilkes snorted. "That's easy to say while you ain't wearin' no bars to prove it. You ain't even American."

"Since we have no idea what country we're in, the matter of my birthplace is irrelevant. However, if it will ease your mind, I am a naturalized citizen of the United States as well as an officer of its armed forces. Now, unless someone outranks me, I—"

Wilkes gave the major's shoulder a shove. "Not so fast, limey. You may have the rank, but I got somethin' more important . . . *strength*." His three friends took a step closer to his back to emphasize his point. "I'll be giving the orders from now on."

Major Cookson had no intention of backing down or using violence to maintain his authority.

"This is really quite unnecessary under the circumstances. Until we determine the logistics of our situation, arguing over power is a waste of time and energy that could be better spent investigating our surroundings."

A subtle stir among the people behind him was followed by the four convicts easing back a bit. For a moment it appeared that they were giving in to the major's logic, but their attention was focused on someone behind him.

Julie's breath caught in her throat as she watched Logan McKay position himself to Cookson's right. His additional inches of height and shoulder breadth might have been threatening enough to a bully like Wilkes, but the look of promised danger in McKay's dark eyes cinched the matter.

"I think you're right about wastin' time, Major," Wilkes said. "We'll let you do the orderin' . . . for the time bein'." His last words were accompanied by a narrow-eyed glare at McKay.

As Wilkes and his cohorts backed away, the major finished the sentence he'd begun earlier. "I suggest you all do what Corporal Gianni ordered. Check every inch of this building for the exit. That includes inside the animal stalls. If we got in, there has to be a way out. In the meantime, the flight crew should report to me for a debriefing."

Logan turned to walk away, but the major murmured, "Stay," so he stayed. Logan wondered how the man could look so damned dignified standing at attention in a pair of pajamas. Personally, he felt ridiculous.

The pilot, copilot, and navigator walked up to Cookson and saluted.

"At ease," the major said, returning their salute, though he didn't relax a muscle. "Name and rank, please."

The oldest, a black man about Logan's age, responded first. "Lieutenant Nathan Boswell. I was the pilot."

"Lieutenant Jeremy Fleischer, copilot."

Logan thought he didn't look old enough to be weaned from his mother.

The third, a young man with a glazed look in his eye, had to clear his throat twice before any sound would come out. Even when it did, it was barely audible.

"L-lieutenant Edward Smith, flight navigator."

"What do you remember?" Cookson asked Boswell.

The pilot delivered a concise report that ended with the plane being sucked through a hole in the clouds toward the sun.

"It was as if someone else were flying the plane. I had no control whatsoever at the end."

Fleischer and Smith confirmed his statements.

"Thank you," Cookson said with a nod at Boswell. "Let me know if anything else comes back to you."

As soon as they walked away, the major turned to Logan with the same no-nonsense expression he had used with the men. "I hope a verbal thank-you for your timely intervention will suffice. I believe prostrating myself at your feet in gratitude might diminish the troop's confidence in me."

Logan was caught off guard by the man's admission and dry humor, and almost smiled before getting control over it. With a face as serious as Cookson's, he replied, "Let's just save that show for when morale gets really low . . . say, about an hour from now." Logan hesitated, then asked the question on his mind. "Why the honesty with me, Major?"

"Please call me Geoffrey, and since I might need your support again in the future, I thought it best to be truthful with you. It's not that I'm a coward, mind you; I'm simply a realist. That man Wilkes would have attacked me and, given his greater size, undoubtedly would have caused me considerable pain. I'm an engineer, not a fighter, but my stepping forward seemed to be the best way of maintaining order until we find out what's going on. You apparently carry a lot of weight with Wilkes and his pals. In case my leadership is required for more than the next hour, I hope you will consent to continuing to back me up."

Logan decided the man's honesty deserved the same in return. "I get the idea that you don't know who I am, so let me introduce myself. The name's Logan McKay. I was a chief master sergeant before they sentenced me to life at Leavenworth. Want to know why?"

Geoffrey met Logan's challenging stare. "Not particularly. For the moment I know as much about you as I need to."

Logan was about to tell him how wrong he was when Captain Evans walked up to the major and saluted. Logan's chest muscles immediately contracted, but outwardly he controlled any reaction. He couldn't help but notice how she kept her eyes fixed on the major, and didn't once glance at him.

"Major Cookson, I'm Captain Julie Evans, formerly head nurse at the fifty-third mobile hospital unit. It seems that I'm the second highest-ranking officer here, so I wanted to put myself at your disposal. The nurses have spoken to each of the patients, and I was certain you would want to receive a status report."

"Of course, Captain. I welcome your assistance."

"It makes no sense," Julie said less formally. "But every single patient has had a miraculous recovery. There's not even a scar to show that any of them were recently wounded or burned."

Logan automatically touched the scar over his eyebrow. It was still there, which proved once again that he couldn't come out ahead, even in the Twilight Zone.

Geoffrey slowly rubbed his jaw. "I heard a number of suppositions about what happened, but they were all from men. Since I've always been a believer in feminine intuition, I'd like to hear your opinion, Captain."

Julie frowned and shifted her balance from one foot to the other. "Well, sir, it sounds a bit crazy, but when I first came to, I thought we might all be dead. After seeing the patients, that idea doesn't seem so far-fetched."

Logan had had the same thought, but it wasn't until she said it aloud that he came up with a way to test it. He had been so relieved to be free of his restraints that how it had come about wasn't all that important.

While Julie and Cookson discussed the possibilities, Logan walked over to a post, picked off a thin splinter of wood, and peeled away a few slivers until one end came to a sharp point. Squeezing the middle finger of his left hand with his thumb and ring finger, he brought blood to the surface of the fingertip, then jabbed it with the splinter before he chickened out. He had been knifed and shot without a whimper, but needles had always made him queasy.

As blood oozed out of the tiny puncture, he swallowed hard and returned to the two officers. "Sorry to have to blow a hole in the death theory, but I'm pretty sure people stop bleeding once they're dead." He held out his hand to show the fresh wound.

Though Julie looked at his finger, she had yet to look at his face. Logan knew he should let it go, but he just couldn't. "If you still have doubts, Captain Evans, I'd be happy to give you a prick." Her gaze lifted abruptly and he was treated to a pink flush across her fair cheekbones. "Then again, maybe you'd rather do it yourself." He held out his makeshift needle.

"No, thank you," she said, ice dripping from her words. "One *brave* soldier shedding blood for the cause is quite enough."

Logan raised an eyebrow as his stomach twisted beneath her sarcasm. "Maybe you would have preferred me to slash an artery or two."

She raised her chin a notch. "Maybe I—"

"Ahem." Geoffrey noisily cleared his throat. "Without jumping to any rash conclusions, can I assume you two are acquainted?"

"Barely," responded Logan.

"Hardly at all," answered Julie.

"I see," Geoffrey said with a nod. "Then I don't need to worry about any personal conflicts getting in the way here. Until we get to the bottom of this situation, you are second in command, Captain Evans, but Sergeant McKay will act as my adjutant."

Logan was certain she wanted to protest, but all she said was "Yes, sir. If I may be excused now, sir?" As soon as Geoffrey nodded to her, she turned on her heel and strode away.

Julie restrained the urge to feel her cheeks. She

didn't really need to touch them to know they were hot. Nor did she need to check her pulse to know that it was racing. Logan McKay was not the first man to make a suggestive remark to her, but for some reason he was the only one whose comments she couldn't ignore or laugh off.

Besides the fact that she had made the mistake of caring too much, there was another reason he managed to embarrass her. Whereas most men used sexual innuendo to make a safe pass, Logan used it like a sharp weapon, poking it at her to make sure she kept her distance. She had misinterpreted it to mean that he was actually needier than the average man she dealt with. Her caretaker instincts automatically had her trying harder to get through to him in spite of the blows he repeatedly delivered.

She had thought he wouldn't remember her, but it was quite clear that he did. And even though she had made a point of not speaking to him, he still found it necessary to provoke her. Before she could give it more thought, Robin walked up to her.

"Hey, what's with the face?" Robin asked quietly. "Did you find out we really are dead, or is it something worse?"

Julie smiled despite her dismal mood. "Something worse than death?"

Robin shrugged. "Sure. It could be that Private Higgs is right—that we were snatched from the plane by aliens and taken to their planet on a spaceship."

Julie rolled her eyes. "How does he explain the

fact that there are Earth-type horses and cows in here with us? Did the aliens abduct them also?"

"Absolutely," Robin said with exaggerated seriousness. "The aliens wanted to create an environment similar to what we humans were accustomed to. Apparently Higgs's aliens are a little fuzzy on certain details. Anyway, he says this barn is actually like a cage in a zoo, and alien tourists are watching us through the one-way windows at this very moment."

"You're right," Julie said with a grimace. "There are some things worse than death. Like being forced to spend time with men like Private Higgs or Wilkes. Can you just imagine what might happen if we were all stuck in here together for very long?"

"Yeah. World War Four. Except this time we don't even have the limited privacy of a latrine."

Julie made another face at her friend. "I've been trying not to think about that. Or about food. Or water."

"You're not the only one, believe me. But something the darling major said stuck in my head."

Julie smirked. "I think the darling major is just plain stuck in your head."

"True," Robin admitted with a wink. "I thought he was luscious the first time I saw him, but when I heard that English accent, I almost wet my pants."

"How can you think about a man at a time like this?" Julie knew her question was rhetorical; there was always room for thoughts of handsome men in Robin's mind.

Robin cocked her head as if giving Julie's question real consideration. "It's hard, but some things are worth the extra effort." She grinned and wiggled her eyebrows, then straightened her expression again. "Anyway, what I was going to bring up before you sidetracked me was what the major said about the animals. They look healthy. Somebody must be in charge of giving them food and water and letting them out. So I'm willing to bet that whoever, or whatever, put us in here, will take care of us too. It's just a matter of being patient until they show themselves."

Julie nodded. "It sounds logical, but I'm worried about how far some of these men's patience can be stretched." Her gaze sought out Wilkes to see what he was up to, but before she located him or any of his friends, all six of her nurses joined her and Robin. Their worried expressions mirrored her own.

Darcy, a young woman with blond-on-blond frosted hair and a courageous air that made her seem larger than her petite body, spoke first. "No one has been able to find a way out."

Kara, Darcy's closest friend, stood silently behind her, as usual, staring at the ground. She was as timid as her friend was brave. Kara was a good nurse, though, and that was what mattered to Julie.

Sunny, a brunette whose nickname perfectly suited her bright personality, rather than her drab appearance, offered her information next. "There doesn't even seem to be a loose board anywhere that could be pried away to make an opening. It might be possible with a tool, but no one's found anything usable."

The "Three Musketeers," Trish, Mandy, and Charlene, had nothing to add, but Mandy gave voice to what they were all thinking. "I'm scared, Captain. More scared than the time the sniper was taking potshots at us."

"At least then we knew where we were and who the enemy was," Trish said.

Just then the group was expanded as two more women walked up and saluted Julie. She automatically returned the salute and waited for them to identify themselves. They obviously knew who she was, or at least they knew of her superior rank.

"Warrant Officer Alicia Samples, helicopter pilot," said the taller of the two. With her statuesque form and long blond hair, she looked more like a model than a pilot.

"I thought you ought to know, someone just found a supply of tents, cots, and bedding in the tack room. Looks like someone's expecting us to make ourselves at home."

The other woman had a Polynesian look about her. "I'm Lee Tang," she said. "Ninth Infantry. We hope you don't mind our joining you, but in case you haven't noticed, there are ten of us and over a hundred of them."

Julie looked at her curiously for a moment before realizing that she was referring to the male-female ratio. It was a fact of life in the field, something each woman dealt with in her own way. She had told Robin she was concerned about physical needs such as food, water, and relieving oneself.

She hadn't given a thought to the kind of physical needs that might drive a man like Wilkes.

Suddenly she was filled with a new fear, but she knew better than to let the other women see it. After all, she was a captain, the second in command. They were expecting her to take care of them and, as always, she would do everything in her power to do that. She introduced herself, Robin, and her nurses, and suggested they all use first names under the circumstances.

"There's no reason to worry about something that's not an immediate problem," Julie stated firmly. "I agree that we should be aware of the situation, especially considering the fact that twenty-nine of them are convicted felons. However, I'm sure the rest of the men can be counted on to behave in a civilized fashion. Besides, we'll probably find out what's going on here any minute and—"

A creaking noise coming from one end of the barn caught everyone's attention. Very slowly a large section of the wall opened outward like a giant door.

With each inch the door opened, sunlight filled more of the barn. Julie was torn between racing for the opening and being afraid to find out what was beyond the barn. For several seconds it looked as though the fear of the unknown was keeping everyone else from moving as well.

"Captain Evans, I believe our place should be on the front line."

Julie turned to see Major Cookson and Logan waiting on her. To the women she said, "Stay back until we see what we're facing." She then posted herself on the major's left as they strode toward the opening. With each step others fell in behind them until Julie felt a bit like the pied piper. Cookson halted them at the edge of the barn and waited for the door to complete its swing.

Julie's heart pounded in her chest as she prepared for the worst and hoped for the best. When the outside world finally came into view, it was not clearly one or the other. The warm air temperature suggested it was summer. The position of the sun said it was midday. Her first guess might have been that they were on a farm somewhere in middle America.

Except the ground cover and tree leaves were royal blue and the sky was celery green.

And the large gathering of Oriental men waiting for them to exit was evidence that they were not the only humans in this place—wherever it was.

Chapter 3

Julie, Logan, and Geoffrey walked cautiously out into the yard. Scanning the group of men a second time, she noted that there were a few who were not Oriental, but they all bore the same expression of wonder. Within seconds the rest of the soldiers and nurses filed into the yard. Their verbal reactions ranged from the spiritual to the obscene. As the two groups stared at each other, it was impossible to tell which looked more surprised.

"Hello," Geoffrey said to break the stalemate.

The group of men smiled slightly, bobbed their heads, and replied, "Hello."

"Does anyone speak English?" Geoffrey asked.

A very old, bald-headed man limped forward, leaning heavily on a wooden cane. He offered a toothless grin. "I do. And a few others. Don't use it much, though. Mostly learned to get our ideas across without words." His speech was slow and subdued, and his gaze wandered as if he were distracted.

"Please, sir," Julie said, "could you tell us where we are?"

His eyes focused on hers, then widened with

gradual awareness. "A woman?" He squinted at the crowd behind her. "Never had women that I recall. Never had so many arrive at once either. Not quite sure what to do about that." He frowned a little as he seemed to struggle with his thoughts for a moment, then his toothless smile was back in place. "But they will. They always take care of any little problems. Must get back to work now." He turned and motioned for his people to get moving.

"Wait!" Julie cried, and the old man stopped and looked back. It occurred to her that he could be senile, but what about the rest of them? Standing there with passive smiles and vacant gazes, they reminded her of well-fed sheep—contented, slow-moving, and almost mindless.

"Oh, yes," the old man said as he hobbled around again. "You asked me a question, didn't you?"

Julie could tell he had no recollection of what she'd asked. "Where are we? How did we get here?"

"I wish I could tell you, my dear, but can't. I think I arrived here about ninety years ago, but I'm not certain. The people here then didn't know where they were either."

"What's the deal, Major?" a soldier shouted, then several others added their own questions.

"What kind of place has green sky?"

"How'd we get here?"

"How do we get back home?"

Logan turned around and, with no more than the slash of his narrow-eyed glare across the nervous crowd, silenced the voices.

Julie didn't see Geoffrey acknowledge Logan's assistance, but somehow she knew he did.

"As you can hear," Geoffrey said to the old man, "we would appreciate any information you can offer. I am Major Geoffrey Cookson of the United States Army. We were all on a plane heading to the United States from Japan, when a storm—"

"Yes, yes," the old man interrupted. "A storm. Always a storm. Thunder and lightning, then the bright light, then waking up in the barn. Sometimes a plane. Sometimes a boat, but always a storm, and always near Japan. I was on a fishing boat off Guam myself. The rest are gone now." Again he appeared to mentally drift away, then return. "I am Duncan, the eldest of this lost tribe." He waved a frail hand toward the men behind him. "You'll have the rest of your lives to meet everyone else. Must go to work now." He started to move away once more.

Julie's worried gaze darted to Geoffrey, but Logan spoke up. "You said *they* take care of problems. Who are *they*?"

Duncan shook his head. "Don't know that either. Just know they're out there, past the invisible wall, and they take care of any problems." He crooked his finger for Julie to come closer. When she did, he whispered, "I think they're fairies."

The more Julie was hearing, the less she understood.

"This is getting nowhere fast," Logan muttered to Geoffrey. "And the animals at your back are starting to show their teeth."

Julie was quickly beginning to realize that decision-making was not one of the major's strong points. His decision to keep a man like McKay at his side had been her first clue. She offered a suggestion when Duncan tried to leave again.

"Duncan, you said you have to get back to work. Perhaps we could help. There are an awful lot of us. If we broke up into groups, and you assigned an English-speaking person to each group, we could be shown what it is you do here and give you a hand."

Duncan smiled broadly. "That's a fine idea, young lady. Lots of strong backs. Must work to eat. Must eat to work." He called five men forward and repeated Julie's suggestion.

"I'll take the women and go with Duncan," Julie stated. "We nurses are known for our endless patience." Her remark won a smile from the major, but Logan had an objection.

"You'll take ten men with you too," he said while his eyes scanned the crowd for candidates.

Julie automatically bristled at his authoritative tone. He had no right to give her orders. "That won't be necessary."

Logan's gaze slid to hers and held. "I say it is."

Julie lifted her chin and crossed her arms. "Listen, McKay. That evil eye of yours may work on the men, but it doesn't intimidate me one bit."

Geoffrey cleared his throat before Logan could counter. "I believe the sergeant made a valid suggestion, Captain. If what Duncan said is true, and these men haven't seen women for years, there's no telling what difficulties you might encounter. My recommendation would be to select ten of your patients. They would be most apt to be protective of you."

Julie still didn't believe the women needed men with them, but at least the major explained his reasoning rather than just giving an order, and unlike McKay, he *was* a superior officer. Besides, Willy and some of the other patients would probably prefer to be with the nurses. "Yes, sir. I'll select ten to take with us."

Before going their separate ways, Geoffrey had one last thing to say. "I want to assure you both that although I have been a bit out of my element thus far, I am quite good at strategic planning. Once we gather sufficient information, I'm sure we will find a solution to this peculiar dilemma. In the meantime, I appreciate the assistance."

Julie thought it took quite a man to admit his weakness and decided right then that she liked the major. As she gathered the women and chose the men to stay with them, she noted that Logan put Wilkes in his own group and split up the other troublemakers. Though she abhorred the macho tactics he'd used so far to maintain control, she could see that his methods had some merit under the circumstances. But she wondered just how long Wilkes would be held off by hostile glares before he tested McKay's strength. Then again, maybe Wilkes was intimidated so easily because he'd already tested McKay and learned what Julie had—that his rough appearance went all the way to the bone.

"Now what?" Robin asked as soon as Julie came near.

"We follow the leader and pry anything out of his fuzzy mind we possibly can." She led her group to Duncan. "We're all yours, Duncan. Where to?"

The elderly man beamed as he was surrounded by young ladies. "I used to work in the fields, but can't keep up anymore. I'm in the kitchen now, with the other old ones. Women's chores are all we're good for these days."

Robin raised an eyebrow, but Julie quickly touched a finger to her lips. Duncan would never have heard of the women's movement, and this was not the time to explain it.

A whinnying sound caught Julie's attention, and she turned to see three of the other groups climbing into horse-drawn wagons. "Where will they be going?"

Duncan squinted at the wagons. "Could be the orchards. Plenty of ripe fruit needs picking. Corn's ready too. Could be either."

Since Julie couldn't see any orchards or fields, she guessed the farm was very large. "And what's beyond the farm?"

Duncan started his slow hobble again. "Don't know. The farmland ends at the invisible wall."

Julie and Robin shared a skeptical glance. "You mentioned that before," Robin said. "Can you describe it?"

"Can't describe something invisible. It's just there and you can't walk through it, dig under it, or climb over it."

Robin leaned toward Julie and murmured in her ear. "Sounds like one of those force fields in science fiction movies. I think we should bring Higgs in as a consultant. He's probably been right all along."

Matching their pace to Duncan's, they were only moving along an inch at a time, but Julie could see they were headed toward another large wooden building similar to the barn. Four smoke-spewing chimneys protruded from the corners of the roof.

Beyond the large building were rows of smaller ones. Every structure, including the barn, was painted white with red doors and roofs. The area looked like a cross between an army unit and summer camp.

Duncan pointed at the smaller buildings. "Men sleep in those. New people have to build their own. No hurry, though. Rainy season's over and colder weather's not due for months."

"You have regular seasons?" Alicia, the helicopter pilot, asked.

Duncan stopped and took a few breaths before answering. "Lived in New York before I set off to see the world. We had seasons there. This place always reminded me of California. Never liked California." He started moving toward the buildings again. "Kitchen's in the big house. Necessary room too. Don't have a separate room for women, though. That might be a problem."

Robin snorted. "*Might* be a problem? I'll guarantee it. How many men live here?"

"Fifty-four . . . no, fifty-three . . . Moishe passed on a few months ago."

Robin made a face at Julie. "Fifty-three, plus a hundred seventeen more. All using the same bathroom facilities? We've got to find a way out of here fast."

"Excuse me, sir?"

Julie turned to see Willy coming up alongside her. Duncan paused again to listen to the young man.

"My name's Willy. Me and these other guys, well, we were half dead on the plane, and now we're walking around like nothing ever happened to us. We were hoping you could tell us how, or why, or something."

Duncan sighed and looked at each of the men. "Half dead, eh? Knew they could fix a broken bone good as new or heal a bad cut. Guess they could have fixed you fellas up before putting you in the barn."

"Do you mean the ones you think are fairies healed these men?" Julie asked.

Duncan nodded and gave her a wink. "Don't know the how or why of it, but when someone here gets sick or hurt, they go into the tack room in the barn and close the door. A while later they come back out all better."

Robin voiced the question in everyone's mind. "What does the sick person say happened to them?"

"No one ever remembers," Duncan mumbled and got moving again.

"Here we are," he said as they reached the big house. Willy quickly opened the door and held it while everyone entered.

Inside were a dozen elderly men performing a variety of chores, but one thing was instantly noticeable. There were no appliances. A hearth was in each corner with large caldrons hanging over the smoldering fires. The man doing dishes was working a hand pump to get water.

Not only had they been dropped into a strange world, it wasn't even the twentieth century here.

Once the elderly men heard how many more people would be eating with them, they welcomed the extra hands.

Before they were put to work, however, they were offered a snack of bread, cheese, and some fruits that tasted like apples and pears but had white and pink skins. Everyone agreed that it was possibly the best food they'd had since they entered the army. The water they were given was lightly carbonated and was so refreshing they each had a second cup. Darcy declared that it had to be from a mountain spring, but Duncan knew only that it came through the pump.

As soon as they had their fill, Julie made sure each person had an assignment while she stuck by Duncan. She could tell he was tiring of all the questions, but she prodded him a bit further.

"You said you'd been here about ninety years. What about the others?"

Duncan rubbed his earlobe. "Hard to say. Some have been here as long as me. Some only a few years."

"You must have been very young when you arrived."

He considered her words a moment, then shrugged. "Was twenty-four. Never thought I'd see sixty, let alone pass a hundred. But they don't let you die so easy here. Just keep fixing a body until it's too old to wake up one morning . . . like Moishe." He stared at a spot on the floor. "Going to sleep and not getting up. That's the only way to leave this place."

Julie waited for him to say more on his own, but after a few seconds the placid expression returned to his wrinkled face.

"Must get to work now," he said and took her to the table where another man was shucking ears of corn.

As her fingers peeled away the husks, her mind tried to make sense of what she'd seen and heard so far, but she only came up with more questions.

Julie decided it was easier to believe in aliens than fairies. But if aliens were in control here, and they had the technology to create a force field, why weren't any appliances in this kitchen?

The other thing that didn't jibe was the attitudes of the men in residence. She could understand how the older men might accept being in this strange place, especially when some of them, like Duncan, had been here for nearly a century.

But what about the others? Her first impression of them had been that they were like sheep. Or maybe robots. If they had been transported to an alien planet, these men could be machines instead of humans. Yet she recalled Duncan's comment about the wall. At one time someone must have tried to scale it or dig under it for him to say it couldn't be done. A robot wouldn't attempt to escape.

Another explanation could be that they were all

tranquilized, but their pupils appeared normal and though their movements seemed a bit slow, they were smooth and coordinated. Rather than exhibiting symptoms of being drugged, she would describe them as being incredibly complacent.

Had they all given up? Or were they simply too afraid to face whatever power was out there?

Logan tipped the clay jug to pour himself another cup of the cool water. It wasn't that he was still thirsty, he just had never tasted anything so . . . clean. That word replayed itself in his head as he realized *clean* was the best description he could come up with for this whole weird place. The water, the air, the whitewashed buildings, even the animals and the men—everything looked too clean and fresh.

As a kid growing up in one of the lousier neighborhoods of Detroit, he hadn't believed there were places in the world where the sky was actually blue. As far as he knew, streets and sidewalks always had garbage all over them. He had seen pictures of cleaner, more colorful places in books at school, but he doubted they were real. For him the world was dirty and gray, a place to survive rather than appreciate its beauty.

Thirty-some years later, his opinion of the world was still pretty much the same, which was why he knew this place—even without the green sky and blue leaves—wasn't part of any world he was familiar with. He didn't belong anywhere this squeaky clean.

Exactly where he did belong was a question he'd

stopped asking himself years ago. As a child he had been constantly daydreaming about being somewhere else. He had always been the good guy fighting the bad, righting wrongs, and saving the world from dark forces. As he aged, his daydreams spilled into real life. Whenever some kid was getting picked on, he just happened to be there and could never resist lending a hand to the underdog.

For his efforts he occasionally received mementos, like the scar on his jaw, when he had stopped three punks from beating a wino and got razor-slashed in the process. Or the scar on his forehead, when he interrupted a man trying to force himself on a woman and learned what it felt like to get hit in the head with a brick.

Despite numerous lessons, however, he never seemed to learn to keep his nose out of other people's business. Fortunately, he grew big enough and became tough enough that his wins soon outnumbered his losses. Eventually he discovered how to cast an impression of danger without having to fight all the time. The strangest part was, the only time he felt right was when he was playing the hero. Otherwise, he always had the feeling he was in the wrong place and time, like he didn't belong where he was.

In high school he had read the story of Don Quixote and come up with a conclusion. He was a Don Quixote, a misplaced hero fighting windmills in a world where windmills were obsolete and there was no Dulcinea to soften the disappointments.

The closest he'd ever gotten to belonging was in

the service, but as it turned out, they had no use for heroes either.

One of the Oriental men came up beside him carrying a bushel filled with pink pear-shaped fruit. He smiled at Logan and, with a movement of his eyes and head, requested his assistance in emptying the fruit into the back of the wagon. Logan gave him a hand, then walked back with the man to help him pick some more. The men here didn't move very quickly or work all that strenuously, but they did keep working—and looked happy about it.

Duncan had been right about there being little use for English, or any other language, for that matter. These men had barely spoken a dozen words aloud. Whatever thoughts they'd needed to express so far had been accomplished silently. Normally that would have been just fine with Logan, but he needed to learn more from them than how to tell which fruit was ripe enough to be plucked. Only verbal questions and answers were going to explain what had happened to them.

Hans, this group's English-speaking guide, was a slightly built middle-aged man from Frankfurt, Germany, who had arrived here when he was in his twenties. He knew very little and didn't particularly care.

That attitude would have seemed odd coming from anyone in this situation, but when Logan uncovered the fact that Hans had previously been a research marine biologist, it made even less sense. When had the man stopped questioning things around him and peacefully accepted a life of performing brainless tasks?

On the way to the orchard, Hans politely answered every question Logan could think of about the layout of the farm, the residents, and how they filled their days. The farm sounded as though it was about a mile square, and the men worked it from sunrise to sunset. Besides their chores, they ate and slept. Nothing else. No entertainment or playing of any kind.

When asked if he or any of the others had ever tried to leave the farm, Hans said everyone tried at first, but they soon realized what a pleasant life they had here and how satisfying it was to put in a good day's work. His dumb-looking smile stayed plastered on his face the whole time he was talking.

As Logan considered the bits of information he'd learned, another question came to him, and he sought Hans out again.

"I'm curious about something, Hans," Logan said as he pulled a piece of fruit off a branch and dropped it into the bushel at his feet. "I can see how important it is for you fellows to do your work. How is it so many of you were standing outside the barn when we came out?"

Hans's smile broadened a bit. "Because it was locked."

Logan could tell that was supposed to explain everything and took a stab at what he meant. "And when the barn door's locked . . . new people arrive?"

Hans nodded. "Once in a while. Not often. Usually it just means Duncan's fairies are at work."

"At work doing what?"

"Trading."

Logan reined in his frustration and forced himself to use the same easy tone Hans used. "What is it they trade?"

"We give them some of the fruits and vegetables we grow, and they leave us things we need but can't make ourselves." Hans caught sight of some ripe fruit on another tree and started dragging his bushel toward it.

Logan picked up the bushel and carried it for him as he asked, "What sort of things?" Hans cocked his head at him with a totally vacant look in his eyes, as if he had no idea what he was talking about. "You said the fairies leave you things you need. Like what?"

Hans's smile came back. "Tools, clothing, sugar. Things we need. Sometimes we put a drawing with the crops so they'll know what we'd like. Other times they surprise us."

Logan wanted to hear more about the fairies, but Higgs chose that moment to do some more fretting.

"Can I talk to you?" he asked, looking nervous enough to throw up.

Logan let Higgs lead him out of the others' hearing range.

"I just want to make sure there's no hard feelings," Higgs said, not quite meeting Logan's eyes. "You know, between us. I mean, I was just doing my job, you know. It's not like I had anything to do with your court-martial."

"Forget it, Higgs. We were all just doing our job."

"Well, anyway, I just wanted you to know, you and the major have my support if you need it. My guess is, Wilkes and his pals aren't the only ones who might cause trouble."

Logan smirked. "Thanks for the news flash." He stopped himself from taking his frustration out on Higgs. "Just pass on anything you get wind of. This situation's bad enough without us fighting among ourselves." He was about to return to Hans, but Higgs stopped him.

"Do you think they're androids?" he asked, glancing at Hans. When Logan furrowed his brows, Higgs added, "You know, robots? Or maybe they're aliens that have taken our shape to gain our confidence."

Logan didn't want to hear what Higgs thought the aliens wanted to gain their confidence for. "I don't know any more than you do, Higgs, but I'll tell you this much. I'd lay odds that these guys aren't the ones we need to worry about. They're just puppets. What we've got to do is find a way to reach the ones who pull their strings."

Higgs glanced from side to side as if expecting to see an eavesdropper. "If it's aliens we're dealing with, I should be able to help. I've read thousands of science fiction novels, you know."

"Thanks, Higgs," Logan said, giving him a pat on the back. "I'll keep that in mind."

As he made his way back to Hans, Logan rubbed his temples. *Damn!* He was getting a headache. Considering the tension he was holding inside, it wasn't surprising that one was coming on. All he needed now to make his day complete was a killer migraine—a blinding, three-day cluster type ought to about do it. Especially since there probably wasn't an aspirin in the whole friggin' place.

What the hell had possessed him to step forward and help the major? He knew when he did it, he'd regret it. The welfare of the men was no longer his concern. The army had spit him out of its womb and forgotten him, much like his own mother had. But he just hadn't been able to stand there and let an ass like Wilkes get the upper hand.

Don Quixote rides again.

So here he was, back to being the one everybody was counting on to make the right decisions and keep them safe.

Well, almost everybody. Wilkes wasn't counting on him for anything but a hard time. Though even that was something he'd have to live up to.

Then there was Julie. She certainly wouldn't count on him for anything. Not if she could help it. In fact, he'd done such a good job of putting her off, she'd probably refuse to ask him for help even if her life was threatened.

Logan was accustomed to life being one kick in the teeth after another, but this little turn of events sure beat the hell out of anything that had come before, including the court-martial. It was the typical sort of trick fate always played on him. He had been spared from life in one prison, only to find himself being held captive in another in which his wardens were either fairies or aliens.

And the only woman in the entire universe capable of twisting him into knots with nothing more than the sound of her voice was there to make sure he didn't have a moment's peace.

Even a cell at Leavenworth was preferable to a lifetime of being within hearing range of Julie Evans yet knowing he could never touch her the way he did in his dreams.

There had to be a way out of this mess, and if it meant taking charge of the whole damn bunch of misfits and puppet people, he'd just have to do it.

Right after he got over the migraine.

Chapter 4

"Assimilation has begun," the elderly domestic affairs adviser Iris of Mergany announced.

Imperial prefect Parisia of Acameir nodded her approval. "Thank you, Iris. Keep a watch for the next few days until the medicine takes effect. I trust you'll advise me of anything problematical."

"I'm sure I won't need to bother you."

Parisia was not so optimistic. "I hope you're right, but I can't help but be concerned. We've never had so many arrive at once, nor have any previous crossovers been in chains or carrying weapons. Perhaps I'm worrying needlessly, but I will feel better once the medicine has adequately adjusted them." The prefect dismissed Iris and motioned to her daughter, Brianne, who had been standing quietly in the rear of the office awaiting instructions.

Brianne had not been her original choice for the post of first aide, but Parisia was now glad her child had nagged her into giving her the chance to prove herself.

As Brianne gracefully moved to one of the chairs on the other side of the desk, her mother's heart filled with pride. She was reminded of herself two and a half decades ago, just before she had conceived her twins, Brianne and Jason. The only genetic characteristic Brianne had inherited from her sire, Delbert, was the jade coloring of her eyes. Otherwise, she looked very much like her mother—willowy, someone once had said—tall and lean, with ivory skin and hair nearly as light. On the other hand, Jason was nearly a duplicate of Delbert, with his dark hair and angular features.

It had recently become apparent that Brianne had also inherited Parisia's organizational skills and leadership abilities. She was going to make a fine prefect one day.

Parisia gave her daughter the necessary time to seat herself comfortably and arrange her long, flowing caftan, then asked for her opinion of the new group of crossovers.

"I share your concern," Brianne answered without hesitation. "It's been eight years since Earth people were last drawn through the gateway to Heart, and almost a century since any females have arrived. But it's the physical appearance of the males that is most troubling to me. The ones who have come before never seemed so young . . . or so . . . *dangerous*."

Parisia angled her head curiously. "Perhaps they just seem so now that you are older and more aware of the differences between Earth men and men of Heart."

"Perhaps," Brianne conceded. "At any rate, their masculinity will be neutralized very shortly and the size of their bodies will no longer be important."

"Agreed. However, I am seriously considering bringing the ten women to us, or at least separating them from the men."

Brianne gave that some thought, then shook her head. "I believe the cost and complications involved in creating a separate, secure environment for them would be harshly criticized by the opponents to your budget proposal. You know Nadia would never go along with such a radical idea."

Parisia gave a slight grimace. "Nadia will take the opposite stand from me no matter what I recommend. Everyone is aware of that."

"Hmph. Everyone is also aware that she is power hungry and hopes to unseat you one day. Unfortunately, Nadia is not the only concern in this matter. Until we have a chance to observe the female crossovers' behavior to be certain that they do not have the volatile personalities of Earth men, I wouldn't risk integrating them into our society. Our cultures are simply too different for them to make a smooth transition."

"I don't fully agree with that, but I will wait a few weeks before making a decision. In the meantime, I'd like to go over another matter that has been brought to my attention. Did you have a chance to see the report that came in this morning from Delegate Koballa?"

"Not yet," Brianne replied. "I spent most of the morning in the Observation Room, watching the crossovers awaken. Did you know, not even an hour passed before a power struggle occurred?" Her eyes grew wide, and she leaned forward in her chair. "One man actually pushed another, and I believe they might have come to blows if another man hadn't interfered!" Realizing that she had become a bit too animated, she resumed her sedate pose. "I found it very interesting."

Parisia refrained from criticizing her daughter's momentary lapse of composure. She had been a very passionate, active child, and although she was now a mature woman, occasionally that child still broke through the adult veneer. There were times she feared Brianne would never fully overcome her excitable nature, but it didn't seem to interfere with her work, so there was really no reason to medicate her yet.

"It's fortunate that you had the chance to observe their primitive behavior firsthand," Parisia said. "Most of our people have seen only old visual recordings. However, I can assure you that in a few days they will be quite normal and not at all *interesting*."

"That's good. They are just a little frightening in their natural state." Brianne frowned thoughtfully for a moment, then abruptly recalled her mother's earlier question. "I'm sorry. You mentioned a report from Delegate Koballa. She's been at the Interplanetary Health Symposium, right?"

"Yes. She just returned. Here's her summary." Parisia picked up a folder and handed it to Brianne. "You can read the entire contents later, but there was one notation I wanted to discuss with you before I spoke to any members of Parliament." She paused a moment to collect her thoughts. "It has nothing to do with the meetings Koballa went to attend. In fact, she clearly states that it is unsubstantiated rumor."

Parisia watched the expression on her daughter's face change from curiosity to concern, and got to the point.

"Do you recall the legend about the time when Heart had only men as rulers?"

Brianne smiled. "Of course. Mythology is a required subject in primary school."

"Tell me what you remember."

Brianne's expression altered to curiosity again, but she began the tale she had memorized as a child. "Once upon a time, all of Heart was ruled by men. Women were assigned the menial chores such as home caring, food preparation, wardrobe maintenance . . . the sort of functions our men perform for us. But the men of that time were barbarians. They fought with one another over the most trivial matters and abused the women's bodies for sport. One day they were visited by beings from another galaxy." She interrupted her narration and cocked her head. "I can't remember what they were called."

"Velids," Parisia said. "Go on."

"Yes, Velids. According to the legend, they looked like giant centipedes as they exited the ship, but once they saw the humans of Heart, they changed their physical appearance to copy them. Never having heard of amorphodites, who are capable of changing their bodies' shape, the men automatically assumed the aliens posed a lethal threat. Rather than attempt to communicate, the men killed the visitors on sight. Before long, another ship of Velids arrived to avenge their people's deaths. Because Heart men believed women were helpless, they placed them and the children in protective shelters during the brief war."

Brianne rose from her chair and slowly paced the office as she continued:

"When the fighting ended and the women left the shelters, they discovered that most of the male populace was dead and the planet had been decimated. Without the men to restrain them, the women's natural superiority surfaced. They used their innate skills to rebuild the cities and reorganize Heart's culture, with the focus on peace and serenity.

"It was clear that the men's violent instincts were solely responsible for the death and destruction. In the restructured society their behavior was controlled, first by physical restraints, later by medication."

Brianne recalled learning something about experiments with genetic alteration, but the results were so disastrous, further attempts to alter the men permanently had been outlawed. They used only the special medicine thereafter.

"As long as men were required for reproduction, they couldn't be eliminated, but the women soon learned how to accomplish conception without having to subject their bodies to invasion as if they were dumb animals."

She returned to the chair and folded her hands on her lap. "I remember asking you what an invasion was. Your explanation was so upsetting I didn't ask another question for days. Did Koballa learn something new about the reproductive process?"

Parisia hesitated a moment before answering. Someday she would have to have another discussion with Brianne about conception, but not today. "No, dear. It's not that. Koballa's report includes information regarding the possible destruction of a humanoid planet in the Templar System."

"That's light-years away from here. The information, if it was factual, would be ancient by the time news reached us."

"Not necessarily. Koballa states that several cultures represented at the conference have now developed faster-than-light travel. Soon no corner of the universe will be out of reach. If we accept that fact, then we must consider the possibility that the information from the Templar System could be current and accurate."

Brianne looked doubtful. She had to see something to believe it. "How was the planet supposedly destroyed?"

Parisia took a slow breath. "An army of giant worm-like beings, with the ability to change shape, attacked unexpectedly, killed every human and leveled the cities."

"*Velids?*" Brianne asked in a shocked whisper. "But they're mythical creatures."

"What if they're not? What if the legend is true and those beings are still seeking revenge against the human race? With faster-than-light travel, might they return to Heart one day in the near future?"

"Oh, Mother, I hope you're wrong."

"So do I. But it brings up a serious question. What will we do if there really is a threat out there? If not today, tomorrow? We've lived in total peace for thousands of years, as have all the other life forms in this quadrant. We have no weapons, no defenses. There has never been a need for such."

"Surely we could request assistance from outside."

Parisia raised her eyebrows a notch. "Request assistance? From one of the more aggressive, male-dominated planets that we have always shunned? I wouldn't count on them hurrying to our rescue after we've consistently refused to deal with them. No, I believe we would be on our own. My question to you is this. Do you think an unsubstantiated rumor is sufficient for me to go before the Parliament and suggest we alter our constitution to permit the creation of a defense system and the manufacture of weaponry?"

Brianne needed to rise and pace again before answering. "If you go before Parliament with a rumor, you could be ridiculed. Worse, suggesting we change one of the basic laws of our people could get you impeached, and Nadia would lead the move against you. However, if you do nothing and the threat is real, our world will come to an end, and protecting your position will have been futile." She stopped and met Parisia's troubled gaze. "If I were the imperial prefect, I would have to argue for self-protection."

Parisia gave her a sad smile. "Good. Because

that's precisely what I'm going to do. But I feel like I'm walking into a cage of hungry she-wolves."

"When do you plan to talk to Parliament?"

Parisia glanced at the calendar on the wall. "Three days. That should be sufficient time for the new crossovers to be fully assimilated before I introduce any new problems."

She didn't tell Brianne what was bothering her more than suggesting Heart develop a defense system. *If* Parliament could be convinced to change the law, who would design it? Who would implement it? She didn't believe a single female on Heart was capable of killing another being. Only men, in their natural state, had the aggressive traits necessary to wage war, and Heart men had been medicated for so many generations, no one knew if the neutralization could be completely reversed. Even if it could, though, Parisia was certain the women would never agree to expose themselves to male dominance, even if it meant survival of the race.

Nadia of Hinac pretended to listen to the inane gossip of the two women who had waylaid her. Her need to keep them as supporters forced her to be polite and feign interest, though her mind was on a completely different track.

She had spent an hour that morning in the Observation Room watching the new crossovers awaken. Some of the observers with her had been repulsed by the barbaric behavior of the Earth men. Others, like the imperial prefect's brat, were intrigued, in the way a child might study an ant colony.

Nadia's reaction was neither of those, though no one else could tell. Outwardly she showed disgust and spoke of how relieved she would be once the medication took effect. Inwardly her pulse raced, her stomach fluttered, and she had to clench her thighs to ease the itch between them.

It had begun when she received news of their arrival. So many of them at once. Some in chains. Some with weapons. The danger was so close she could taste it.

She had given in to the temptation of watching them being taken care of in the hospital, knowing that later she would be obsessed by visions of their large masculine, nude bodies. Tortured by fantasies of how she could use them to satisfy her secret needs—needs that women weren't supposed to have. But the itch had already begun, and she was never able to resist the dark pleasure that followed it.

At a very young age Nadia had learned that the itch was not normal and shouldn't be mentioned, not even to one's own mother. The result of revealing an unhealthy interest in the male gender was medication. It took only a few doses for Nadia to realize she didn't like having her personal strength nullified by the medicine. After that she kept her curiosity secret and became the perfect Heart woman—at least in public.

In private she experimented with different ways to appease the itch. Before long she discovered that she could increase the intensity of the satisfaction by prolonging the build-up. Sometimes she would make herself wait all day before giving in to it. She would ease the throbbing a little by crossing her legs or squirming in a chair, but she would hold off the final burst of sensation until she was nearly crazed with need. That way the sweet darkness was often so powerful, it would last half the night.

There were times when the itch came on by itself, but more often it followed thoughts about men. Like every schoolgirl, she had learned the facts about the male species and why they had to be medicated. In their natural state they posed a severe danger to women. Their strength, aggressive nature, and especially their male anatomy were all structured to dominate.

While the other girls were shivering with distaste, Nadia had trembled with excitement. The characteristics of men that Heart women were so adamant about controlling became the trigger for Nadia's secret fantasies.

Throughout Heart, men were forbidden by law to touch a woman without her permission, and proper behavior dictated that such permission should be granted only in extreme circumstances. Thus Nadia could only imagine feeling their forceful hands on her body, touching all her private, ticklish places.

The day she had learned how animals reproduced and equated the activity to humans, the itch had been so demanding, she had been forced to seek the privacy of the school lavatory to relieve it.

During one of her private experiments she discovered the pleasure she could generate by pushing the hard, rounded handle of her hairbrush in and out of her womanpiece, and her fantasies took on a new dimension.

While medicated, Heart men did not suffer from the malady that made their manpiece swell and harden while their minds emptied of everything except thoughts of relief. While medicated, a man was unable to invade a woman's body with his mighty weapon, even if he was given permission.

Nadia became so obsessed with the idea of using a man's body to stop the itch, one day she ordered her mother's personal servant to remove his clothing so that she could inspect his anatomy. Her examination clearly made him uncomfortable, but his manpiece failed to enlarge, even when she pulled on it.

Since men were not permitted to attend school, he had never been taught the lessons Nadia had. He hadn't known what it was she had expected from him, but he could see he had somehow disappointed her and had been willing to accept whatever punishment she saw fit.

The rush of power she had experienced in response to his submissive attitude launched a whole new series of experiments for her. While the medication tempered a man's masculinity, it also enhanced his need to provide useful service.

After that day she'd spent long hours imagining unique ways a servant could be put to use and ingenious ways to punish him if his performance was less than satisfactory. Unfortunately, she was unable to enact any of her fantasies without risk of being medicated herself.

Though daughters normally remained in their mothers' homes all their lives, Nadia found the arrangement suffocating. By the time she reached her thirtieth year, she decided she needed a home of her own. With her freedom came privacy, and she selected her personal servant with great care. Fulton was completely inexperienced, but especially pleasing to her eye and anxious to be of service. She quickly guaranteed his loyalty to her by utilizing his sperm to fertilize her egg.

Following the birth of their daughter, Chloe, child care was added to Fulton's responsibilities. Only after Nadia was certain of his attachment to the child did she begin demanding more unusual services from him.

As politically ambitious as she was, she had to be very protective of her reputation, which meant she had to be certain Fulton would never speak to anyone about the special services she required of him. Technically he was still her employee, and though he didn't have all the same privileges as a woman, he had the right to change employers if he was unhappy, or felt he was being mistreated. Another employer, particularly one who was a supporter of Parisia, might encourage him to gossip about her, and that could spell disaster.

Unwilling to give up her secret pleasures despite the risk of discovery, Nadia found ways to bind Fulton to her. Through trial and error she learned that he thrived on words of praise about his work and would do absolutely anything for a few minutes of being petted by her. If she criticized his work or ignored him entirely, he would be desperate to make it up to her. Only a handful of times had she caused him physical pain, but the threat of it was always there.

Then, of course, she made sure he knew that if he ever left her, he would never be permitted to see Chloe again.

All things considered, their association had gone along rather smoothly for the last five years. But recently she'd become bored with the predictability of his behavior, and had begun thinking of hiring another young, trainable man.

If only there was a way she could acquire one of the Earth men! Several of them had been especially appealing to her, and the dark-skinned men were so different from any she'd seen before. Then there was that tall, dark-haired man with a scarred face, who would undoubtedly be the lead character in her fantasies for weeks to come.

For now, however, Fulton and his limited abilities were all she could count on to ease the itch that the Earth men had caused.

As soon as she entered her home, she let him know the mood she was in by her greeting. "Fulton! Where are you, you lazy creature?"

"In the kitchen," he replied. As she strode into that room, he gave her a hesitant smile. "I've made your favorite sweet to go with your tea."

"I don't want tea," she snapped. "I called to tell you I was coming home for a bath, not tea. If you don't start paying better attention when I give you instructions, I am going to replace you. Do you understand me?"

Fulton frowned and bowed his head. "I'm sorry, Nadia. You didn't say how long it would take for you to get home, and I was worried that the bath water would cool if I prepared it too soon. I'll get it ready immediately." He took a step, then paused and looked back at the teakettle. "Shall I pour you some tea since—"

"I said I don't want tea, you dolt! *Go* before I lose my patience entirely." As Fulton hurried from the kitchen, Nadia's pulse quickened. He had been on the verge of tears. In fact, he was probably in her dressing room sniveling away while the water ran. He was primed to do anything she ordered, and she was aching for much more than the usual bath. There probably wouldn't be a better time to try out her new creation.

As she considered how she could introduce it to Fulton, she broke off a chunk of the sweet he had baked for her and placed it in her mouth. Rich chocofine superbly blended with black shamberry melted on her tongue. Though Fulton was beginning to bore her in some ways, his culinary skills assured him a permanent position in her household no matter how often she threatened to get rid of him.

She finished the sweet and headed for her bath. She had designed the spacious dressing room with her unique needs in mind. The walls and closet doors were mirrored, and the floor was covered with plush black carpeting. On one side of the room was an oversize black tub with gold fixtures, and on the other side was a gold velvet chaise wide enough for two people to lay on at the same time. The few women who had seen the room questioned such extravagance for something so private. They preferred to show off their luxuries. But Nadia had always been a little different from other women.

As she entered the dressing room, she smelled the perfumed oil rising with the steam. Fulton stood next to the tub, awaiting her. As usual, he had undressed so that his clothing would not get wet while he assisted her. She gave his ample body a lingering look. He was taller, heavier, and broader across the shoulders than she, but he lacked the hardness that she noticed about the Earth men. Looking at his short dark hair, she decided to focus her attention on that feature and pretend he was the scarred crossover that had fascinated her.

"You may remove my robe," she stated in a harsh tone to remind him he had yet to make up for his earlier failure to please.

In the mirrors she watched him move around her, carefully drawing back the hood of her robe and untying the bow at her throat without touching any part of her. With the same caution he undid the fastenings down the front of the garment and slipped it off her body.

As he hung up the robe, she reminded herself that the longer she could put off the physical contact, the better the reward would be. "Now brush my hair out. Slowly."

One at a time, he removed the pins that kept

her waist-length black hair wrapped in a braided crown around her head. With unhurried strokes he brushed it out until it hung around her like a satin cape.

Nadia was always fascinated by her own transformation from civilized woman to primitive creature. "That's enough. You may take my slip and briefs. Carefully."

She hadn't needed to say that. She knew he would take the utmost care not to touch her flesh until she gave him the specific order to do so. As he removed her briefs, she wondered if he noticed how damp her crotch was today and whether his dull mind ever figured out what that meant. She doubted it.

"You may touch my hand to help me into the tub. And make sure my hair doesn't get wet."

As she submerged her body in the deep water, Fulton placed a pillow behind her head and draped her hair over the back of the tub. Normally the hot, perfumed water would instantly start relaxing her, but today the itch was too strong to be calmed so easily. Fulton dipped a washcloth into the water and held it out to her.

"I'm quite worn out today. You do it." He pressed the cloth to one of her feet, but she kicked it away. "Not with the cloth. Use your hands. The way I showed you before. Remember, the doctor said I have poor circulation and should be vigorously massaged to improve the condition." She closed her eyes and smothered a sigh as his fingers closed over the toes of her one foot and squeezed. It would take some time for him to get to her abdomen, but he had learned the routine well, and it would be worth the wait.

One leg, up to the hip joint. The other leg. One arm, then the other. Her nipples were tightly puckered long before his palms pressed over them. He kneaded her breasts and rolled the nipples until her breath came in gasps. "Go on," she whispered, and his fingers slid down over her stomach and into her womanpiece.

Instantly she felt the first streak of pleasure and gripped the sides of the tub. "More," she said, spreading her thighs so that he could fit his whole hand over her. "Faster," she demanded, gyrating her hips in the opposite direction of his motions. When the explosion came, she bit her lip to keep from crying out. It would not do to let him know how very well he had served.

She rested in the tub awhile, but the itch was still nagging at her. This was definitely the day to teach Fulton a new trick.

She gave him permission to help her out of the tub and towel her off. While he was on his knees, drying her feet, she ran her fingers through his hair. His hopeful gaze leaped to hers. "Did I hurt your feelings before, Fulton?"

He lowered his eyes again. "I deserved your criticism. I wasn't attentive."

She stroked his cheek and neck and noticed how he angled his head for more. Continuing to pet his face, hair, and shoulders, she softened her voice to complement the gentle touch. "But you usually are, and I shouldn't have been so stern with you." She eased him forward just enough to tickle his nose with her pubic hair, and he giggled in response.

"I tasted the sweet you made me. It was excellent. You really are very good most of the time. You can't help being slow about some things. I should be more patient." His lips parted, and she felt his hot puffs of breath against her womanpiece. A little more attention and he wouldn't question anything she ordered, no matter how outrageous it was.

"Would you like to rest on the chaise with me?" His gaze darted to the golden lounge, then back to her. She didn't know what he liked more, her petting or the feel of velvet against his skin. To give him both at once was the closest he could come to ecstasy.

She considered reminding him that this was a very special privilege that he would never be granted from another employer. But he knew well that, since it was so distasteful for a woman to touch or be touched by a man, her gift to him was extremely rare and should be cherished. His payment for the privilege would continue to be silent loyalty and total devotion.

"Before we rest, though, there is another service I require . . . something you've never done before, but it was prescribed by the doctor to . . . stimulate my circulation from within. Remain on your knees while I get what I need."

She opened one of the closets and brought out a drawstring bag. As she withdrew her creation from the pouch and saw the bewildered expression on Fulton's face, she nearly changed her mind.

What she was intending was terribly daring. Then she felt the insistent beating at the base of her abdomen and decided the risk would be worth it.

She had no way of knowing what a swollen manpiece looked like, but having once seen a pair of horses copulating, she assumed it wasn't much different for humans. With a little ingenuity, some leather strips, and her favorite ceramic hairbrush handle, she had made an artificial manpiece for Fulton.

As she knelt in front of him and strapped the invention around his hips, his expression turned fearful, but she scraped a thumbnail over his nipple and glanced purposefully at the lounge, and he forgot any objection he might have had.

Positioning herself on her knees before him, she thought to imitate what the horses had done. Fulton shifted his hips back and forth as she instructed, but the result brought her little satisfaction.

It was better when she made him lie on his back and mounted the piece from atop, yet she still required manual stimulation to feel the pleasure.

Certain there had to be a way to make her creation work properly, she tried several different positions before she found one that sent a tremor through her. Symbolically, his lying on top of her was completely unacceptable, but physically, his lower body rubbing so intimately against her was extremely titillating. Fulton required more practice—that much was clear—but this new method of seeking pleasure was worth a little effort.

She held off the mind-numbing release as long as possible, but eventually it overwhelmed her. She was so pleased with Fulton and her invention, she spent much longer than usual with him on the chaise. Her fingers tickled and scratched his flesh until he whimpered with a mixture of pain and pleasure. She toyed with his private parts in ways she had never thought to do before.

The expression on his face was one of excruciating pain, but the shivery bumps on his skin revealed an appreciation for his torment. Nadia wallowed in the raw power his torture stirred in her, and the itch started up all over again.

Suddenly his entire body was racked with shudders, and a tiny drop of clear fluid seeped from his manpiece. If she didn't know it was impossible, she might have thought he just had a sexual experience.

She was about to order him to massage her one more time when she noticed he had gotten teary-eyed again. His weepiness was really becoming quite tiresome. Waving him away, she didn't bother to conceal her annoyance. "Get up, you fool. Go fix my tea now. I'll have it in the sitting room."

The moment he left, she proceeded to take care of the itch herself. Visions of the Earth men filled her mind, and she wondered how close Fulton and her invention had come to the real thing. As delicious waves of sensation flooded through her, she knew she would never be truly satisfied until she could make the comparison firsthand.

All she had to do was come up with a reason why she should be permitted to make contact with one of the crossovers, preferably the big, dangerous-looking man with the scars.

Chapter 5

Julie stretched and wiggled her tired fingers. After two hours of husking corn, the boring task was finally completed. It might have been less tedious if she could have kept Duncan talking, but he had nothing more to say. In fact, it was unnaturally quiet throughout the kitchen. Normally her nurses were so talkative, she had to hush them.

She got up and walked over to Robin and Sunny. They had been helping the dishwasher, but that chore was finished as well.

"It's too quiet," Robin murmured the moment Julie sat down with them.

"I know," Julie replied. "Duncan said these men don't talk much, but what about our people?" She gave it some thought. "Maybe everyone's suffering from post-traumatic shock."

Sunny nodded, her usual smiling face clouded with worry. "I know I am. I keep thinking this must be a bad dream, but I can't make myself wake up. Nothing we've heard makes any sense."

Before Julie could respond, Kara and Darcy joined them. As Darcy sat down beside Julie, she asked, "So, how do we get out of here?"

"I wish I knew. Duncan insists that no one has ever left here unless they die of old age."

"Swell," Robin said. "But I can't buy that. I absolutely refuse to live out my days like some hippie in a sixties commune."

"At least the communal bathroom facilities are more up to date than this kitchen," Sunny said, trying to find a bright side.

Kara nudged Darcy and made a face that prompted Darcy to speak. "We want to go home, Captain. Our families are expecting to pick us all up at airports today and tomorrow. They're going to think we're dead."

Julie patted Darcy's hand and put on her most reassuring face. "We'll find a way. These old men may have been cowed by whoever's in control of this place, but that doesn't mean we have to be."

As the women tried to console one another about their loved ones waiting for them at home, Julie fell silent. She had loved ones too—sort of. Surely they would miss her a little.

She had been only three when her young parents divorced, and she had very little recollection of that time. Her memories began when she was in grade school. Both parents had remarried and had children with their second spouses. Julie lived with her mother's new family during the school year, but most holidays and summers she stayed with her father's family.

Some of her friends at school were envious of her because she had two families and always received twice as many gifts. She never admitted how envious she was of them. Yes, she had double everything, and was treated well by both families, but she was always the outsider—the stepdaughter or stepsister. She often felt more like a visitor than a member of either group.

Through the years she did her best to make everyone love her and appreciate her presence. As the oldest child, she automatically took on greater responsibilities. Taking care of the young ones was what prompted her to go into pediatric nursing.

But nothing she did ever changed the fact that she didn't really belong in either home. She dreamed that someday she would have a family and home all her own.

Last year she had finally been able to purchase a cozy town house. As for a family, she had given up that dream. If Mr. Right hadn't popped into her life by this time, there wasn't much chance of it happening in the future.

A rumble of wagon wheels outside alerted the kitchen staff that the field workers had returned. Julie and the others pitched in to help fill plates of food while the incoming men lined up at the water pump to wash. Since there was a shortage of tables and chairs inside, a lot of people carried their dinners outside and sat on the grass. When Julie saw Major Cookson heading out the door, she got her own dinner and followed him. Robin stayed right behind her.

"Would you mind if I joined you, Major?" Julie asked once she caught up with him.

"Not at all, but please call me Geoffrey," he said pleasantly.

She smiled in return. "And I'm Julie. This is my friend Robin."

His hands being full, he simply nodded his head. "How do you do?"

Robin smiled and held his gaze. "I do very well, thank you. And how do you do?"

Geoffrey's only response to her obvious flirtation was to clear his throat and turn away. "Shall we sit over there?" he asked, looking at a spot under a tree. As they seated themselves, he caught sight of Logan coming out of the big house. "McKay!" he called. "Over here."

Logan turned toward Geoffrey's voice, but the squiggly black lines in front of his eyes blurred his vision. He just hoped he could find the latrine before he heaved his guts all over the ground. Suddenly a light flickered in his left eye, and he knew the migraine had reached its next level. Any second now he would feel the pickax lodge itself in the left half of his head.

Julie watched Logan sway and bump into the wall of the house. A moment later the glass he was carrying slipped from his grasp. Without hesitation she rose from the ground and started toward him.

"Sergeant McKay?" When he continued staggering around the corner toward the back of the house, she picked up her pace. "Logan! What's wrong?"

Whether it was the pounding migraine or the sound of her voice saying his name, he couldn't take another step. Closing his eyes, he leaned back against the wall and slid to the ground.

"Are you ill?" Julie asked, dropping to her knees beside him. His eyes were squinted shut and his upper lip was dotted with perspiration. She placed her palm on his forehead to check for fever, but he jerked away from her hand.

That abrupt movement caused him to groan aloud and press his hands against his temples.

"Headache?" she asked softly.

"Migraine," he whispered. "Just leave me alone."

Julie clucked her tongue, and continued to speak in a gentle voice. "I will *not* leave you alone. Is there anything that helps?"

His voice remained a harsh whisper. "Medicine was in my bag . . . wherever that is. Aspirin helps a little. And ice."

"Hmmm. I'll go find Duncan and see what he's got. Will you be okay here for a few minutes?"

He didn't bother to answer. It was taking all his concentration not to throw up on himself. The setting sun was drilling a hole through his eyelids, but the effort it would take to find shade was beyond him. He just crouched there, helpless as an infant.

It seemed that Julie had been gone quite a while, but he knew from previous experience, she'd be back. She couldn't resist fussing over a man incapacitated by pain.

"Logan?"

That voice! He covered his ears to shut her out.

"I need you to get up and walk a little ways with me." She grasped him by the arm and tried to lift, but he didn't budge. "Don't be stubborn. There's a tent set up for you with a cot and lots of soft pillows. It's dark in there. I couldn't get any ice, but Duncan gave me a powder that might help."

The pillows and darkness did it. Logan mustered sufficient strength to open his right eye and pull himself upright. She hadn't been completely honest about it being only a little ways. Despite his limited vision he noted a number of soldiers erecting tents in the area. Each thud of a hammer forcing a stake into the ground was like a pin being poked into his brain, but he was in no condition to stop them.

Julie led him away from the construction and past the small wooden shelters to a tent that had been set up by itself. She held the flap open as he entered, then closed it except for a sliver after she was inside.

The simple act of eliminating the brilliant sunset went a long way toward relief for Logan.

"Sit down on the cot, but don't lie back yet," Julie ordered. "There's a bucket there if you need it. My stepmother used to get migraines that made her nauseous, so don't try to be a tough guy if your stomach's queasy."

Whether it was her words or the sight of the bucket, his stomach overruled his mind. When he was finished, she handed him a glass of water to rinse his mouth, then removed the bucket. Efficient as always.

He started to lie down, but she stopped him again. "Wait. Take the powder first." As she mixed it with the water, she explained, "Duncan says this is all they have. It doesn't sound very strong, but it tastes like ground aspirin. I figured it's worth a try."

While he drained the glass, she arranged the pile of pillows so his head and shoulders would stay elevated. "Okay, lie back now and try to relax."

He might have been able to do that if she hadn't sat on the cot next to him and slipped her hands behind his neck. Instantly his fingers clamped around her wrists and held. "What are you doing?" he asked through gritted teeth.

"There are pressure points in your head that will release your endorphins, which are natural pain-killers. Would you rather suffer or let me touch you?"

He groaned and released her wrists. What he couldn't tell her was that tolerating her touch caused another kind of suffering. He groaned again as her fingers worked some kind of magic, pressing and rotating two spots at the base of his skull. From there she went to the points behind his ears, the sides of his head, then on to his face.

The pain was still there, but the sharp edge had been slightly dulled, making room in his mind for more awareness of her. He didn't need to open his eyes to see her. She was a permanent fixture in his memory. He knew he should send her away, but the migraine and her gentle treatment had sapped his willpower.

He relaxed a bit more as she massaged the tension out of his neck and shoulders. Now he felt her hip pressed against his, how her forearms brushed lightly over his chest as her hands manipulated his muscles. His fingers curled into his palms to keep from stroking her back and urging her closer until he—

He reminded himself that he was allowed to do that sort of thing only in his fantasies. This was real life, and it wasn't personal. She was a nurse caring for a patient, just as before. Nothing else.

Julie could see by his clenched jaw that he was still in pain, though somewhat more comfortable. A wicked thought briefly crossed her mind that he probably deserved whatever pain he was in, but she immediately banished it. Who or what he was didn't matter at the moment—only that he was ill and needed her attention.

It occurred to her that she could massage his neck and shoulders better without his shirt in the way, but she cancelled that idea. As unreasonable as it was, in spite of everything, she was still having a hard time ignoring the fact that Logan was a man. He was just so big, so hard-muscled . . . so masculine.

Of all the men she had treated, most of whom she had seen completely naked, he was the only one who had ever made her want to forget that he was a patient. For that reason she had always been extra careful when she changed the dressing on the wound in his thigh and *never* helped him bathe. Somehow that would have been too intimate with him.

Forcing herself to think back to when her step-mother had migraines, another technique came to her. She moved her fingers from his neck to his hands so suddenly, his eyelids flew open.

For several seconds his gaze snared hers, and

the desperate need she saw in his eyes stunned her. But she had seen that look in his eyes once before, and it had turned out to be false. She steeled herself against that look by recalling his most recent rude remarks to her. She might be obliged to *take* care of him, but that didn't mean she had to care.

She lowered her gaze as she massaged his wrists, then the palms and backs of his hands. To distract herself more than him, she explained, "Sometimes by stimulating the circulation in the extremities, the pressure in the head can be decreased."

Yes, he thought as he closed his eyes again. He definitely felt the blood abandoning his brain and collecting in his lower parts.

Robin picked up two pillows and a stack of linens and headed for where she had last seen Geoffrey.

When Julie unexpectedly had left her alone with him, she had thought it was a nice bit of luck. Then the oddest thing happened. She couldn't think of anything to say. Not even one funny joke to entertain him. And he hadn't helped the situation any, sitting there with his perfect posture, eating dinner with his perfect manners. As soon as his plate was clean, he excused himself, very politely, and set about organizing work details to get everyone settled for the night.

That was when she realized the only way she was going to get to know the major better was by working with him, and she did so want to know him better.

After circling the big house, she finally spotted him helping Willy erect a tent.

"Hi, Willy," she said cheerfully. "Did you get linens yet?"

Willy grinned. "Sure did. But if you run into the guys distributing cots, I could use one here."

"You got it. Geoffrey, do you need anything for your tent? If you point it out, I'll be glad to make sure you're set up."

Geoffrey smiled politely. "I haven't gotten to mine yet, but thank you for the offer." He returned his attention to the stake he was pounding into the ground.

Robin wasn't willing to give up that easily. "In that case, just point out where you'd like your tent to be, and I'll see to it that it's set up. I have nothing else to do. The linens are all distributed."

He finished setting the stake and stood up. "All right, then." He looked around the area a moment. "I think it would be best if I was in the midst of the men. Any place you pick will be fine."

Robin nodded and took a few steps away when he spoke again.

"Robin? A moment please."

She turned and faced him with a soft smile that she knew disarmed the average male.

Geoffrey's gaze darted away from hers, and he cleared his throat. "I, uh, was wondering if we should check on Julie and McKay."

Robin arched an eyebrow at him. "Check on them?"

He covered his mouth and coughed as if it would help him get his words out. "Yes, um, I mean, he seemed ill, and I sensed some antagonism between them, and—"

"And nothing, Major," Robin interrupted defensively. "Julie is a dedicated nurse who would take care of Attila the Hun if he was in pain. If anyone can get your bodyguard back at your side, it's her." She thought she saw Geoffrey's fair cheekbones pinken and regretted her choice of words. "I'm sorry—"

"It's quite all right," he said quietly. "I didn't make myself clear. I was concerned about your friend's welfare . . . being alone with him for such a long time."

Now it was her turn to blush. "Oh. Well, there's no need to worry. Julie can handle the worst of them. And believe me, she has."

"She does seem very capable."

Robin laughed. "If the war had gone on any longer, she probably would have made general!" His smile seemed more genuine this time, so she hoped he had forgiven her rash comment. "Well, I guess I'll go see about your tent now."

For several seconds Geoffrey simply stood there, watching Robin walk away. Slowly he refilled his lungs with the air her nearness had stolen from him. She wasn't a woman. She was a fantasy come to life. If she had been homely, he could have conversed with her easily. Instead he had been tongue-tied, as he always got around beautiful women. And Robin Pascal was undoubtedly the most beautiful woman he had ever seen, which made her the most dangerous to his well-being.

"Geoffrey!"

He turned to see Julie hurrying toward him. "What's wrong? Is McKay—"

"No, no," she said, waving her hand quickly. "He'll be fine, eventually. He has a bad migraine, though, and from what he told me, without his medicine it could last for days."

"Days?"

Julie nodded. "But it's not necessary. Duncan gave me some medicinal powder they use for minor discomfort. He said that in cases when the powder isn't enough, the injured or sick person is sent to the fairies for treatment."

"Yes. I was told the person goes into the barn and comes out cured, but with no recollection of how it happened."

"Right. It also sounds like the fastest route to whoever's in control here. So, why not test it ourselves . . . with Sergeant McKay? Who knows how long it might be before someone else falls sick?"

Geoffrey rubbed his chin. "If he was in good enough shape to defend himself, I wouldn't think twice about sending him into unknown territory, but under the circumstances . . ."

"McKay already volunteered," Julie said, putting a quick end to Geoffrey's vacillation. "In fact, as soon as I mentioned Duncan's fairies to him, he came up with the suggestion himself. Not only does he want to find out what's going on here, he said he'd try anything that would get rid of the migraine."

The expression on Geoffrey's face made it clear that he hated having to make the decision, but he did it anyway. "All right. I'll get McKay and help him to the barn while you find Duncan."

Ten minutes later, the four of them were standing in the open doorway of the tack room at the back of the huge barn.

"How does it work?" Julie asked Duncan.

"He just goes inside, closes the door, and tells them what's ailing him."

"Tells who?" Geoffrey asked.

Duncan almost looked exasperated. "The fairies, of course."

"You mean, you can see them when you're in there?"

"No. They're invisible. Like the wall."

"What if—" Logan began, then pressed his temples to shut out the excruciating pain uttering those two words had caused. Taking a slow breath and maintaining the pressure, he tried again. "What if someone goes in with me?"

Duncan shook his head. "They don't help the sick person unless he's alone and the door's locked tight from the inside." His smile faded as an old memory came to him. "Tried that myself once. A long time ago."

"Okay," Logan said, stepping into the room. "Let's get on with it."

As Geoffrey and Julie backed away, Duncan said, "Just throw the bolt on the door and say your problem out loud."

"We'll wait for you right here," Geoffrey added.

Although Logan thought the idea of telling a bunch of saddles and harnesses that he had a migraine was completely ridiculous, he locked the door, turned around, and voiced his complaint. When nothing happened immediately, he sat on the floor to wait. It was all he could do to keep from closing his eyes, but he didn't want to miss whatever was coming despite the pain.

Several minutes later, a hissing sound, like air being let out of a tire, drew his attention upward, but it stopped before he could discern what had caused it.

The ping of the transmitter next to Nadia's bed surprised her. It was rare for her to receive a call in the evening. She touched the red button on the top of the small white box. "Hello?"

"This is Simone in Observation."

Nadia's attention perked up. "Yes?"

"By coincidence, not long after you called, something occurred."

Though Nadia was tapping her fingernails impatiently on the table beside her, she replied with only slight interest. "Can you tell me about it?"

After a slight hesitation Simone spoke again. "Not really. Too many ears, if you know what I mean. I get off in half an hour. Why don't you come by for a visit?"

"That sounds fine. See you shortly." Nadia touched the red button again, then bounded from the bed to her closet. She didn't bother to call Fulton to help her dress. She needed to hurry, and he didn't know the meaning of the word.

What could possibly have happened to prompt Simone's call so soon? She had called the woman earlier and requested that she be kept up to date

regarding the new crossovers. Nadia had insinu-
ated that there could be a problem that might reflect badly on Parisia, and any small occurrence
could be important. Fortunately, Simone was one
of the women who believed that Nadia would eventually be in a position of great power, and would
personally benefit later if she proved ingratiating
enough in the meantime.

Unfortunately, Simone was nearly as ambitious
as Nadia herself, which could eventually become
a problem, especially when Simone had a natural
advantage. Nadia was tall, large-boned, dark-haired
and dark-complected, with a prominent nose that
openly proclaimed her hawklike disposition. Simone was petite and fair with tiny ringlets of
honey-colored hair framing an innocent face. She
was femininity and grace personified, the ideal of
every Heart woman.

Nadia managed to reach the Observation Room
as Simone was signing out for her break, but she
still had to wait a few more minutes until they
walked out of earshot of the relief operator.

"One of the crossovers came in for medical
treatment," Simone said in a conspiratorial tone,
even though no one was around.

"Male or female?" Nadia asked in the same
voice.

"Male. Rather dangerous-looking, too."

"Oh?" Nadia's interest increased another notch.
"Can you describe him?" As soon as Simone
began, Nadia was positive it was the same man
she had been intrigued by that morning. "What
was the problem?"

"Headache, he said. He did look uncomfortable."

"Were normal procedures followed?"

Simone nodded. "He was anesthetized and taken to the sanatorium. I happen to have a friend who's on duty there tonight. If you're interested, I'm sure she wouldn't mind filling us in on his condition and treatment."

Nadia managed to conceal her excitement beneath an indifferent façade. "I have nothing better to do this evening."

At the sanatorium, Simone's friend, Olympia, informed them that the man's headache was caused by a severe chemical imbalance in his brain, and though there was no way of determining what had caused it, the medic was able to correct the problem. She could not be certain, however, that the imbalance would not reoccur. As a precaution, vital signs and brain activity were being monitored for two more hours before returning him to the commune.

"He is unconscious, isn't he?" Nadia asked.

"Of course," Olympia replied.

"Would it be possible for me to get a look at him?" Nadia asked as casually as possible.

The woman pressed a key on the numerical board in front of her, then turned the monitor toward Nadia and Simone.

Nadia inhaled sharply as she stared at the screen. It *was* him, just as she had suspected. "You were right, Simone. He does appear to be extremely dangerous."

"There's no need to worry," Olympia said. "His room is completely secure."

"Thank the sun for that," Nadia said, pretending to be greatly relieved. Actually, she was racking her brain to come up with an excuse to get into that room. After her experiment with Fulton that afternoon, her curiosity about the Earth men was increasing by the hour. But no reasonable explanation came to her. After a few more seconds of studying the image of the man's body, she had no choice but to leave unsatisfied.

"Thank you for your help, Olympia. Perhaps I'll be able to return a favor one day in the future. Simone, I'll speak to you later." With a formal nod to each of the women, she headed back home.

Somehow she was going to gain possession of that man. Regardless of the danger he posed, she wanted him before the medicine completely stripped away his masculine qualities. Based on his size and the dosage he should be consuming daily, she estimated that she had three days at the most to come up with a viable scheme and implement it.

After that the scarred man would be as mellow and impotent as Fulton.

Chapter 6

The click of the bolt being pulled back on the tack room door instantly drew Julie and Geoffrey to their feet. Robin, who had brought Julie's uneaten dinner, then stayed for the vigil, remained on the floor until Logan actually appeared.

Julie could see he felt better even before he spoke. His usual bored expression was back.

"Headache's gone," Logan said as he walked up to them. "But I have no idea what happened to me."

"Think, man," Geoffrey prompted. "There has to be something. You were in there for four hours."

Logan shook his head. "I was awake and miserable one minute, then I was waking up without a headache the next. I don't even remember falling asleep, but I obviously did."

"Any kind of aftereffects?" Julie asked.

"No," Logan answered. "In fact, I feel like I just had a great night's sleep."

Robin glanced at Julie. "Maybe it's some kind of mind control."

"Whatever it is," Geoffrey said, "we don't know anything more then we did before—that someone with advanced technology is in control here, and this barn is some sort of way station between them and the farm."

Logan looked back at the tack room and frowned. "I think we can assume they're keeping tabs on us too. I'd say the first step should be to tear this building apart."

"Right," Geoffrey responded. "Considering the number of mouths there are to feed, we'll have to continue to do a fair share of the work, but a few less hands won't matter. In the morning your team can concentrate on the barn. I'll put my team on examining the wall."

"And keep the women in the kitchen all day?" Robin asked in a falsely sweet tone. "I don't think so."

Julie spoke before Geoffrey could reply. "If I might make a suggestion, it might be best to rotate chores. Everyone's going to want to feel they're contributing to an escape plan."

"Quite right," Geoffrey said. "Preparing a rotation schedule will be the first order of business in the morning."

"With my help," Robin amended. "If that's okay with you, Julie."

Julie gave the major a chance to object, but he only cleared his throat. "That will be fine. And now, if I don't get a little sleep, I won't be much good for any kind of chore."

The others agreed that there was nothing more to be accomplished that night. As they walked out of the barn, a star-studded sky lit their path, and the rustle of leaves was the only sound in the air.

Everyone had apparently given in to fatigue. Just before they split up, Logan asked, "Could I have a word with you, Captain?"

Julie gave Robin a sign to give her a minute.

"Come on, Geoffrey," Robin said with a smile. "I'll show you where I put your new home, then I'll come back to guide Julie to ours."

Julie grew tense the moment they walked away, leaving her alone with Logan. While he was ill, she could forget about the fact that he was a murderer and a traitor to his country. But he wasn't ill now, and she was much too aware of how much bigger he was. It seemed as though he sensed her nervousness, for he just stood there looking at her, as if daring her to run away. She made herself stay perfectly still and meet his gaze. And when he stepped closer, it took all her courage to stand her ground and not show the slightest trace of fear.

Slowly he extended his right hand toward her. "I just wanted to say thank you," he said in a low voice.

It took her another moment to realize that he was only trying to shake her hand. By the time she did, he had withdrawn his hand and walked away. She hadn't meant to be rude. His gesture had simply been a shock. It was completely out of character for him to say thank you for anything.

"Sergeant McKay?"

He stopped and looked back at her.

"You're very welcome."

His response was a casual salute.

"He's a strange one, isn't he?" Robin said, coming up behind Julie.

Julie turned and shrugged. "He was a patient of mine once. I didn't understand him then either."

For fear of disturbing anyone, they kept silent as Robin led the way to their tent. All of the women and most of the men were bunking two or three to a tent, partly for a sense of companionship and partly because there were only half as many tents as there were people. The caretakers must have assumed they would sleep in pairs. There was probably some sort of clue in that, but she was too tired to figure it out.

A candle lantern burning inside the tent allowed Julie to see what Robin had accomplished while she was with Logan. Their cots were made up and a few changes of clothes were stowed beneath each. Since they were relatively close to several other tents, they kept their voices to a whisper.

After Julie thanked Robin for setting them up, she said, "Considering the unreality of this whole situation, we're fairly well settled in."

"Yeah. When we get back we can all send thank-you notes to the Pentagon for training us to adapt so well."

Julie pulled off her shoes and examined one. It was stretchy, like a one-size-fits-all slipper sock, but the expandable sole was made of a harder, rubbery substance that was similar to the bottom of a sneaker. "Whoever our caretakers are, they're quite ingenious."

"About some things," Robin amended. "About others they're practically prehistoric. If they can heal a man with severe burns, why do they need to barter for food? Why have a semi-modern lavatory but a kitchen from pioneer days?"

"Good questions. Now I have one for you. If the men we met today didn't have to work the farm or prepare food the old-fashioned way, what would they do all day?"

Robin gave it some thought, then said, "I think we can rule out socializing. They barely talk to each other. Maybe they'd just sit and stare at the green sky like a bunch of zombies."

Julie shook her head. "I don't know. They seem to take pride in working, and no one I saw today tried to shirk their responsibilities. That in itself is odd."

Robin laughed. "Yeah. That many men and not even one goof-off. Back to Higgs's theory that they're all androids."

Julie gave a sigh and lay down on her cot. "We'd better get some sleep while we can. Who knows what hour the sun rises in this place."

Robin blew out the candle and settled between the soft sheets. "Mmmm. Maybe I'll get lucky and this will all turn out to be a weird dream."

Julie was about to respond when several voices shouting obscenities broke the stillness outside. As she and Robin quickly pulled their shoes back on, she could tell both men and women were involved in a furious battle over something, but the cause wasn't clear. They hurried outside at the same time everyone else did.

At the center of the commotion Wilkes and Lee Tang circled each other—she in an offensive karate pose, he clearly defensive. On the ground, one of Wilkes's pals lay holding his crotch and moaning in pain. Standing guard over him was the beautiful Alicia Samples, and she looked furious enough to do him more damage if he dared to rise.

"What goes on here?" Geoffrey shouted as he shoved his way through the crowd.

"Stay out of this, limey," Wilkes growled. "The bitch wants to play rough, and I'm going to oblige her." He swung a meaty fist toward her face, but she instantly blocked it with her left forearm and followed with a powerful right punch to his diaphragm. As his body folded forward under that blow, she spun around, leaped into the air, and delivered a kick to his jaw that sent him sprawling beside his friend.

Lee stood poised to continue the fight until she was certain he had given up. Leaning over his barely conscious, pain-contorted body, she said, "Thank you so much for obliging me, asshole. Let's do this again sometime." An angry flame still glowed in her eyes as she turned toward the major and defended her actions. "These two guys intercepted Alicia and me coming back from the latrine. When we told them we weren't interested, they got nasty. We only defended ourselves from assault." Her narrow-eyed gaze scanned the circle around her. "And we'll do it again if we have to."

Logan cut the tense silence from the back of the crowd. "Show's over, everybody. Back to your tents. Except Gianni, Higgs, and Evans." After a moment's hesitation, all but a handful of people drifted off. Robin remained despite his order.

Geoffrey grimaced at the two men on the

ground, then asked Julie, "Would you mind seeing to them?"

"Wilkes's jaw cracked," Lee stated without remorse. "I felt it go. Other than that, they'll recover . . . eventually."

A few seconds later, Julie confirmed Lee's prognosis. "We should put Wilkes in the tack room and let our caretakers check on him."

"Good idea," Logan said. "That'll keep him out of trouble for a few hours. Who knows, maybe he'll remember something I couldn't."

Geoffrey explained the procedure to Higgs, Gianni, and Wilkes, and the two MP's helped the patient to his feet. As they headed toward the barn, Lee and Alicia "assisted" Wilkes's cohort back to his tent.

"This problem isn't going to go away," Logan said to Geoffrey. "We may have to assign guards for the women."

"I beg your pardon?" Julie demanded. "In case you missed it, Lee and Alicia did just fine without a man to protect them."

Logan looked down his nose at her. "That was one on one. What do you think will happen when Wilkes comes out of that tack room in one piece again? He's going to want blood, and he probably won't care if it's his attacker's; any female will probably satisfy him. Only next time he'll make sure he's got better backup." To Geoffrey he said, "I'll move my tent next to the women's, and tomorrow we'll split them up on two teams. You and Gianni take half, and I'll take Higgs and the other half."

Julie had the strongest urge to object just for the sake of opposing him, but her common sense kept her quiet. She didn't resent the protective measures as much as the fact that *he* had given orders for them. As hard as it was for her to accept, the one person in this entire group most capable of leadership and commanding obedience seemed to be the last one deserving of that position—a murderer and traitor who should be serving a life sentence in prison, not controlling the lives of others.

And yet as he and Geoffrey walked away to set about moving Logan's tent, she wondered why he was using his talents to maintain peace and order rather than behaving like Wilkes, whose crimes weren't nearly as serious. She shivered at the thought of what could be happening right now if Logan had chosen to side with the other criminals instead of Geoffrey.

"Like I said before," Robin murmured, guessing at Julie's thoughts, "he's a strange one."

"Don't tell me you're interested in him too?" Julie smiled to hide the queasy sensation that touched her stomach as she thought of Robin going after Logan.

"Hell, no!" Robin said with a laugh. "He's the kind that never lets a woman push him around, and I'm the kind that likes the top." She wiggled her eyebrows at Julie and made her laugh. "I'll stick with the shy, moldable type like Geoffrey."

"What's this?" Julie said with feigned shock. "You still find him attractive after an entire day? This sounds serious."

Robin made a face at her. "Very funny. I've met the man of my dreams and you finally develop a sense of humor." She looked out into the dark for a glimpse of him, then sighed. "The truth is, he hasn't even noticed I'm alive."

"I doubt that! If anything, you might be too alive for him."

Robin's eyes opened wide. "Quiet, reserved little me? Hmmm. You could have a point there. I suppose I could tone down my aggressiveness just a bit. At least until I can get past his defenses."

Julie knew better than to try to talk Robin out of something she'd decided to do, but she secretly hoped Geoffrey didn't give in to Robin too easily. Best friend or not, Robin could benefit from running up against a man who didn't instantly fall at her feet. Maybe she could even learn to appreciate him for something other than good looks and an English accent.

They returned to their tent and settled down for what was left of the night, but it took Julie awhile to fall asleep. She had spent a lifetime examining each of her thoughts and deeds, always looking for a way to perfect any flaw that might prevent her from being loved as much as all the other Evans children. Thus, it was quite natural for her to analyze the peculiar reactions she'd had to Robin's comments.

Why did she care if Robin was interested in Logan?

Because he was dangerous and she feared for her friend's well-being. She played with that explanation a moment, and gave it some credence, but she knew that wasn't the whole of it. What she had felt was closer to jealousy than fear.

Did that mean *she* still had an interest in Logan herself?

Absolutely not. If anything, she experienced a momentary pang of jealousy at the thought that Robin—with her sensual beauty, lush figure, and terrific sense of humor—could get through Logan's shell and find the heart she'd been unable to locate with her vast experience at softening up tough guys.

Yes, that's all it was. A tiny pinprick in her professional pride.

Then what about the other feeling, the one that followed Robin's reference to Logan's sexual preference?

She acknowledged that it felt like desire, but that was impossible, completely unacceptable.

There was nothing wrong with being a little curious about him, however. He had the kind of body that any healthy woman might want to get to know better.

Yes, that's what that was. Simple feminine curiosity. She certainly didn't desire Logan McKay. She couldn't.

And if her body didn't agree . . . well, she simply wouldn't permit such disobedience.

Parisia maintained a show of calm control throughout Iris of Mergany's report. No other imperial prefect of Heart had ever been faced with so much turmoil at one time. The past twenty-four hours had been terribly upsetting for her, but her normally sedate domestic affairs adviser was practically undone.

Parisia had not thought attending the monitors during the night would be necessary. A clear tactical error on her part. The barbaric Earth men apparently required continuous observation. She now realized that the men in chains might not have been slaves after all. They might have been bound because they were even more dangerous than usual. And she had been responsible for releasing them among the medicated innocents of the Earth commune. Another tactical error.

Should she take some decisive action immediately to correct her mistakes, or wait the full three days for the medicine to take effect, then reevaluate?

"Despite the distance and lack of sound," Iris continued, "the visual scanner of the sky monitor provides evidence that two of the women were forced to defend themselves against the men, and did so quite efficiently."

"Do you think we should bring the women here?" Parisia asked.

"Oh my, no," Iris instantly replied. "They would never fit in."

"Then you believe they should be left to fend for themselves against all those men?"

Iris hesitated a moment before giving her advice. "I don't believe we have a choice, and in a few days they will be as safe as we are among our own males."

Parisia sighed. "I suppose you're right, but I don't feel good about it. After all, they are females, and we must never forget our foremothers' oath to protect every member of our gender from male abuse."

"But that oath wasn't meant to include barbarian races," Iris protested.

"Are you sure they're as barbaric as the men? Or have they just learned how to deal with violence in the only way available to them? If you'll recall, our ancestors had to keep their men bound or imprisoned for centuries before the medication was perfected. Throughout history women have done what they have to do to survive in worlds dominated by men."

Frowning, Iris conceded a bit. "As always, you have managed to make me doubt my own convictions. Yet I still believe you should leave those women be for now."

Parisia nodded. "And I agree . . . for now. But we will discuss this matter again before I speak to Parliament the day after tomorrow. Was there anything else?"

Iris's frown deepened. "It's about Nadia. An observation tech, Simone, informed me that Nadia is showing an unusual amount of interest in the new crossovers. She actually left her residence last evening and went to the sanatorium to get a look at the man with the headache. My guess is, the tech is playing both sides of the political field, but she denied any knowledge of how Nadia learned about the patient. You might consider having Simone relocated to a less sensitive post."

Parisia shook her head. "No. Leave her where she is. As long as she believes we don't suspect her of duplicity, she might be of use to us at some later date."

That made Iris smile. "Very good. You never know when we might want to pass a little misinformation on to Nadia."

"McKay?" Julie called from inside the tack room. "Could you come here, please?"

His team had begun examining the barn, inch by inch, right after breakfast. In the three hours since, no one had been able to pry even a sliver of wood off the walls with any tool they tried. Nor had they discovered how the outside door had been sealed, then automatically opened.

Logan stood in the doorway holding a cup of water. "Yes, Captain?"

She immediately noticed his relaxed posture, then saw his expression. He was almost smiling. "Are you all right?"

He drained his cup. "Never felt better. Just a little thirstier than usual, but that happens to me after a migraine. What can I do for you, Captain?"

He had just said more words to her at one time than he had all together during the last three weeks of his stay at the hospital unit, and it flustered her. "I . . . I, uh . . . please call me Julie. Everyone else seems to have dropped formality."

"Fine. Did you need something?"

His unusual congeniality was playing havoc with her composure. "Yes. I . . ." She had to pull her gaze away from his before she could remember what had been on her mind when she called for him. "We have to be missing something in here. I thought if you acted out what you did when you came in with the migraine, you might recall something else."

He shrugged. "It's worth a try." Imitating his previous actions as closely as possible, he stepped inside the tack room, pulled the door shut, and threw the bolt. "It's only a guess, but it's probable that locking the door works like an alarm to let them know someone needs medical attention, in which case you might get to experience the miracle firsthand."

"No. Duncan said they never take anyone unless they're alone, so that's out. But it also suggests that they must be able to see into this room to know whether it's only one person." She scanned the solid walls and ceiling for the hundredth time. "I just don't see how, though. Okay, so you bolted the door. Then what?"

"I turned around and said, 'I have a migraine, a very bad headache.' They must be able to hear what is said in here as well. Anyway, I stood here for several minutes, but nothing happened, so I sat down." He lowered himself onto the straw, set down his cup, and leaned against the bolted door. His gaze returned to her face and stayed there.

Julie had seen plenty of male patients look at her that way before—as if she were some sort of angel. She knew enough not to take it seriously. But Logan shouldn't be looking at her that way. Not now. "Are you sure you're feeling all right?"

He laughed. "Of course. Why?"

"You . . . you don't seem . . . normal." It was the

best explanation she could come up with. "Never mind. What happened after you sat down?"

"Some more time passed. The next thing I knew I was flat on my back, waking up like I'd had twelve hours of good sleep."

Julie shook her head. "If nothing else, at least Wilkes's recollection is the same as yours."

Remaining on the floor, Logan closed his eyes. His brow furrowed as he struggled to remember when and how he had been rendered unconscious. Suddenly his eyes opened and he stared at the ceiling.

"What is it?" Julie asked, following his gaze to a wooden beam in the ceiling.

"I was gassed," Logan declared, rising to his feet with his eyes still focused overhead. "I don't know why I forgot it, but it just came back to me. I heard a hissing sound right before I blacked out. It seemed to have come from up there." He pulled her over to where he was standing. "Look up. See that dark knothole in the wood?"

She could see the impression he referred to, but failed to see his point. She watched him pick up a long piece of straw and point it toward the knothole, but he was about two feet short. "Here," he said, handing her the straw. "You try it."

She couldn't understand how he thought she could reach it if he hadn't until he bent down, circled her thighs with his arms, and lifted her into the air. "McKay!" she scolded, quickly grasping his shoulders for balance.

"Now try it," he said with a grin.

She felt the strength of his arms beneath her

bottom and knew he wouldn't drop her, but his warm breath wafting across her breast made her tighten her grip on his shoulders nonetheless.

"I won't drop you," he assured her in a husky voice. "See how deep you can make it go."

Her cheeks flushed hot, and she felt his low chuckle all along her body.

"The *straw*, Julie."

Despite his words, his eyes told her she hadn't misunderstood what he was really thinking about. Since a response would probably only further her embarrassment, she proceeded with his experiment. Without meeting any obstruction, she was able to feed the straw completely into the hole. "It appears to be a tube," she told him as she extracted the straw and dropped it on the floor. "Your assumption about being gassed is probably correct."

Rather than acknowledge her comment, his mouth brushed back and forth over her taut nipple.

"*McKay.*" She meant to sound offended, but his name came out in a whisper that revealed too much of what he was making her feel. His mouth treated her other breast to the same light touch, and she forced out the words her mind demanded she say. "Put me down, McKay." But her back arched into him instead of away.

He let her slide down his body a few inches so that their eyes were now level. "Call me Logan."

She could feel his heart pounding hard against her own and told herself to run. His hold on her was supportive, but not so restraining that she couldn't escape—if she wanted to.

Her hesitation made him clarify his terms. "I'll put you down after you call me Logan. Say it the way you used to when I was your patient and you wanted me to believe you cared."

The intense longing in his voice, accompanied by the need so visible in his eyes, stripped her of what little sense she had left. *"Logan."*

His lips came to hers, then left again with a tenderness that made her heart ache. Her fingers combed the lock of hair off his forehead as she repeated, *"Logan."*

Once more his mouth met hers, softly, as if he feared her rejection. When she didn't retreat, he murmured something unintelligible and pressed a bit harder. She felt the muscles in his arms tremble slightly, so she wrapped her legs around his waist to keep from slipping away. Intent upon the depth of emotion he was pouring into the simple, closed-mouth kiss, she barely noticed when he descended to his knees with her on his lap.

His lips grazed her cheek and caressed her ear. When he spoke, she felt his words more than she heard them.

"You can't know how many times I've fantasized about holding you like this." He continued planting butterfly kisses down her neck, up her throat, and moved to her face. "I'd see your angel eyes and hear your angel voice, and you never, ever left me to go take care of someone else."

His claims made no sense, and yet pure honesty laced each kiss. The hand easing up and down her back, his fingers threading through her hair, every touch gave proof that having her in his arms filled him with innocent wonder. Though she knew she shouldn't believe him, she asked, "You fantasized about *me*? Like this?" She felt the vibration of his muffled laughter.

"Like this." He lowered her onto her back and stretched out beside her. "And this." His fingers explored her face as his dark eyes made seductive promises. "In my fantasies you open your mouth for me. You stroke my tongue with yours and let me taste you for as long as I want."

She pulled his head down to hers and whispered against his lips, "Like this?" His groan of pleasure assured her that she was living up to his fantasy. For her, however, he surpassed any fantasy she had ever had of what the perfect kiss would be like. Time passed without either caring while the kiss went on and on.

Finally Logan raised his head and said, "Like that."

He had her trembling with a need for more than deep kisses, and with a brazen smile she asked, "And nothing more?"

His return smile was equally suggestive. "Sometimes that was enough."

"And other times?"

He took a deep breath and dragged his bent leg up across hers. "Sometimes I need more. You touch me. And you ask me to touch you."

Although Julie felt his arousal throbbing insistently against her thigh, so far he had done nothing more aggressive than enticing her to make a choice that would please them both. "Like this?" Her fingertips caressed his cheek, trailed down and up his arm, and settled on his chest.

His adoring gaze held hers, and he whispered, "And more."

"Show me." She closed her eyes when he guided her hand down below his waist to confirm just how hard he was straining to control his desire for her. As she learned the width and length of him, she made the request he awaited. "I'd like you to touch me too, Logan."

Her breath caught in her throat until his hand slowly found its way to her breast. Cupping her in his palm, his thumb teased the hardened peak through her shirt as his mouth returned to hers for a kiss that could only be described as reverent.

He made her feel things she didn't know were possible, and yet she wasn't surprised. She had believed from the first that there was something special about Logan. She was torn between wanting this sweet torture to go on forever and the desire to rush headlong toward the magical burst of satisfaction she instinctively knew he could give her. To her immense relief, he made the decision for her by slipping his hand beneath the waistband of her slacks.

"I love you, Julie."

His words brought back a painful memory, but she couldn't hold on to it. As she tried to respond, he found the core of her womanhood, and her only answer was a gasp of pleasure. She wanted to feel him in the same way, but his experienced touch brought her to a peak so quickly, she could only lay there, melting, dying, feeding on kisses that had finally, thankfully, become demanding and urgent.

"Logan!" Geoffrey shouted through the door, then pounded on it for good measure. "Are you in there, man?"

Chapter 7

Logan's hand stilled as both his and Julie's heads jerked toward the door in shock.

"Sh-ssh," Logan sounded. "He'll go away if we don't answer him." His mouth returned to hers, and his fingers resumed their exciting play between her legs.

For several heartbeats she was more than willing to complete what they had begun. Then she heard Geoffrey's voice talking to someone just outside, and the sensual haze began to lift from her mind. Ending the kiss and moving his hand from her body, she whispered, "We have to answer him. If we don't, there's liable to be a whole crowd out there waiting for us to come out." He tried to pull her close again, but she managed to resist this time. "No. Logan, please. I'll die of embarrassment."

That seemed to make an impression on him, and he took a deep, calming breath. "I'm in here," he said loudly enough to be heard through the door. He and Julie sat up and started extracting straw from each other's hair. "Just running an experiment."

"Have you seen Julie?" Geoffrey asked. "She's nowhere around."

"She's in here too," Logan replied, his eyes still making love to her. "We're almost finished. We'll be out in a minute."

"Right. I'll meet you outside. Lunch is on and I need to discuss something with the both of you."

Julie made a move to rise, but her legs weren't ready to support her. She closed her eyes and tried to regain control of her body.

Logan wrapped his arms around her and stroked her hair. "I'm sorry. This should have waited until we were assured of privacy. After lunch we can—"

"No," Julie protested, her head bobbing up from his shoulder. Sanity abruptly returned like an icy blast of wind. "This . . . this shouldn't have happened. I don't even know how it did."

Logan eased back from her and frowned. "What do you mean?"

"You . . . I . . . I'm not sure what I mean," Julie stuttered as her mind tried to form an excuse for her reckless behavior. "It must be this crazy situation. We're both under a lot of stress, and—"

"I'm not feeling any stress," he countered with an easy smile. "In fact, I don't remember ever feeling so relaxed."

"You're doing it again," she said, rising to her feet and stepping back from him.

"What?"

"Smiling."

He stood up and kissed her nose. "Of course I'm smiling. I just had my own personal angel in my arms."

Her heart wanted to believe the look of utter devotion on his face, but her mind was insisting that something was wrong. "That's not why. You were smiling before. I wondered about it when you first came in, but then—"

His smile turned sexy and he bent to kiss her mouth. She almost gave in, but at the moment his lips touched hers, she moved away. "I have to think. Please. Just give me some time to work this out."

Logan's fingers stroked her cheek. "I've waited this long for you. I guess a few more hours won't matter." His hand slid around to the back of her neck and urged her closer. "I'll give you the time you need, but I need something from you to tide me over. Just one more kiss, angel. Please."

She knew she should deny him, but her head angled beneath his, and she couldn't resist one more quick flight to ecstasy. Much too easily her body responded to him, and the one kiss became several more. Only when both of them made an effort to remember that Geoffrey was waiting were they able to compose themselves enough to leave the tack room without clinging to each other.

Simone wasn't at all sure what she should do. The scene she had just witnessed on her monitor had her very confused. She had learned the facts of primitive male behavior long ago and thought they were quite clear. But the man in the tack room hadn't appeared cruel or violent. Nor had the woman looked repulsed or in pain. If anything, she seemed to be enjoying the way he was touching her and pressing his mouth to her face.

Watching them had caused the most peculiar feelings, a discomfort of sorts, especially in her womanpiece, yet it wasn't entirely unpleasant either.

Should she tell Nadia, or should she simply make a note of the incident in her report to Adviser Iris? Nadia would be furious if she wasn't informed of such an unusual occurrence. But if Iris learned that Nadia was aware of it, she would know that Simone had to be the one who had given out the information. Simone was the only one on duty at the monitors.

After a few minutes' consideration, she decided it was a situation in which she could only come out a loser. The only way around it was to edit out the scene, as if it never had happened. Before she erased it, however, she played the recording twice more to get a better understanding of what the pair were doing. Nothing in her education explained it, and yet she was certain their actions and dialogue had some importance.

"I can't put my finger on it," Geoffrey told Logan, Julie, and Robin as they ate lunch. "But something is going on. I expected Wilkes to cause trouble this morning. Instead he was pleasant and worked as hard as everyone else. And when Lee Tang passed right by him in the kitchen just now, the look on his face was practically contrite."

"He's not the only one that's acting different," Robin injected. "Now, don't get me wrong here, but some of our men were giving me the eye yesterday. You know, like they were ready whenever I was."

Julie noted the way Geoffrey grimaced at Robin's comment, then kept his eyes glued to his plate as she went on.

"Today, though, those same men smiled nicely without any hint of sexual interest. I know it sounds conceited, but I'm a realist. I know what most men think when they look at me, and those thoughts were noticeably missing today."

Julie met Logan's gaze and knew his thoughts. Something strange had happened to them as well, but neither was ready to discuss it with the others.

"How do you feel, Geoffrey?" Julie asked. "Anything that you'd describe as unusual?"

"I feel fine," he answered with a smile. "If it's something in the air, I don't think it's affecting me."

She prompted him a little further. "Would you say you feel relaxed? Comfortable?"

He chuckled. "Very much so. I slept better last night than I have in years, even with all the excitement."

"Logan's very relaxed too," Julie stated, then glanced at him for confirmation. His smile said all that was necessary. "Robin? How about you?"

Robin pressed her forefingers to her temples, closed her eyes, and hummed in a monotone for a few seconds. "All systems are A-OK," she said, imitating a computer voice synthesizer. Then with a thoughtful expression she amended her report.

"Now that you mention it, though, I feel pretty relaxed also."

Julie nodded. "Same here." Mentally she acknowledged that for her, it was more than being relaxed. What she had just permitted with Logan suggested that her entire defense system had broken down. "Now, I want you all to think about that. Is there any reason we should be at ease? Yesterday at this time we were nearing hysteria. Don't you think it's strange that no one—not a single person—is worried about our situation today?"

Logan's smile had faded as he realized how right Julie was, and yet it still didn't worry him overmuch. "Did any of you see Higgs this morning? He was the worst yesterday."

"I did," Robin said. "I didn't give it a thought at the time, but he wasn't even trying to bend anyone's ear. He seemed perfectly content to go quietly about his work."

"Just like everyone else," Geoffrey said, his eyes narrowing with concern.

They were silent for a moment as they drew the same conclusion. Julie said it aloud. "Whatever causes the residents here to act like robots must be affecting us as well."

"In another day or two," Robin said, "we could all be just like them. We might even give up the idea of getting out of here."

Logan forced himself to remember what his attitude had been twenty-four hours ago. As good as he felt at the moment, he knew that wasn't the case then. He would never have acted on his desire for Julie yesterday, and he definitely would not have spouted his private thoughts to her. It was as if all his personal barriers had been stripped, leaving him vulnerable—and mindless. Just like the puppet people.

"Okay," he said in a voice that was almost back to normal. "We're being relaxed in some way. How?"

"The food?" Robin offered.

"The water?" Logan asked, immediately thinking about how many gallons he had consumed already.

"I was being facetious about the air before, but we shouldn't rule that possibility out," Geoffrey said. "Or sonic waves either."

Julie sighed. It could be anything. "Obviously we can't stop breathing or absorbing sound. And we might be able to fast for a day or two, but eventually we'd have to eat and drink again. The only way we'll be able to avoid whatever it is, is to locate the source. And only our caretakers have the answer to that."

"True," Logan stated. "But at least we can fast as long as possible while we step up our escape plan."

"We have an escape plan?" Robin asked in surprise.

Logan laughed. "That's Geoff's department. He claimed he's a master of strategy."

Geoffrey made a face. "I believe I did say something along those lines." He rubbed his chin as he organized his thoughts. "All right. Let's start with what we know. The barn is a go-between, but it's impregnable. An ill person can get out of here, but only if he's alone, and then he's gassed first."

"We might be able to block the flow tube without them knowing it, so the patient could stay conscious," Logan suggested.

Geoffrey shook his head. "But that would still be only one person."

"Sometimes a single man can be more effective than a whole squad," Logan reminded him.

Again Geoffrey contradicted him. "Only when he knows what he's up against."

Robin brightened with an idea. "What if a whole squad was in the tack room, but hiding? You know, create an optical illusion for whoever is watching so that they think there's only one man in there?"

"Excellent idea," Geoffrey said with a grin. "When all the candles are extinguished, it's completely black in there. We could set it up in darkness, during the night, then surprise them."

Julie played devil's advocate. "At most you could hide only a dozen people in there, and we have no weapons. That's not much against an unknown power. I think we should hold off trying that until we're positive there's no break in the invisible wall where the whole company could get through at once."

Geoffrey nodded. "That would be preferable, but from what we've been told, I don't have much hope of our finding such a break. At any rate, the team examining the wall will be reporting back this evening. We should work on the tack room plan this afternoon and have it ready to go if the findings on the wall are negative. We could try it tonight. Agreed?" He met each of their eyes.

"Agreed," they replied in unison.

"Robin and I can spread the word about fasting," Julie said.

Geoffrey gave another nod of agreement. "I'll start working on the optical illusion. Logan, are you willing to head up the squad?"

"Of course. Besides, I'm probably the best decoy we've got since they already treated me and shouldn't be suspicious if I claim to have another migraine."

"Good. Then I'll leave it up to you to select the others that will go with you."

Logan accepted with a thumbs-up sign. To Julie he said, "Don't worry about our being unarmed. There's plenty of things around the farm that could be used as weapons. It won't be the first time I've had to improvise."

"That's it, then," Geoffrey said.

As they each got up and threw out the remains of their lunch, Logan motioned Julie aside, but she spoke before he could. "Before you say a thing, I want you to know that what happened was obviously a result of whatever is being done to all of us. I don't blame you, nor do I hold you responsible for anything said. And I hope that you will forget my behavior as well."

Logan looked down into her eyes in hopes of seeing a spark of the desire that had been there before, but she had successfully erased any trace of it. Instead all he saw was a woman who had made a terrible mistake and wanted to forget it ever happened. "You took the words right out of my mouth," he told her, though what he had originally intended to say was quite the opposite. Without another word he turned and went about his assignment. He should have known better.

For a few seconds Julie was tempted to call him back. There was something in the way he looked at her that made her think she had hurt his feelings, but she knew his expression was no more genuine than the tender, respectful way he had treated her, or the beautiful romantic words he had spoken. He had been manipulated to behave that way by some unseen force. It was very similar to the way the narcotics in the hospital had altered his personality. Only this time she had been affected as well.

How else could she have forgotten who and what he really was? Now that she was aware of the cause, though, she could make certain nothing like that ever happened again.

What a terrible shame, a little voice in her head whispered, for nothing like that had ever happened to her before.

As she struggled to dismiss the entire episode, another unsettling realization sunk in. More than likely, a caretaker had observed her moment of weakness. How could she have freed her inhibitions so completely that she forgot about the possibility that they were watching that room from the instant Logan had bolted the door? It wasn't logical, but the thought of the love scene being enacted for some alien's amusement was more upsetting than anything that had happened so far.

Throughout the rest of the day they both performed the tasks agreed upon. At one point Julie
felt as though someone was watching her. She
turned around and met Logan's gaze. Again she
read something so vulnerable in his eyes that she
had to stop herself from going to him. When he
realized she was looking back, he hardened his expression and turned away. She fortified herself
with the hope that their plan would be a success
and things would soon be back to normal. Or at
least as normal as they could be in this strange
place.

All of the soldiers and nurses were cautioned
about the food and water before dinner. The fast
caused some half-hearted grumbling, but everyone
was too relaxed to make a serious fuss.

When the team that had been examining the
wall came in, their report was a confirmation of
Duncan's statements. The invisible barrier began
at one rear corner of the barn and ended at the
other. The back wall of the structure was apparently part of the barrier. There was no interruption
or detectable weakness around the entire perime-
ter. It couldn't be scaled and went far higher than
anything they could construct to climb over it.
They had dug a twenty-foot hole, but the wall appeared to be bottomless.

They now had no choice but to attempt an escape through the tack room.

Geoffrey had selected five men and women to
assist him in preparing the hiding places within
the room. In case they were being observed, one
person at a time went into the tack room to fetch

or return an item and did their best to make their actions appear innocuous.

When everything was in place, Geoffrey met with Logan's team, which consisted of nine other men, Lee Tang, and Alicia Samples. Logan and Geoffrey had decided that the major should stay behind. Each was given a diagram of the tack room and an assigned spot so they would be able to find it in the dark. The tube would be blocked only when the maneuvers began.

Taking advantage of what was available on the farm, each member of Logan's team had at least two weapons. Knives, cleavers, pitchforks, hammers, and a variety of other implements had been scavenged by sundown.

As any good leader would, Logan warned them of the risks involved. For all he knew, they could be about to face an army of alien beings whose minds were all the weapons they needed. They could be charging into a situation more dangerous than anything they'd faced in the Orient. Their escape attempt could result in retaliation that would make their future even bleaker than it already was.

He gave each person the option to back out. No one did.

Since they had no way of knowing if activities outside the tack room were observed, it was decided that everyone else should retire to their tents as they had the night before. If anyone was watching, everything should appear to be normal.

Tension mounted throughout the evening as the time for action approached. Julie knew part of the reason was anticipation, but she hoped it also meant that whatever had been relaxing everyone was losing strength. She asked one person after another if they could tell any difference since they had stopped eating and drinking, but no one could be positive. Finally she sought out the one individual who seemed to have been the most drastically altered. Standing outside the circle of men and women around Logan, she waited for him to notice her, then asked, "Could I speak to you a moment?"

He excused himself from his team and walked away with her.

When she was certain no one could overhear, she stopped and looked up at him. "I want to wish you good luck."

He accepted her wish with a stiff nod. "You could have said that in front of everyone else."

She flinched at the harsh edge in his voice. "You're back to normal, I see."

With a negligent shrug he said, "More or less. At least I'm in control of what I'm doing. But then, adrenaline's been known to counter some pretty strong drugs."

"You think that's what it was? A sedative of some kind?"

"I think that's the best bet considering how I feel after ten hours of no food and water. If it was the air or sound, I doubt if adrenaline would make this much of a difference."

"That's what I was thinking also." There was more she had wanted to say, but it no longer seemed appropriate. They were back to being hostile strangers. "Good luck, then," she said and held out her hand.

He hesitated a second before taking it, and when he did, he held it considerably longer than necessary. She tried not to think about how that simple contact caused her heart to pick up its pace or how warm and strong his hand felt enveloping her own. But she could not ignore what she saw in his eyes. He had claimed he was in *better* control; now she understood what he had not said. He still wanted her.

What she didn't understand at all was that she wanted him as well.

Immediately after Iris of Mergany had received the report of the unusual amount of activity in and out of the tack room that afternoon, she assigned a second technician to the monitors. It could be nothing, but she didn't want to take any chances. They were both instructed to keep her posted and take no decisive actions regardless of how routine it seemed to be.

Now it appeared that her precautions were warranted. The visual showed the first man who had been brought over the day before. He was again claiming to have a terrible headache. Had she not ordered the techs otherwise, they would have automatically opened the door to bring him over.

"Do a slow scan of the entire room," Iris said. The one candle lantern he had carried in with him didn't provide much light, but it was sufficient to confirm that he was alone. "Fine. Transmit the anesthesia."

The first tech flicked the proper switch, and almost instantly a red warning light appeared on the panel. She directed the computer to run a check on the system.

Iris watched the man on the screen slump over as he should have, and thought the light was a false alarm. A few seconds later, the system check was complete and a message flashed across the screen announcing a blockage in the pipe. But if it was blocked, the man should still be conscious.

"Bring up a life-signs report."

The tech pressed a series of keys, and the visual of the man blacked out. Instantly a white rectangle was drawn on the screen, in which the letters *A* through *L* were printed along the inside edges.

SPECIFY LIFE FORM OR PRESS ENTER FOR ALL

Iris stared at the words on the monitor and counted the letters. There were eleven other people inside that room! Neither she nor the techs had seen them. How very ingenious of these Earth men. She could hardly wait to share this information with Parisia.

"It appears that our new crossovers had thought to surprise us ladies," Iris declared. "But due to your diligence we have a surprise for them. Do nothing. Eventually they'll tire of their cramped quarters and give up. We will have to be even more observant for the next twenty-four hours in case they have any more ideas for escaping the commune. After that, though, we should be able to return to our normal routines. Just continue to keep me advised as you have, and pass the instructions on to your relief in the morning."

* * *

By midnight Nadia's frustration level had reached an all-time high. Knowing Fulton was merely a weak imitation of a man prevented her from seeking any relief with him. What she wanted was the real thing, and there were over a hundred of them practically at her fingertips. Practically.

Therein lay the problem. Two different men had been taken to the sanatorium and neither time could she gain access to them. With each hour that slid by, her chances of experiencing the ultimate pleasure decreased a little more.

Nor had she come up with a single plausible reason why she should be allowed to make personal contact with any of the new crossovers.

There was only one thing she could do, but the risk of discovery was extremely high. If she was caught, her career, possibly her life, could be ended.

On the other hand, if she didn't try it, there might never again be such an opportunity. She could die of old age and always regret having passed up her one chance to reach nirvana.

From what Simone had told her that evening, they had doubled the observation staff, but they were concentrating primarily on the tack room. There was a good possibility that she could quickly pass through the barrier at a point far from the barn and the momentary disruption in the force field would go undetected.

After all, who in their right mind would purposely enter the commune? Perhaps if she was in a different frame of mind, she wouldn't either. But frustration, curiosity, and anticipation had control of every bit of reason she possessed.

Exchanging her nightgown for a black, hooded, floor-length caftan, she became a figure that could slip into the night and walk through walls.

Higgs was so frustrated, he wanted to scream. He burned up a little nervous energy by kicking the loose stones on the ground.

It just wasn't fair! He was a military police officer. He should have been chosen to serve on McKay's advance team like Gianni. Instead he'd been assigned to patrol the area outside the barn and around the tents to make sure everyone stayed put. He figured this was McKay's way of getting back at him for being his guard, but hell, that wasn't his fault. He tried to explain his position, but no, McKay had to be the kind to hold a grudge.

On top of that, Higgs was hungry and thirsty. He knew the orders to fast were justified; he was back to feeling as jumpy as he always did. It was just so hard to ignore an empty stomach and dry throat. Hopefully it would all be over any minute and—

He thought he saw something in the distance. The stars and crescent moon were partially clouded over, yet it was bright enough for him to see a shape moving across the open field. His duty might not have been on the front line, but he did have a job to do nonetheless. Picking up his pace, he headed for whoever it was who dared to disobey the major's order.

"Halt," he shouted when he was about fifty feet

from the shrouded figure. "Who goes there?"
Rather than stop or identify himself, the person
kept walking toward him.

Higgs's empty stomach did a somersault, and he
took a step backward. It had only just occurred to
him that this might not be one of his kind but one
of them, and he didn't even have a weapon to defend himself. "Who—who are you?" he asked,
nearly strangling on the words.

The figure stopped a few feet away and pushed
back the hood, allowing Higgs to see that it was a
woman. She was at least six inches taller than he,
with a plain face except for a rather large nose.
With a slight shake of her head, black hair cas-
caded loose and settled down past her waist. He
was momentarily distracted by all that beautiful
hair, but he quickly regained his fear. "You're not
one of us," he stated unnecessarily.

"No, I am not," Nadia replied in a deep, velvety
voice. "I am from beyond the barrier. You may call
me Parisia. I have come to copulate with you."

Chapter 8

Higgs almost swallowed his tongue. "Co-co-cop-ulate? W-w-with *me*?"

"Are you not an adult male from Earth?"

"Yeah, sure, but—"

"Then we will copulate." She unfastened the caftan and let it drop to the ground at her feet.

Higgs gaped at the voluptuous body being offered to him, but he was too frightened to respond in a normal manner. "Uh, Parisia? Couldn't we, uh, get to know each other a little first?"

She took a loud, exasperated breath that caused her large breasts to jiggle. He noticed, but it struck him that maybe she was tricking him in some way. Like, maybe she could read his mind and make her body appear to be the kind that would normally drive him up a wall with lust when really she looked like a lizard or something equally gross.

The woman slipped her fingers into the dark patch of hair between her legs, and his lower body gave a hint of response regardless of what she truly was.

"What is it you wish to know before you proceed?" she asked while readying herself for the act.

Higgs racked his brain for a coherent question. "Uh, you said your name's Parisia. Mine's Higgs. Ray Higgs. Where are we? How'd we get here? Why are we confined to this farm? How many of you are there beyond the wall? Are you human or—"

"Enough! I have no patience for this 'getting to know each other.' I will answer one question only, then we will copulate . . . or you will be punished."

Higgs gulped as he imagined all sorts of horrible punishments that she might subject him to. If he was going to have sex forced on him by an alien, only one question was really important. "Uh, are you, uh, human, like me?"

"Yes," she hissed impatiently. "I am as human as you, perhaps more so. Now remove your clothes before you anger me further!"

Higgs's hands shook as he shed his clothing as quickly as possible. He had always known this was going to happen to him someday. How many hundreds of stories had he read about alien abductions and their abusive treatment of the humans they chose to study? Almost every report referred to experimentation involving the sex organs. Good God! He was about to become a sex slave to an alien, possibly even father a baby mutant for her.

As the cool night air shriveled his manhood even more than her threats had already, he wondered what sort of punishment she would deliver if he tried but couldn't.

The woman scowled at the useless appendage drooping between his thighs. "You are not engorged. Are you not stricken with madness at the sight of me?" She lifted her heavy breasts. "Do these parts not interest you enough to make your manpiece grow?"

Higgs watched her toy with her nipples, pinching and twisting them between her fingers, and felt another twitch of interest. "You have a beautiful body, Parisia, really. It's just that you, uh, caught me by surprise, and I, uh, never had to do this under orders before."

"Oh?" she asked with a curious expression. "How would you usually become ready?"

He couldn't believe this was happening. Not only was she planning to take advantage of him, she needed lessons in how to do it!

For the umpteenth time in his young life, he thanked God for his mother's best friend, Celia, who, upon accidentally glimpsing his excessive endowment, had taken it upon herself to tutor him in subjects never covered in the classroom, such as how to find the hot spot Dr. Grafenberg had discovered. Thinking of "Aunt" Celia helped calm his fears enough to say, "Well, uh, gentle persuasion goes a lot further than orders in this kind of situation."

"Explain how this gentle persuasion works."

"Well, uh, first there's usually some kissing, then some touching, and, uh, it helps if you use your mouth too."

She reached down and squeezed his genitals.

"Ouch! Easy does it." He took her hand and demonstrated what he meant. "Gently." His shaft extended an inch. "You see? That works better."

"Yes. I understand the touching. Show me these other actions you require."

He pulled her head down to his and closed his eyes. If he could just block out what she was for a few minutes, his body would take over after that. She was momentarily shocked when he pushed his tongue into her mouth, but she caught on quickly enough. And she moaned with pleasure when he moved his mouth to her breast and used his tongue and teeth on her there. He *could* do this after all. She tasted like a real woman to him, and that was the only thing that mattered at the moment.

When his fingers slipped into her thatch of tight curls, he was the one shocked by how damp she already was. He inserted one, two, then three fingers as far as he could, and her only response was a frustrated cry. At least he was assured that she could take all he had to give, which he had often been told was more than the average man could boast of.

Handling him the way he'd shown her, she brought him to a respectable size, but he knew he could do even better. "Now your mouth," he told her, then explained exactly what he needed her to do. He anticipated her surprise, but her hesitation was brief. A minute later he gave her points for being the fastest learner in the universe.

And a few minutes after that, he was able to deliver what she had come to him for. As she squealed and bucked beneath him, he forgot what she was and enjoyed the free ride. But once they were both satisfied, he felt cocky enough to demand answers to the questions he'd asked before.

"I do not wish to converse," she declared in her authoritarian manner. "We will copulate again."

"That's easy for you to say," Higgs replied. "You sure don't know much about this. If you're human, how come you don't know about men's bodies?"

She made a growling sound of irritation. "Our men are not capable of performing this function." She examined the softening flesh of his genitals. "What is required for you to become engorged again?"

He was fairly sure he could manage it again, but he was now clearheaded enough to bargain for his service. "It takes a little time and a lot of the kind of attention you gave me before. But in exchange I want some answers."

Her eyes opened wide. She was clearly not accustomed to making deals. "Do not forget that I can punish you for your insolence at any time. However, you pleased me well enough. I will answer another question after we copulate again."

Higgs needed only a reminder of punishment to weaken his flash of confidence. "Okay. But understand, it won't be so fast this time, and there's no way I'll be able to go a third time, no matter how much you threaten me."

"Understood. Proceed."

She needed no further instructions this time, and even improvised a bit, much to Higgs's surprise. Her enthusiastic efforts had him ready for another bout much sooner than he'd thought possible, but when it was over, he insisted there was no way he could do it again that night.

She was disappointed that her fun had come to

an end so quickly despite the fact that he had warned her in advance. "How long before you are able to function again?"

"A day," Higgs answered without thinking.

"Then I will return at this time tomorrow. You will be here when I arrive, and you will teach me more about this."

"More?"

"Don't think to hide anything from me. I will know if you do. I wish to study every position of copulation and method of inducing pleasure."

It hadn't occurred to Higgs that she would demand a rematch. Then he recalled that some abductees swore that their alien captors came for them more than once. If he was to be studied, however, he wanted to get something in return. "What about my questions?"

As she rose and picked up her caftan, she said, "One more question tonight. You may ask another tomorrow if I am satisfied with your performance."

Higgs figured one question was better than none. He knew her name was Parisia, she claimed to be human, and there were men among her people, but they were impotent. "Okay, one question. Uh, where are we?"

Fastening her gown, she answered, "This is Heart, the twin planet to your Earth."

"A parallel universe?" Higgs exclaimed. "But how did we get here? Did the storm create a gateway of some sort and our plane—"

"Cease. I have answered your one question. If you wish more information, you will be here tomorrow night . . . prepared to please me in some new fashion."

He watched her remove what looked like a cigar from her pocket and point it at him. Before he could avoid it, she sprayed a mist in his face.

Instantly his eyes blurred and he tried to wipe them, only to discover that his hands didn't respond. In fact, his entire body was frozen stiff!

She had one final order for him before she departed. "Until I tell you otherwise, do not drink any of the water or eat any food cooked in it."

Nadia ran as fast as she could toward the barrier. At the medium setting she had used, the paralyzer sprayer immobilized a large creature only for a few minutes. She had kept the canister of deterrent after her last safari into the wilderness, though at the time she hadn't any idea that she would be using it on a very different sort of beast. Hopefully, it wouldn't harm the man in any permanent way.

Her lungs burned from the unusual exertion, but she didn't dare slow down until she reached the barrier. Barely pausing to extract a thin rectangular box from her pocket, she created a narrow opening, hurried through, and closed it again. That box was another object she had kept without reason, except as a souvenir of her stint with Protective Services. The tool's main function was to detect, repair, and reinforce any weakness in the barrier, but it could also work in reverse to cause a flaw just as well.

Now that she was safe, she stopped to catch

her breath. She couldn't believe how splendidly the adventure had gone. Closing her eyes and hugging her body, she wallowed in the remnants of pleasure still tripping through her. What was most exciting about what she just experienced was knowing she could have more whenever she liked. It simply required a certain boldness and relying on her intuition to hone in on the Earth male's fears as well as his natural urges.

She hadn't found the scarred man as she had hoped, but Ray Higgs was quite adequate for her purposes—at least until she tired of him.

She recalled how she had called herself Parisia and laughed aloud at how mortified the imperial prefect would be if she learned how her name had been used. Nadia thought it made a delightful private joke, but it was also a slight precaution against being correctly identified if Ray Higgs ever managed to reveal her activities to anyone.

As she neared her residence, she considered taking a long, hot bath to soothe her strained muscles and cleanse the man's leavings from her body. She could wake Fulton and—no. She didn't want that half-man's hands on her tonight. Not after having the real thing. She would see to her own bath, and her need, which was already creeping back to life.

Tomorrow night couldn't come soon enough for her.

Higgs slowly regained control of his muscles along with his vision. He was so anxious to tell someone about what just happened, he'd taken several steps before realizing that he was still naked. Between his nerves and natural lack of co-ordination, it took him longer than usual to get himself clothed and headed toward Major Cook-son's tent.

Geoffrey heard someone approaching and got up from his cot. He was disappointed to see that it was only Higgs.

"I'm sorry to disturb you, Major, but this is of urgent importance."

"Come in," Geoffrey said, immediately wondering how long it would take to get the man out again. He was tense enough waiting for news of Logan's team without having to deal with Higgs. He lit his candle lantern and made himself ask, "What's the problem?"

"It's the water! There's something in it."

"That possibility occurred to us. That's why you were ordered not to eat or drink anything all day."

"It's not the food. She only told me not to drink the water."

Geoffrey could see Higgs was upset over something, but he was making less sense than usual. "She who?"

Higgs waved his arms in the air and tried to pace within the small tent. "A female alien, from beyond the invisible wall. I was just with her out in the field."

Geoffrey turned away so Higgs wouldn't see his look of disbelief.

"I'm telling you, she came for me. She . . . she wanted to . . . she forced me to—to *copulate* with her . . . right out there."

Geoffrey couldn't hold back a chuckle at that

one. "Are you trying to tell me you were just raped by an alien woman?"

"Twice!" When he got only another laugh at that, he tried harder to be convincing. "She was *huge*, and strong, and she tortured me first, and she had a weapon that paralyzed me."

Geoffrey nodded with feigned comprehension. "An amazon used a stun gun on you, then took advantage of you while you were helpless."

"No, no," Higgs said, getting more frustrated by the second. "She used me first, then paralyzed me while she ran off."

"Just out of curiosity, Higgs, how did you happen to be in the condition necessary to be used?"

"She—she must have used some sort of mind control. I couldn't resist."

Higgs clearly believed what he was saying, but Geoffrey could hardly accept the truth of such an outrageous tale coming from a man who had been whining about aliens and androids from the moment they'd arrived in this place. There was a strong possibility that this was just another attempt by Higgs to get others to accept his point of view.

"I'm not crazy, Major," Higgs insisted. "She said her name was Parisia, that there were humans on the other side of the wall, and that their men don't . . . function like Earth men. This is a parallel planet to ours. Actually, she said it's a twin planet called Heart."

"Heart?" Geoffrey asked sarcastically. "I suppose it's a coincidence that Heart is an anagram of Earth."

"Maybe. Why not? Maybe it's not an identical

twin. It could be like Earth, but twisted—like the green sky and blue grass, and men that can't have sex. But you don't have to believe me. You can see her for yourself. She said she was coming back tomorrow night for more. The last order she gave me was not to drink the water. I'm sure that had to be because there's something in the water that would relax me too much to be able to service her!"

Geoffrey was no longer certain that Higgs was off his nut. The more he talked, the more believable his story seemed. He needed another opinion. "Come with me," he said and led him to Julie and Robin's tent.

The flap to their shelter was pulled back, but he didn't presume to enter unannounced. Standing to the side, he spoke in a hushed voice. "Julie? It's Geoffrey. May I speak to you?"

"Of course," she replied, and a moment later she and Robin stepped outside.

Geoffrey's gaze automatically took in the fact that Robin's long legs were exposed below the large shirt she was wearing. He had to work at concentrating on why he was there. By focusing his attention on Julie, he was able to get back on track. "Higgs just came to me with an interesting story, and I'd like you to hear it from him."

Higgs shifted from one foot to the other and looked extremely embarrassed, but he managed to relate his experience to the two women. Geoffrey noted that it came out in better order this time and with more colorful description. Also, the alien female had become more monstrous and terrifying with the second telling. Whatever truth there was to Higgs's claims would probably be completely obscured in exaggeration by the fourth or fifth time he told it.

Julie tried not to be influenced by the skeptical expressions on either Geoffrey's or Robin's face. They were in a strange world, and she didn't think any story should be dismissed, no matter how crazy it sounded or who was telling it.

When Higgs finally ran out of details of his close encounter, Julie asked, "Is there a possibility that you had a hallucination? If they could tranquilize us without our being aware of it, couldn't they also administer a hallucinogenic?"

Higgs shook his head. "No way. It happened. I'm positive."

Geoffrey had another thought. "Is there any way it could have been one of our women and you mistook her—"

"Geoffrey! That's ridiculous," Robin stated with annoyance. "There are only ten of us, two of whom are with Logan's team and another two of whom are standing here."

"Robin's right," Julie said. "I'd vouch for the other six. None of them are thinking of fun and games right now."

Geoffrey shrugged. "I'm just trying to cover every possibility. No offense meant."

"None taken then," Robin said with a smile of forgiveness. "So what's the verdict?"

Julie looked at Geoffrey, but he was waiting for her to speak. "I think we have to assume it happened as Ray said. In which case, we can trust the food and fruit juice but not the water."

"Thank God!" Robin said with a laugh. "I'm starving! How much longer are we supposed to pretend everyone's tucked away for the night?"

Geoffrey glanced at his watch and made a face. "Logan's team went into the tack room nearly two hours ago. We agreed to give them until sunrise before taking any further action. But I have to admit, I'm worried."

Julie wished he hadn't said that. It made her identify the queasiness that she'd felt for the last hour—a combination of worry and guilt. Now she wished she had spoken the kind of words she'd meant to say to Logan before he left. It might not have meant anything to him, but it would have made her feel better now.

After Geoffrey and Higgs said good night a second time, Robin and Julie went back inside their tent to wait for sunrise. Sleep was out of the question.

In spite of her support of Higgs's story, she still thought his mind might have been playing tricks on him. The drug, or whatever it was, obviously had the power to drastically alter one's personality. It had turned a murdering, thieving traitor into a gentle Romeo, complete with a fabricated memory of sensual fantasies and delusions of unrequited love. It had turned her into a horny twit who lacked the ability to see through blatant lies. Someone who could set aside her moral values and all inhibitions and think only of pleasure.

That considered, Higgs's eight-foot-tall, sex-starved invader could have seemed completely real to him.

"I think he's attracted to you," Robin said, abruptly breaking into Julie's thoughts.

With her mind on Logan, Julie automatically thought that was who Robin was referring to. "It was just the drug. Nothing else."

"I don't think so. Right from the start he kept his eyes on you. He barely glanced at me. The only time a man *doesn't* look at my legs when they're showing is when he's in love with someone else, or he's a homosexual. Dear Lord! You don't think he is, do you? I mean, wouldn't that be simply *too* depressing?"

Julie squinted at her friend. "What are you talking about?"

Robin sighed. "I don't mean he looks like it or acts like it, but I've missed the mark before. And he is very gentle and soft-spoken for a man. If he's a homosexual, that could explain why I haven't been able to get through to him."

"Wait a minute," Julie said, holding up a finger. "Who do you think is homosexual?"

"Geoffrey. Who did you think I was talking about? Higgs?"

Julie chuckled at the face Robin made. "No. I'm sorry. I guess I was giving you only half my attention."

"That's all right. I'm not making any sense anyway. This waiting is driving me nuts."

"Me too," Julie admitted. "I can't help but wonder where they are and if they're safe, or in trouble, or—" She wouldn't say her worst fear aloud.

* * *

Logan opened one eye a crack to peek at the candle in the lantern. Judging by the short stub left to be burned away, he guessed that it was nearly dawn. He was proud of this team. No one had moved or made a sound in hours. Unfortunately, it had all been a waste of effort. Somehow the caretakers had figured out what they were up to and had chosen to ignore them. He hated to think what that meant.

A lifetime of imprisonment. Of course, he'd been facing that anyway, and the farm was considerably more pleasant than Leavenworth would have been. *Being drugged and having no defenses.* Although, he had to admit, the time he'd spent with Julie while both their defenses were down was like a taste of heaven. It was only after their minds cleared, and they both remembered that he wasn't good enough for her, that he was sorry he'd been given that taste. At least with the drug in his system, he didn't feel the ache in his chest.

All in all, he wasn't sure which was worse—remaining on the farm and becoming one of the puppet people, with Julie, or returning to his own dismal world without her. It wasn't as confusing when he put it that way.

"Okay, everybody," he said, stretching his arms and legs. "There's no sense putting in more time here. They didn't fall for it."

A harmony of groans accompanied the unbending of stiff bodies.

"Damn!" Gianni muttered. "I think I need some

medical treatment for real now. How do you think they knew?"

Logan shook his head. "For all we know, they could have heard us planning it. The main problem is that we have no idea how closely we're being watched. But it was worth a try. And we'll keep on trying till we get out of here." The sad faces around him brightened a little from his attempted pep talk, but it was hard to sound optimistic when he didn't believe a word he was saying.

As he had estimated, the sun was just topping the horizon when they exited the barn. In a matter of seconds they were surrounded by people who were relieved to see them unharmed and anxious for a full report. However, the relief was quickly buried beneath the news that the mission had been a complete failure.

Geoffrey took advantage of the gathering to tell everyone that they could resume eating but should continue to avoid the water. If they felt at all unusual after eating, they were to notify Julie immediately.

The hungry crowd practically tripped over one another to get to the kitchen. Refortified, there was barely a complaint uttered when Geoffrey gave out the day's chore assignments. Though he knew they all needed to get some sleep, he requested a meeting with Logan's team, Julie, and Robin.

At the last moment he asked Higgs to join them, rather than having him spread his story to everyone else just yet.

Geoffrey waited until all the other teams departed, then gathered his group under one of the large shade trees near the big house. As soon as they were settled, he asked Logan to open the discussion.

"Actually," Logan said, "you heard all there was to report when we came out of the barn. Everyone was in place. I heard the hissing sound and pretended to fall asleep. We waited as planned, but nothing happened. They had to have known we were up to something."

"There is another possibility," Higgs said. He paused for Geoffrey to acknowledge him before continuing. "They might have come for you, and you may have attacked, but they overpowered you, then replaced your memories with what they wanted you to remember, which was that nothing happened. They might have that much power."

Logan rolled his eyes. "Look, Higgs, I've had just about—"

"Hold off on that," Geoffrey cut in. "I think you need to hear something first." He still wasn't entirely convinced that Higgs' tale was true, but he also wasn't convinced otherwise. "Go ahead, Higgs, tell them what happened. But, please, try to stick to the basic facts without your assumptions. I'd like everyone else's opinion without being influenced by your superior knowledge of extraterrestrials." As he had hoped, Higgs took that as a compliment and proceeded to give a fairly concise report that was only slightly more enhanced than the story he'd told Julie and Robin. If nothing else, he provided a much needed boost to the team's spirits.

Gianni laughed the loudest. "Right! Out of all

the men stranded here, she picked you to teach her about sex!"

"You were lucky it wasn't a male who came for a few lessons," Lee taunted.

"If you were so damn good," another prodded, "how come she didn't abduct you and take you home in her spaceship with her?"

"Oh, sure," Higgs whined. "You can all laugh, but you wouldn't think it was so funny if you were the one forced to strip and play stud-horse to the creature from the black lagoon."

Geoffrey cleared his throat to stop the not-so-good-natured teasing. "That's enough everyone. I can vouch for the fact that Higgs was near hysteria when he came to my tent. *Something* happened to him out there, and considering the fact that we're sitting under a green sky, it's certainly possible that he was used by a woman from outside the farm." He covered his mouth with his hand, but couldn't quite conceal his smile. "I do apologize, Higgs. I am trying to believe your story, but you must see how difficult it is to imagine."

Higgs's tight expression showed that he didn't see any such thing.

"Okay," Julie said. "No matter how hard it is to imagine, this is all we've got. I've been thinking about it for hours, and I keep coming back to one thing. This woman warned Higgs not to drink the water. By tonight, if everyone is still feeling perfectly normal, we should know whether the warning had basis. If so, we have to consider what else she said."

"Yeah! And you know what that was?" Higgs

asked in a challenging tone. "She's coming back for me. She'll make me do it again. And she threatened to turn me into dust if I didn't have something new to show her. Maybe you should all come and watch. Then you'll see that I didn't make any of this up!"

"That's it!" Gianni exclaimed, fighting a grin. "We'll all go watch Higgs perform, and when he's got the alien blinded by desire, we grab her. Maybe if we threaten never to let her use Higgs's body again, she'll take us to her leader."

Everyone burst into another round of off-color joking, but Geoffrey put a quick stop to it by saying, "It could work. If Higgs distracted her sufficiently, we might be able to capture her."

"A hostage?" Logan asked, still looking somewhat amused.

"Have you got a better idea?" Julie countered, then was immediately sorry she had, for it brought his attention to her. As much as she wanted to lower her gaze, she didn't allow herself to be such a coward. Finally he was the one who looked away to speak to Geoffrey.

"The only other thing that's come to me would be for one man to go into the tack room with a mask of some kind to prevent him from inhaling the gas. We could stage another fight and have the loser appear to have a broken nose or something, like Wilkes's jaw. That way the mask wouldn't be noticed for what it really was."

"They have too much power," Higgs declared. "I didn't stand a chance, and I was only facing one of them."

Logan ignored him. The differences between Higgs and himself weren't worth wasting breath on. He kept his eyes on the major until the man was obliged to make a decision.

"We'll try to capture the woman first," Geoffrey said after a few more seconds of silent deliberation. "If that fails, then I'll consider sending in one man, but only as a last resort."

Contrary to the old adage, keeping their hands busy for the remainder of the day did not make the time go faster. At sundown, Julie and the other nurses took a poll of everyone's mental condition. They were bored with the menial tasks and anxious for action. No one could be described as relaxed.

On a personal basis, she could attest to the fact that in spite of numerous glances passing between her and Logan, neither was overcome by lust. Her defenses were firmly in place, and apparently, his indifference was as well. The only emotion she was suffering from was lingering embarrassment.

Geoffrey's advisers gathered without his having to call them.

Julie made her report first. "I don't think there's any question about it. The only thing we have all avoided is the water, and everyone is behaving normally."

"If by normal," Logan added, "you mean Higgs is so antsy he's making my skin itch, and Wilkes is preparing to go ten more rounds with Lee Tang, then I agree. The drug, or whatever it is, must be in the water."

Geoffrey nodded. "Of course, this is only supposition, but if we hadn't stopped drinking the water yesterday, I believe we would all be totally passive by now."

"Just like the puppet people," Logan said.

Robin made a face. "We'd probably be bedding down now, perfectly content to sleep until it was time to work again. *Ick!* What a horrible thought."

"Correct," Geoffrey said. "We would have given up on any escape attempt and our caretakers would still expect that, which gives us the advantage of surprise."

Logan agreed. "It's probably also safe to assume that they'll be lowering their guard once they're certain their drug has taken effect."

"Which means we need to act the way they expect us to," Geoffrey stated. "Slow-moving, little or no conversation, early to bed, early to rise. This meeting is to be the last of its kind. We'll have to be extremely discreet from now on."

Higgs couldn't stay silent another moment. "If you capture the woman tonight, none of that may be necessary. I could tell she was somebody important. Used to giving orders, you know. They'll probably agree to anything we want to get her back."

"Are you still willing to go through with this?" Geoffrey asked Higgs.

"I'll do whatever I have to," he replied seriously, despite several snickers from the others.

"Then, unless anyone has thought of an alternative," Geoffrey concluded, "we go with the hostage plan." He waited a few seconds, but no one spoke up. "That's it, then. We all retire to our tents except Higgs, who will be patrolling the area as he did last night. The cloud cover is with us tonight, but that field is still wide open. It's going to be very difficult to sneak up on her without her seeing us."

Logan offered his advice. "The clothes we have are all light colors, but the blankets are dark. If we're lying on the ground, covered by the blankets, we should blend in with no problem. At midnight my team will crawl out of their tents, camouflaged by the blankets, and position themselves in a horseshoe around the spot where Higgs is to have his rendezvous. Once he gets her good and distracted—preferably naked and disarmed—we'll close up the ends of the horseshoe and move in."

"What about weapons for us?" Alicia asked.

"No weapons," Geoffrey said. "Take ropes to tie her up, but I don't want to risk any accidents that might reduce our bargaining power."

Logan went over the timing and each person's positioning and movements. "Any questions?"

"Should I give some kind of signal when I see her coming?" Higgs asked. His unintentional pun earned another round of chuckles, and after he got the joke, he laughed with them. "I'm serious," he protested in vain. "I could whistle to let you know she's approaching, then say something appropriate when it's a good time to move in, like . . . *now!*"

"It works for me," Lee said with a grin, and everyone else agreed.

Geoffrey shook hands with each member of Logan's team, wished them luck, then they straggled off to their tents to try to get a few hours' sleep before beginning another vigil.

At the appointed hour, Logan's team stealthily

slipped out of their tents and started creeping toward the field. Higgs had to keep reminding himself to walk slowly and ignore the dark mounds slithering their way across the ground. As he meandered repeatedly along the same patrol path he had set for himself the night before, he kept his gaze focused on the spot where he had first noticed the woman in the field.

What if she doesn't come back? He would never live it down. *Why couldn't she have chosen someone else, like McKay or Wilkes?* No one would have laughed at them. *What if she does show up, and I can't do it?* It was one thing for a couple of guys to share the same whore in front of each other, but this was different. Geez! He was going to have to do it in front of the whole squad!

He did a quick check of his male anatomy to make sure it hadn't disappeared altogether. He had to forget about how many people were watching and counting on him to make good. He decided his best bet was to call up one of his favorite fantasies and concentrate on that.

Keeping his attention on the field, he pictured two gorgeous cover models driving along in a terrible thunderstorm. Suddenly their car stalls out, right in front of his house. Since his parents are out of town, he's the only one home. By the time the two girls knock on his door to ask for help, they're both soaked, their thin T-shirts clinging to their perfect, braless breasts.

As his mind automatically replayed the part of the fantasy when they exchange their wet clothes for towels and proceed to show him their apprecia-

tion, he felt his body quickening. If Parisia came—
no, *when* Parisia came for her next lesson, he
would simply close his eyes and pretend she was
one of his models.

Despite his positive attitude, however, when another hour passed and she hadn't shown up, all
his worries resurfaced. He glanced up at the black
sky and wondered if he was going to get rained on
now as well. As he passed near one of the mounds
on the ground, it spoke to him.

"Psst! Higgs. Isn't it about time for Wonder
Woman to show up for her date?"

Higgs was about to shoot back a smart reply
when he saw a figure in the distance. He walked
a few steps more until he was fairly sure it was
her. Puckering his lips to make the promised an-
nouncement of her approach, he realized he hadn't
been told what tune to whistle. The only song that
came to his mind was "The Star-Spangled Ban-
ner," and that seemed a little disrespectful. Telling
himself that what he was about to do was in fact
his patriotic duty, he licked his lips and whistled
the opening bars of the national anthem.

Holding on to the mental picture of his two
blond models, he prepared himself to confront
the enemy.

Chapter 9

"Nice to see you again, Parisia," he said when she was close enough for him to confirm her identity. "I didn't drink any water, like you said. What's in it anyway? Some kind of tranquilizer?"

"Something like that," Nadia answered brusquely. She had been dying for this hour to arrive all day, and she had no intention of wasting one more second than necessary on foolish conversation. She was more than ready to get on with it, but she remembered the procedure from the previous night and knew he required certain actions before he could deliver what she needed. "You may ask your question after, and I will answer, as I did last night . . . if I find your performance satisfactory."

"Oh, I think you'll be satisfied with what I'm going to show you. And I have a big surprise for you at the end."

There was something different about him tonight, Nadia noticed. He seemed more sure of himself; he was even smiling at her with a hint of mischief. The pulse between her legs throbbed a bit stronger as she anticipated what he might have planned for her. Her fingers grasped the neck closure of her caftan.

"Wait," he said, taking her hands in his and lowering them to her sides. "Part of what I have to show you is the undressing."

Nadia had been undressed by Fulton a thousand times and couldn't imagine how it could be done differently, but she was willing to give the Earth man a chance to surprise her. "Go on."

Her first surprise was that he didn't immediately remove her caftan. Instead he ran his hands through her hair, over her face, and down her clothed body. He continued to stroke her in that manner as his mouth pressed to hers—kissing, he had called it. Shortly after his tongue began its interesting little dance in her mouth, she felt the urge to touch him back in the same ways and was rewarded with an approving murmur from him.

The removal of their clothing took place an inch at a time, and more touching and kissing accompanied the gradual exposure of naked, tingling flesh. The law against men touching women in her world was fundamental to their way of life. And yet Nadia couldn't help but wonder why women would deny themselves this delicious entertainment. How could they believe something that felt this good was detrimental?

As Ray Higgs's mouth closed over her nipple, concern over the other women's beliefs fled her mind. She only knew that nothing had ever been as exciting as what this man was doing to her, and

she didn't care if she was the only female in her
world who knew about it.

So caught up in a whirlpool of sensation, she
noticed but didn't care why he tossed her caftan
far from where she was standing. All that mattered
was that he lowered her to the grass and was rubbing his naked body against hers. She parted her
legs for his entrance, but received her second surprise instead. As he buried his face in her womanpiece, she squealed with shocked delight. The
notion streaked through her brain that she could
teach this trick to Fulton; then, in the next instant,
only one thought remained. *More.*

She was lost to the desperate hunger he aroused,
fed, and aroused again. She climaxed several times,
and yet she still felt the clawing need to have his
manpiece ramming into her body.

She heard herself cry out to him, begging and
pleading in a way no woman of Heart would ever
demean herself, and finally, thankfully, he gave her
what she demanded.

"Now!" he shouted.

"Yes!" she cried back. *"Now! Now! Now!"* The
explosive release hurled her to the very edge of
consciousness, where her weightless body spun out
of control in a sea of darkness. As she floated back
to awareness on wave after wave of pleasure, she
felt the man abruptly shift his position so that he
was straddling her hips and pressing her shoulders
to the ground in a most peculiar fashion.

All of a sudden her hands were yanked over her
head, her legs shoved together, her wrists and

ankles bound so quickly, she was immobilized before she was fully alert.

"What is the meaning of this?" she screeched indignantly. "Release me this instant!" She glared up at the man she had mistakenly assumed was under her control, then realized too late that they were no longer alone.

"Ride's over, sweetheart," Higgs said with a grin. "Time to pay up."

"Okay, Higgs," Logan said. "We'll take it from here."

Higgs glanced at him, then the others. A surge of pride flooded through him when he saw their expressions. He had finally won their respect! As he rose to his feet, he was aware that their gazes dropped to his sex, which hadn't yet gotten the message that the game had been cut a few seconds short. He had successfully restrained himself to make sure he didn't get too distracted to do his duty.

As he turned to get his clothes he found himself facing Lee and Alicia. Both their eyes widened with feminine interest as they discovered what a number of other women had—that the little man was *not* built proportionately all over.

Logan shared a look of amazement with the other men as they watched the two beautiful, independent women assist the hero into his clothes, then offer to escort him back to his tent—with Sergeant McKay's permission. Logan gave it, but told them to let the major know they had their hostage.

As they saluted and walked away smiling, Logan

thought that the last three days had held more surprises than the previous three years! With a shake of his head, he got back to the business at hand. "Gianni, check her clothes for that weapon Higgs mentioned."

"You have no right to take what is mine!" she squawked. "I order you to release me! You will all be severely punished for this impertinence!"

Logan decided they would be better off with their eardrums left intact and promptly rectified the problem. He pulled off his shirt, twisted it into one long band, and covering her mouth, tied the muffler behind her head. Her first reaction was incensed shock, but as she checked out his bare chest, her nostrils flared as if catching an intriguing scent, and a predatory gleam filled her eyes. She was clearly considering taking him on for dessert. He hoped all of her kind weren't as hungry for men as she was, or he was going to have one hell of a time convincing his team to fight for their freedom.

His gaze shot to Gianni to see what was taking him so long and caught the man staring at the woman with his mouth open. Despite her bindings she was managing to move her thighs and hips to relay her message of sexual need loud and clear. "Gianni!"

Gianni's attention jerked back to the robe in his hands. He pulled two objects out of a pocket and passed them to Logan.

No longer doubting Higgs's claims about anything, Logan deduced that either the cigar-shaped thing or the cigarette case-shaped thing was a weapon. He turned them in his hands, but carefully avoided touching anything that looked like a button or trigger. "Cover her up . . . before any of you catch whatever she's got. Don't untie her, though, just wrap her up in that thing."

It took several men to handle the order, but she was soon trussed up like a large black sausage.

"Well," Logan said, "I think it's safe to assume she doesn't have any of those super mental powers Higgs warned us about." Standing at the woman's feet, he asked her, "How is it that you were going to punish us?" Her eyes were so easy to read; they were now filled with loathing. He pointed the flat, rectangular box at her chest. "With this?" No reaction. "Or this?"

The second he raised the silver cigar, her eyes squeezed shut in expectation of something bad. "Very good. Of course, I don't know how to use this thing, but I'll bet if I pushed this little slide up and down or pressed this button on the end, I'd figure it out eventually." She definitely didn't want him to do that. "So, what do you say? Would you like to be cooperative or shall we play trial and error?"

Her narrowed eyes shot out lethal threats, but she appeared willing to hear more, so he explained. "Cooperative is where we take the muffle off your mouth, but you talk only to answer our questions. And you do answer our questions—truthfully—or we move on to door number two."

Before she could indicate her choice, Geoffrey, Julie, and Robin arrived. "You haven't missed much," Logan said to Geoffrey. "Higgs exaggerated a little about her size and powers, but everything else is pretty much the way he described."

Geoffrey appraised the bundled-up female on the ground and noted the furrow of tension between her eyes. He guessed that Logan and his team had frightened her sufficiently that she would welcome a friendly voice. "I am Geoffrey Cookson, of the United States, Planet Earth. Higgs said your name is Parisia, that your people are human like us, and that we're on a twin planet called Heart. Is that correct?"

She tried to say something that came out only as muffled noise, glared at Logan, then mumbled again.

"It sounds like she wants to talk to you, Geoffrey," Logan said. "Must be that British accent of yours. Okay, lady, you've got one chance to play nice. If you behave and answer our questions, you might get home in one piece."

Her eyes widened at his implication that she might *not* get home again. Then she slowly nodded her agreement to his terms. Logan retrieved his shirt and helped her into a sitting position.

Nadia's mind worked frantically to come up with a means of escape. She had to get back before dawn, at which time someone might witness her passage through the barrier. If her little excursion was discovered, she would be chastised and humiliated, her plans for the future irreparably damaged. She understood that the Earth women had no power over their men, so she couldn't depend on them to assist her.

Looking from one man to the other, she had the

feeling that the blond man could be manipulated, whereas the scarred man exuded too much hostility to be of use to her. Directing her response to Geoffrey Cookson, she said, "Ray Higgs spoke the truth."

Geoffrey hunkered down to her level to make his interrogation seem less threatening. Her features relaxed as soon as he did so, and he smiled to calm her fears a bit more. "We mean you no harm. We only want information."

Nadia smiled back and spoke in a tone that she meant to sound cooperative. "I will tell you whatever you wish to know, but only if you treat me in a civilized manner. Untie me, allow me to dress, and return my property to me."

Geoffrey ignored her order. "If we are truly on another planet, how did we get here?"

She guessed that he might be more pliable if his peers were not observing him so closely. "I prefer to speak only to you. Send the others away."

Geoffrey glanced at Logan and noted his disapproval of that idea. "If you wish to be left alone with one man, it will be him," he told her, pointing at Logan. "And I assure you he's not nearly as patient as I am."

She might have given it a try, but the minutes were ticking by, and she had no more time to waste. She emitted a loud sigh of disgust. "I should have known it was impossible for men to behave in a civilized manner. What is it you wish to know?"

Geoffrey began his list of questions by repeating his first one. "How did we get here?"

Since she had no idea how extensive his scien-

tific knowledge was, she decided to stick as close
to the truth as possible rather than try to fabricate
answers and risk being tripped up in a lie.

"You came through a gateway. As far as we can
tell, there is a magnetic field that flows between
the northeastern hemisphere of Earth and the
northwestern hemisphere of Heart. Apparently the
magnetic pull goes only one way, from your world
to ours, and it causes a problem only when there
are violent electrical storms in the fields on both
worlds at the same time. When that happens, a
gateway opens and whatever or whoever is in the
eye of the earth storm is pulled through. Fortunately, the precise conditions required for such an
incident have been rare."

"It sounds like Higgs was right about that Dragon's Triangle business after all," Logan said to
Geoffrey. "But how did we land here in one
piece?"

Nadia waited for Geoffrey Cookson to indicate
that she should answer the other's question. "Once
you were through the gateway, your pilot regained
sufficient control to land your craft."

"Why doesn't anyone remember that?" Julie
asked.

Nadia assessed the woman who spoke without
the man's permission to interrupt. Perhaps she had
some power after all. "A short-term memory depleter. We find it is best to keep our existence as
secret as possible. May I ask you a question now?"

Julie looked to Geoffrey and received his approval. "All right."

"Why do you allow these barbarians to abuse

one of your own kind? Do you have no control over them at all?"

Julie wasn't certain which question was more surprising—that this woman considered them sisters of some sort or that she assumed the men could be controlled. "As second in command, I fully endorsed the actions of our men. By imprisoning us here, it is you who have abused us."

Nadia arched an eyebrow. "Release me and I will make arrangements for all the women here to be freed. You would have happy lives, unburdened by the demands of any man."

Geoffrey brought the interrogation back on track. "Higgs said your men are impotent. Is it your people's intention to use us as breeding stock?"

Nadia laughed aloud. "Introduce your primitive genes into our society? What a ridiculous notion! Our men's bodies provide the sperm necessary for reproduction without the barbaric act of copulation."

Logan snickered. "You didn't seem to find it so disgusting a few minutes ago."

"If you don't need us for reproduction," Geoffrey countered, "what was the purpose of your visits?"

Nadia paused to form a credible answer. "I needed to experience this physical contact for a scientific experiment I am conducting."

"Why didn't you use one of your own men?" Logan asked.

"Contact between men and women on Heart is unacceptable."

"Hold everything," Robin interjected. "I'm beginning to get a very interesting picture here. A minute ago you offered to free the women to get yourself out of here, but not the men. And you keep referring to men as though they're some inferior species. Is it possible that your men are not only impotent, they're slaves?"

Nadia eyed her with curiosity. This one sounded as though she found the idea of keeping men as slaves quite attractive. "Slavery is against the law. Our men are servants."

"Hot damn!" Robin said with a laugh. "Talk about an upside-down world. Green sky, blue grass, and women in charge."

"Heart is much safer than your world," Nadia said, "where men wage wars and fight one another in their own homes. We have no such violence here."

"How do you know Earth is like that?" Geoffrey asked.

She shrugged. "We question crossovers when they first arrive, before their memories are depleted."

"Are your people all forced to drink the water? Is that how you keep them so peaceful?" Logan asked.

Her eyes narrowed warily. "Higgs told you about the water?"

"Of course," Geoffrey said. "But we had already guessed that we were being tranquilized by something."

"I see. You should have all been fully assimilated by tonight. No previous crossovers ever figured it out in time." Panic turned her stomach as she realized that her warning to Ray Higgs made her responsible for this uprising. The sexual pleasure she had discovered wasn't worth the price she might yet have to pay. How could she have known that Earth men could be so devious? No wonder her people kept them medicated.

She glanced at the western horizon and noted a hint of the approaching dawn. "Please. I have answered your questions. Allow me to leave now. I have important duties to attend to this morning."

"I regret any inconvenience," Geoffrey replied. dropping his friendly tone. "But you've barely begun to answer our questions. You claim your world is peaceful, but surely someone must break a law from time to time. What sort of enforcement agencies do you have? Police? Militia?"

Nadia frowned. She wasn't familiar with those terms, but she understood the meaning. "Laws are enacted and enforced by Parliament."

"And who heads up Parliament?" Geoffrey asked.

"The imperial prefect, Par—" She abruptly recalled her lie about her identity. "Nadia of Hinac is the ruler of all the provinces on Heart."

"What is your position?"

She hesitated again. As she feared, one lie was leading to another and starting to get complicated. "I am Parisia, representative of Acameir."

"Would the imperial prefect have the power to free all of us?"

"Not alone. The majority of Parliament would have to agree to it, and that would never happen."

"Nevertheless," Geoffrey said, "We would like to meet with your ruler."

Nadia gaped at him in shock. "That's impossible! Even if you were freed from this commune, no man may speak to her other than her personal servant."

Logan frowned at her skeptically. "Then you'll have to come with us and make the proper introductions."

She gasped. "Never! I couldn't do that. No Earth person is permitted beyond the barrier."

"That's why you're going to be our escort," Logan told her.

"No. I refuse to assist you. I—I will remain here in the commune rather than betray my people."

Geoffrey brought her attention back to him and spoke with feigned innocent curiosity. "You said none of us are permitted beyond the barrier. What if someone did get through? Are there guards around the wall?"

Nadia smirked. "That would be an unnecessary use of womanpower. No one can penetrate the barrier from this side, and even if someone did, their action would be picked up on the monitors."

"And after that?" Geoffrey asked, then saw that she didn't understand. "If someone broke through, how would that person be stopped?"

Nadia opened her mouth to reply, but nothing, not even a lie, came to her. Since no one had ever managed to escape from the commune, she was not aware of any procedures to deal with it. "That information is confidential. I do not have access to it."

Logan's instincts told him that was a blatant lie. By her reaction to the question, he'd bet his Crations that there was no one on the other side prepared to stop an escapee from this funny farm. "Tell me something you do know, lady. If it's impossible to penetrate the barrier from this side, how did you get out of here last night?"

Her gaze dropped to the control box in his hand before she could stop herself. She tried to hide her mistake with a cough, but he wasn't fooled.

"This?" he asked, holding up the box. "Would you like to be nice and explain how to use it?" She only glared at him. "No problem. I'm sure we can figure it out. Geoffrey?" He handed him the box. "This should be a piece of cake for an engineer."

Nadia's panic was nearing the surface. "You must not fool with the controller. Improper use could have disastrous results."

Geoffrey turned the box over in his hand and studied the three red buttons and the numbered dial. "It would be better if you instructed me—"

"Never! I have answered your questions, but I will not help you invade my home. I have made my decision—I will remain here in the commune."

Julie thought perhaps it was time for a feminine approach, and she knelt down beside the woman. "Parisia, my name is Julie. You wouldn't want to remain here any more than we do. You said slavery is forbidden, and yet we are being held captive and required to work in the fields to provide food for you. Surely you must see how wrong that is." She refrained from mentioning the service required of Higgs.

"We don't need the food," Nadia replied defensively. "The farm is merely the best means to keep the Earth men busy and self-sufficient."

Julie cocked her head thoughtfully. "Busy? As in, busy hands are happy hands? Is that why they're still farming and cooking by century-old methods? To keep busy?"

Nadia was duly impressed by this woman's deductive reasoning. She definitely showed signs of intelligence. "Precisely. Their days are so filled with mundane chores that they couldn't possibly get into mischief."

"And the more modern bathroom facilities?"

"Hmmmph! We would never leave sanitation up to men."

"One more question," Geoffrey said. "How closely are we being observed?"

Nadia gave him a sly smile. "Closely enough."

"Are we being watched now, out here?" Julie asked. When the woman didn't respond, she reminded her; "Your freedom depends on your cooperation. We wish to know how much your people are aware of what we say and do."

Nadia thought about it for a moment, then decided the truth could not make things any worse than they already were and it might just help. "There is a sky monitor that views the entire farm from a distance. The cloud cover tonight has probably obscured the picture."

"And inside the buildings?"

"Only the barn is monitored for sight and sound."

Julie nodded thoughtfully. "So, when someone goes into the tack room with a medical problem, they are seen and heard by someone. Correct?" She felt Logan's gaze on her, and her stomach clenched with renewed embarrassment.

"At the moment there are observation techs on duty around the clock, though that is not usually necessary. Your avoidance of the medication has caused a number of inconveniences," Nadia said with obvious annoyance.

Logan motioned Geoffrey aside and Julie and Robin followed, leaving the rest of the team to guard their captive. As soon as they were out of the woman's hearing, Logan said, "My guess is, she's told the truth for the most part, but either something she said is a lie or she's holding back an important bit of information."

"Agreed," Geoffrey said. "For one thing, she said the magnetic pull goes only one way, but polarity can be reversed. If we got here, we should be able to get back."

"Why would she lie about that?" Julie asked.

Geoffrey shrugged. "Maybe her people just want to keep their world secret, so they don't allow anyone to go back to Earth to talk about it."

"I'm not so sure," Julie said. "I had the feeling she was stating facts as she knows them. If there is a way back, she may not be important enough to have that information. But that makes me wonder about something else. We haven't heard a single story about anyone from outside the farm coming to visit before. Why now, and why would she be the one given permission to make contact?"

"Maybe she didn't have permission," Logan murmured, then realized what had been bothering him. "That's it! She's here illegally. I'd bet on it. She was dying to get back one minute, then willing to stay forever the next. I'd say she definitely did not want her ruler finding out she was here. Now all we have to do is figure out how to use that to get what we want."

Robin was first with a suggestion. "We could promise to release her after she got us out of here and directed us to where we could find that imperial person."

Logan added, "If she's telling the truth about there being no police or guards, we could probably take over the palace or whatever it is, before they knew what was happening."

"And what if she wasn't telling the truth?" Geoffrey asked. "If they were able to get us off the plane and corral us here without us having any memory of it, they could do it all over again. We'd be right back where we started.

"No, I think we need to stick to the original plan and use her as a hostage to negotiate our release. Perhaps if we prove that we can behave in a civilized manner, they might be willing to deal fairly. Any aggressive action on our part will only serve to confirm that we are the primitives she called us."

"I agree," Julie said. "There's only one part of the plan I think you need to reconsider. From what Parisia said, there's no way her ruler will negotiate with a man, no matter how passively he behaves. Our representative should be a woman."

Logan knew she meant herself, and his immediate impulse was to refuse to let her take such a risk, but a heartbeat later he conceded that he had no right to do that, and he remained silent.

"Are you volunteering?" Geoffrey asked Julie.

"Yes, sir."

"Same here," Robin said. "She can't go alone."

Geoffrey shared a look of resignation with Logan. "I don't like it, but you're right. It will be the two of you, plus Lee and Alicia, just in case you need to defend yourselves. You may as well get started right now. We'll take care of stowing our guest out of sight."

While Geoffrey and Julie went over the plan and the terms she would request, Logan tried to think of one good reason Julie shouldn't go or why he should, but nothing logical came to him. All that remained was to wish her luck, as if she were any other soldier going off on a dangerous mission.

You might never see her again! his heart cried. *Tell her.*

But Logan knew there was nothing he could say that she wanted to hear. "Good luck," he finally said, giving Julie and Robin each a curt nod, then returned to his prisoner as they walked away.

Julie told herself she was imagining things. Logan hadn't looked at her in any special way. He hadn't been about to say something, then changed his mind. It was just tension and the dark playing tricks on her eyes.

"Do you suppose Alicia and Lee are finished tucking in sweet little Ray by now?" Robin asked, grinning and wiggling her eyebrows suggestively.

Julie made a face. She tried not to judge other people by her own moral code, especially after everything she'd witnessed since she enlisted. "Let's just hope they all know the meaning of discretion. The last thing we need now is for Wilkes to find out the ladies preferred Higgs over him."

"*Oooh.* Not a pretty picture. But speaking of discretion . . ." Robin pointed at three figures huddled together in front of a tent. As they walked closer, she could tell it was the trio they had just been discussing. Their approach was instantly noticed.

"What's going on?" Lee asked Julie.

"The four of us are going into the tack room and try to negotiate our release. I think we should have a brief strategy meeting before we go in."

"You got it," Lee said, then turned Ray's face to hers and gave him a quick kiss on the mouth. "Sleep tight, baby."

Alicia waited for him to look up at her. "We'll catch you later, love. Behave yourself till we get back." She lowered her head to deliver a considerably longer kiss than he'd gotten from Lee.

On the way to the barn, neither Julie nor Robin asked, and neither Lee nor Alicia offered comments. Instead Julie summarized what they'd learned after the other two women left with Higgs. "There's no way of knowing if Parisia was being honest or if she's even typical of her people. The best we can do is assume she was truthful, but expect anything."

"In other words, we're going to play it by ear," Robin said with a laugh.

Julie smiled back. "Right. And try to let me do most of the talking so they get the impression I have some control over my people."

Robin saluted crisply. "Yes, sir. You're the bosslady."

"That's what I want them to think. Otherwise, I'm not sure they'll believe I have the power to negotiate. So, no matter what I say, even if it sounds outrageous, back me up. You can argue with me later." She met each of the women's eyes and knew she could count on them. "Ready?"

They all nodded and wished one another luck before entering the barn. Robin lit the candle lantern by the door and led the way into the tack room. Once they were all inside, Julie threw the bolt on the door and spoke the words she and Geoffrey had decided on.

"I am Captain Julie Evans of the United States of America. We have captured one of your people, Parisia, representative of Acameir. We wish to open negotiations regarding her release."

Chapter 10

Simone felt like pulling her hair out in frustration. Didn't these Earth people ever sleep? She had purposely requested a change to the night shift in hopes that there would be less activity in the commune—which translated to less decisions for her to make.

Not that there was any real decision to make here. This was an emergency, and emergencies required one to follow the proper procedures regardless of loyalties. She just wanted to stall for a while in hopes that her coworker, Orleander, would return early from her break and then she could handle the situation. To protect herself, she paused the recorder so that the delay would not be evident.

Nadia would do flips down the halls of Parliament if she heard that Parisia had ventured into the commune and gotten caught. Adviser Iris, on the other hand, would be extremely grateful to anyone who helped cover up a potential security leak about the imperial prefect. Simone couldn't imagine why Parisia would have taken such a risk, but she was certain the reason must be of world-shattering proportions.

Five minutes passed, but the four women in the transfer room hadn't magically vanished from her monitor, nor had Orleander returned. Simone knew she had to act.

She was about to call Adviser Iris when a solution occurred. She didn't have to tell Nadia anything. All she had to do was get her to come to Observation and "just happen" to witness the situation for herself.

Simone dashed to the door and scanned the corridor to make sure Orleander was nowhere in sight, then placed a call to Nadia.

A very groggy Fulton answered on the sixth ring.

"This is an emergency," Simone stated. "I need to speak with Nadia immediately."

"May I tell her who is calling?"

"No, you may not. But rest assured, she will appreciate being awakened after I speak to her."

"All right," Fulton said, not at all convinced that Nadia would reward him for disturbing her in the middle of the night no matter how important the cause. Nearly two minutes went by before he was back on the line. "I'm sorry. Nadia is not here."

"Not there? That's ridiculous. If you are saying that merely to avoid leaving your warm bed . . ."

"I swear," Fulton whined, hearing the implied threat. "I've looked everywhere, even outside. She's not here."

Simone would have questioned him further, but the sound of footsteps warned her that time was up. "If she comes in, tell her to go to Observation. Speak to no one but her about this call, or she will be very displeased with you." Without waiting for his reply, she disconnected from him and called Adviser Iris. The woman answered at the same moment Orleander walked in. Simone gave her a frantic signal to join her at the monitor as she spoke to Iris.

"We have another emergency in the commune, madam."

"Oh, my. I'll be there within the hour—"

"I don't believe this should wait," Simone interrupted. "If you'll turn on your monitor, I'll transmit from here."

"One moment, then."

While Simone waited for the adviser to go to her monitor, she backed up the recording to the point when the four women had entered the transfer room. Fortunately, she was fast enough with the controls to prevent Orleander from suspecting anything unusual.

"Go ahead," Iris said in a tired voice. All remnants of fatigue fled, however, when the young woman on the screen issued her short statement. "She lies," Iris said, more to herself than Simone. "It will take me but a moment to refute her claim." She took a calming breath to organize her thoughts. "As of right now, Observation is under security quarantine. No one is to enter or leave without my express permission, and neither of you is to communicate with anyone but me. Is that understood?"

"Yes, ma'am," Simone said quickly, relieved that she had already made an attempt to reach Nadia.

"Yes, ma'am," Orleander repeated. "Should we put the women to sleep?"

Iris studied the frozen images on her monitor. Their stances were defensive, but courage was evident in each face. They could be dangerous. "Yes, but leave them in the transfer room for now. Adviser Iris out."

With the touch of a key she disconnected from Simone. By pressing a few more, she brought up the view of the Observation Room from the concealed scanner to confirm that Simone and Orleander were the only ones there and that they were following her instructions. She thanked the sun that she had doubled the tech staff, for she truly did not trust Simone.

Once she was certain the situation was temporarily put on hold, she placed a call to Parisia's private line.

"Hello?"

It sounded like Parisia, but Iris had to be certain. "Security precautions please." In the blink of an eye she had a visual of Parisia on her monitor, then the palm of the prefect's hand was flattened on the screen. Iris's computer verified that it was indeed the imperial prefect, but she and Parisia had devised one other fail-safe. She asked, "What happened on the twelfth day of June, 1969?"

Parisia moved her hand away from the screen. That question had made her smile when they'd chosen it; now, knowing that it signified a critical security breach, it filled her with anxiety. "My daughter, Brianne, cut her first tooth."

Iris gave an audible sigh of relief. "I apologize for disturbing you, but we have a problem." She relayed as much as she knew so far and what actions had been taken. "Obviously they have not captured you, but somehow they know your name. What makes it doubly confusing is that the woman referred to you as a representative rather than the imperial prefect."

"There's something else that's not quite right," Parisia said, rubbing her eyes. "From what we know of these people, doesn't it seem rather odd that they would choose women rather than men to confront us?"

Iris nodded slowly. She had been too concerned about Parisia to analyze the situation fully. "It does seem unlikely that they would send women. Unless they knew something about the structure of our society."

"It can only mean one thing, Iris. They *have* captured one of our people and convinced that person to reveal certain information about us. But who? And how?"

"I will have the four women taken to the sanatorium and isolated. If you'll meet me there, we can question them together."

Nadia glared at the three silly girls that had been assigned to guard her. She had tried being friendly, demanding, and threatening. She had offered every bribe she could think of to entice them to help her escape. Obviously the scarred man had chosen them to guard her knowing that they were immovable.

At least she had been allowed to dress properly, and though her hands and feet were still bound, she was somewhat more comfortable. She lay on the cot and turned toward the side of the tent. There had to be a way to save herself. Escape appeared unlikely for the moment, but she was certain that eventually an opportunity would avail itself. If she couldn't get the controller back, she could always go through the transfer room. If her timing was right, Simone would be the tech on duty, and she could be convinced to keep a secret—for the right reward.

She recalled Simone telling her she would be working nights now, and it was already nearing dawn. The best thing to do was pretend to be docile long enough for her guards to give her a little freedom. Then by nightfall she could make her break.

But what if the men who captured her figured out how to use the controller in the meantime? What if they escaped from the commune and told someone about her presence? It wouldn't be long before her absence was connected with the escape in spite of her using Parisia's name.

She laughed at the route her thoughts had taken. Earth men didn't have the intelligence to analyze the controller or manage a successful escape. There was no real reason to fret. Just in case, however, she started to create a credible excuse for why she had ventured into the commune.

A short while later, she was satisfied that she was prepared for every possibility and allowed herself to go to sleep.

Logan flopped onto his stomach and punched his pillow one more time. Years in the service had accustomed him to grabbing an hour of sleep whenever and wherever he could. He was an ace at shutting out distractions and ignoring uncomfortable surroundings to get the most out of a catnap.

So why was he having so much trouble taking advantage of the rest time he'd been granted and badly needed?

He knew the answer; he just didn't like admitting it, even to himself. His quixotic instincts had him wanting to protect Julie regardless of the fact that she didn't want his protection and probably didn't need it.

As long as he had kept her classified as an unattainable fantasy, thoughts of her had never kept him from sleeping. But now, after having held her, touched her, *tasted* her, and discovered exactly how she looked when she was filled with wanting him, the reality and the fantasy was all mixed together.

He couldn't help but wonder what it might have been like if he and Julie had met before— His thought stopped there. Before what? Before he was born maybe? There had never been a time in this life when he would have belonged in the same world as Julie.

What if she didn't come back? What if the people on the other side of the wall decided to keep her and the other three women over there and leave Parisia here? He shifted to his side to consider that possibility. He doubted that would happen, but if it did, he felt certain either Geoffrey would figure out how to use the device that had got Parisia through the wall, or Parisia herself would eventually break down and help them escape.

One way or the other, Logan was betting their present circumstances would soon be changing. He just wished he had a crystal ball to see whether that change would be for better or for worse. The only thing he knew for certain was that even life in paradise would be torture if Julie was within reach yet untouchable. And as long as she believed he was a lowlife murdering, drug-dealing traitor, she would remain untouchable.

Of course, he could always tell her the truth, but since there was no one here to back up his story, why waste the breath? It would be his word against everyone else's—just as it had been at his court-martial.

Julie, Robin, Lee, and Alicia awoke on the carpeted floor of a very large unfurnished room. There were no windows, only a closed door in the wall across from them. Julie rose and walked toward it, but was stopped halfway there by an invisible barrier.

"Well," she said, turning back to the others, "I don't know if we've made progress or not. We've gone from a walled-in farm to a cell."

Robin stood up and stretched. "I wonder how long we were out. I feel like I had a really good night's sleep."

"That's how Logan and Wilkes described their experiences too," Julie reminded her. "But in actuality they were only gone a few hours. At least we didn't wake up still in the tack room. Hopefully this means they're going to talk to us."

No sooner were the words out of her mouth than the door opened and two women dressed in long white robes entered. Lee and Alicia were on their feet in an instant.

One of their visitors was middle-aged and so pale and slender, it seemed that a light breeze would blow her away. Julie thought she looked friendly but troubled. The other was shorter, plumper, and much older. Her worried frown appeared to be a permanent expression.

"Good day," the younger woman said with a near smile. "We understand that you wish to speak with us."

Julie took a step forward and repeated her earlier statement. "I am Captain Julie Evans of the United States of America. We have captured one of your people, Parisia, representative of Acameir. We wish to open negotiations regarding her release."

"That is most intriguing, particularly since I am Parisia of Acameir, and my title is not representative but imperial prefect of Heart. This is my chief adviser, Iris of Mergany."

Julie hadn't known what to expect, but it certainly wasn't that! "The woman we are holding hostage claims that *she* is Parisia and that Nadia of Hinac is imperial prefect."

"Nadia?" the older woman asked skeptically. "What does this woman look like?"

Julie shot a glance at Robin. Someone was lying, but who? "She is tall, full-figured, has very long black hair and a rather large nose."

The two women exchanged whispers, then the adviser said to Julie, "Your description matches that of the woman we know as Nadia, but it is difficult for us to believe you have captured her. Tell us how this happened."

Julie straightened her shoulders, met the older woman's penetrating gaze, then related the facts as if she were delivering a report to a superior officer. She could tell her straightforward delivery was appreciated, but what she was saying was beyond belief.

"Impossible," the woman who claimed to be the real Parisia murmured. "That is too much, even for Nadia."

"I have no reason to lie to you," Julie protested. "And how else would I have learned the names Parisia and Nadia, or known about the gateway, the drug in the water, or that your planet is called Heart?"

"We are not accusing you of lying about having captured one of our women," Parisia said, "but the circumstances are simply too unlikely. Our entire society has been structured to prevent the sort of male aggression you have described. It is impossible to believe that one of our women would not only permit but welcome an invasion of her body."

"All I can tell you is she said she was conducting an experiment, and it was not for breeding purposes."

As the pair whispered to each other again, Julie had the distinct impression that they might not want Parisia/Nadia back. She remembered how that woman had tried to play on their sisterhood, and she thought that angle was worth a try here. "Excuse me?" She waited until she had their full attention. "Surely you wouldn't consider leaving one of your own among all those primitive men."

"What is it you wish in exchange for her freedom?" Iris asked.

"It's very simple," Julie replied. "Send us all home."

"That may sound simple to you," Parisia said, "but it's a request we could not fill no matter how desperate we were to make a trade."

Julie had anticipated that response. "We know you have something called a short-term memory depleter. You could use that on us so that we'd have no recollection of Heart at all."

Parisia shook her head. "I'm afraid you misunderstood. We can't send you back because we don't know how."

"How can that be? You're able to heal critically ill people and build invisible force fields, yet you can't figure out how to make the gateway work in reverse?"

"It's never been considered a priority."

"Well, it damn well should be," Robin interjected, not able to remain silent a moment longer. "How would you like to be stranded a zillion miles away from your home, turned into zombies, and treated like lab rats?"

Julie held up a hand to stop her from continuing. It was important that these women thought of them as equals, and she was fairly sure the way to accomplish that was through intellectual rather than emotional channels. "If you truly do not have the ability to send us home, then at least release us from the farm and give us access to your technology. We have men and women with a wide variety of talents and skills. Given the chance, we may be able to solve the problem for ourselves. Besides that, we need a more stimulating life than what you had planned for us. We don't know what your society is like, but it has to be closer to what we're used to than that farm."

"Anything else?" Parisia asked. Julie ran down her mental checklist. "There may be some minor details as we go along, but there's only one more major request. No more drugs or using any other methods you have to control or alter our behavior. We want our freedom in every way. Our hostage said you are human, so you must know how important individual freedom is. We're asking no more of you than we believe you would ask of us if the situation was reversed."

Parisia slowly nodded. "This is a very grave matter. One that I must discuss with others before taking any action. I cannot make you any promises, but I assure you that I empathize with your position and will try to come up with an acceptable compromise for everyone concerned. It may be some time before I am able to meet with you again, so I will have you moved to a more comfortable room to wait. Your cooperation and patience will be appreciated."

Parisia and Iris weren't gone more than ten minutes when Iris returned. "Come along," she said, holding the door open.

Julie stepped forward, but the invisible barrier stopped her progress.

"Oh my, forgive me," Iris said, then took something out of her pocket. It looked like the small box that had been taken from their hostage. "If you'll all stand back and off to the side, I'll have this out of your way in a moment."

They did as she directed, then watched her point the box at the center of the barrier. A white beam shot out from the box, and with two sweeps of her arm she drew a large X across the wall, then put the device back in her pocket. "You can cross now. It's gone."

Since Julie couldn't see any change with her eyes, she tested the space before her with her hand to confirm that the barrier really had disappeared, then motioned for the others to follow. Iris led them down one corridor, then another, with barely a glance behind her.

Julie was a little surprised that they had gained so much trust so quickly. It was almost as if . . . "Iris? May I ask you a question?"

"Certainly."

"Are you telepathic?"

Iris raised her eyebrows. "No. Why do you ask?"

"You don't seem at all afraid of us now. I thought perhaps you'd read my mind to know that you're safe and we wouldn't attempt an escape."

Iris angled her head at Julie. "I'm not telepathic, but my intuition is usually quite good, and it says you're an intelligent, logical woman. Harming me or attempting an escape would not serve any purpose at this time. Therefore I'm perfectly safe with

you at the moment. Here we are." She opened a
door and waved them inside. "Full illumination,
please." Immediately the room was flooded with
light.

"Very nice," Robin said, scanning the large
room. "We finally found civilization."

Julie smiled as she took in the red, white, and
blue color scheme. The furnishings were all combi-
nations of geometrically shaped cushions and
pieces of what appeared to be lucite, which could
be mixed and matched to serve different functions.
Iris pointed out the bathroom, then slid back a
panel on one wall to reveal a kitchenette.

"Lighting and temperature are voice-activated. If
you are hungry or thirsty, the cooler and cabinets
are stocked with a variety of items. If you wish to
heat something, place the entire tray or container
inside the laser oven." She opened the door to
demonstrate. "The unit will automatically read the
instructions and cook it accordingly."

Iris closed up the kitchenette and moved across
the room to a low table surrounded by cushions.
"This room is normally used as a waiting area for
family or friends of a patient. It's equipped with
the most modern entertainment center available."
She touched the edge of the table, and a directory
listing of options appeared on its surface. "It's
touch-sensitive and self-explanatory. For instance,
if you would like to hear some music . . ."

She passed her finger over that word, and the
room was suddenly filled with the sounds of a sym-
phony orchestra. The tabletop now offered a
means of changing the volume, tone, and musical

selection. Iris gave a quick demonstration of how to use those features, then touched the edge of the tabletop again to turn the system off.

"It is capable of running as many as a dozen programs simultaneously, though I've never figured out why anyone would want to do that." She walked to the door and opened it while they were all still awed by her brief tour.

"As Parisia said, it may be a while before we can get back to you, so please be patient and make yourselves comfortable." A second later she was gone.

Lee went to the door and tried to turn the knob. "It's locked."

"So much for trusting us not to make an escape," Robin said with a laugh. "But at least they're no longer trying to bore us to death. I don't know what I want to test first, the kitchen or the entertainment center."

Julie shut out the other women's voices and tried to focus on what was bothering her about the room. She surveyed every bright, cheery inch before it hit her. There were no windows or timepieces—no way to tell how many hours would be crawling by. She supposed that might be good for some people, but she had always been very time-conscious. Not knowing whether it was day or night, if one minute had passed or ten, added to her already tense state.

She was a little envious of Robin. They were in precisely the same position, yet Robin was having fun and she was fretting. Determined to change her attitude, at least until they got out of this room, she joined the group at the entertainment center.

"What do you think *Fictionvision* is?" Robin asked.

"Let's find out," Alicia said and touched that word on the directory. That list of options was replaced by only two words; *Comedy* and *Drama*.

Lee chose comedy, and a list of alphabetical titles and running times began slowly scrolling along the tabletop. "Good grief! We never had this many choices even after we got satellite. Your turn, Julie. You pick one."

Julie squinted at the flow of printed words. Finally she just closed her eyes and lowered her finger to the table.

They all leaned forward to see her selection.

"*Mother Knows Best*?" Robin read with a laugh. "This should be ripe!"

Before anyone else could comment, the title appeared in script on the blank wall in front of where they were seated.

"Lights out, please," Lee requested to the ceiling, then giggled when her order was obeyed.

Without the lights Julie could see that the images on the wall were three-dimensional. It looked as though they were sitting in the living room being displayed.

Despite the bits of information Nadia had given them about her society, the program still came as a bit of a surprise. The comedy aspect seemed to be at the expense of the bumbling houseman, who meant well but managed to screw everything up so badly that only the wise, long-suffering heroine could straighten it all out when she came home from work.

"You know what this reminds me of?" Robin asked. "*I Love Lucy* in reverse. Do you think this is really how they live here?"

Julie drummed her fingers on the table and accidentally shut off the program. "Bring the lights up halfway," she said, then smiled when it worked. "I could get used to that part, but as to what we just watched, I think we'd have to consider it in the same way as we view our television sitcoms. You know, based in fact but fictionalized and exaggerated to be entertaining."

"That show was more pathetic than entertaining," Lee said with a grimace.

"To us, maybe," Julie said. "But their culture obviously differs from ours. I don't know if Iris did it on purpose or not, but she's handed us a way to study their society. A little while ago we were dealing blind. With this little toy we might be able to learn enough about our opponents to get everything we want." She was satisfied to see the nods of agreement from the others. "As of this moment, ladies, school is in session. Let's begin with the news of the day."

Nadia had said Heart was peaceful and the news seemed to back that up. It contained primarily positive rather than negative news. There were no reports from war zones or famine-stricken countries, no homicides or hijackings, no arrests of drug lords or deaths of innocent bystanders because of a shoot-out in a fast-food restaurant.

What there was was an overabundance of statistics—how many tons of corn had been produced at a profit of so many dollars for such-and-such corporation; percentage comparisons of utility usages on this date over the past twenty years to reflect an improvement of efficiency level; numbers of patients admitted to sanatoriums and for what diseases. Minute details of progress made on a health-research study of some microscopic bacteria was the lead story of the day.

In the field of science, there was evidence that FTL (faster-than-light) travel had been developed in a certain distant galaxy by beings known as the Faxons.

In sports, the Pajanese team was leading the Blue League in the free-style dance competition, and Litay was the forerunner of the Red League. It looked like the finals were shaping up to be the most exciting in ten decades of tournament dancing.

The closing story of the day was apparently meant to be a big shocker. A woman confessed to having taught her son to read. She was sentenced to six months of extreme ostracism, during which the child would be placed in a foster home where he would undergo a series of memory-depletion sessions.

Robin was the first to speak. "Talk about your women's lib!"

"Did you notice there wasn't a single man involved in that whole broadcast?" Alicia added.

"Obviously," Julie said, "Nadia was telling some truths. This is definitely a female-dominant society. We should be able to use that to our advantage."

Lee stood up and went to the kitchenette. "But other than the fact that men aren't equals, these women seem to have a pretty good handle on things. I'm gong to try one of these meals," she said, pulling a tray out of the cooler. "Anybody else want anything?"

They all decided to have something to eat and drink, then returned to the entertainment center. Julie was disappointed that there were no educational offerings for them to study the history of the planet. She would have liked to have known how it could be so much like Earth yet evolved so differently.

"Let's try a drama next," she suggested.

By watching dozens of programs, they were able to draw a few conclusions about life on Heart.

In every instance, regardless of the story line, men were scarcely seen. And when they were portrayed, they were always servants, meekly carrying out the orders of a female. Women ran the government and businesses, constructed buildings, and traveled to other planets. Robotic technology took care of any job that might require excessive strength or dirtying one's hands. The women of Heart, despite their power, highly valued their femininity. Men cooked, cleaned, did laundry, took care of the children, and generally did as they were told.

Julie knew there wasn't much difference between this and how women had once been portrayed on American television, but it was still hard to imagine. A vision popped into her head of Logan wearing an apron, holding a baby on one hip, while stirring the contents of a frying pan.

She couldn't quite hold the image. It was too ludicrous to contemplate. There probably wasn't enough of that strange drug on all of Heart to domesticate a man like Logan. But she couldn't help but think of how interesting it would be to have the upper hand with him for once.

"I can't figure out the politics," Lee said after they'd all seen enough. "It sounds like capitalism, socialism, democracy, and imperialism all got boiled in one pot. But if the whole planet is at peace, it must work."

Alicia hugged her knees to her chest. "These women obviously respect power. Not brute force, but the mental kind. I think they probably do a lot of bargaining and scheming behind the scenes. I'd say power and politics are what keeps their wheels turning."

"And production," added Julie. "There seems to be a lot of importance placed on progress, productivity, and efficiency."

"You know," Robin said, "it all make sense if you consider the one thing that was missing from all those programs—male-female relationships. There wasn't even a hint of romance, let alone love or lust. These women have turned their men into eunuchs who are happy to take care of all the aggravating, time-consuming tasks that keep most of our women too tired or busy to compete in the political or scientific arenas for the first half of their lives. Hell, we might even have a woman president by now, and cabinet too, if no one ever fell in love and put being a wife and mother before her career."

"It sounds reasonable on the surface," Alicia said with a thoughtful frown. "But knowing what it feels like to fall in love or to be held in a man's arms, I don't think many women would be willing to give that up for a more efficient, peaceful world."

"Which brings us to our hostage," Julie stated. "I think we can assume that she wasn't supposed to trespass onto the farm, and from the shocked expressions on Parisia's and Iris's faces, I'd say if she was conducting an experiment, it was strictly personal."

Robin made a face. "It sounds like our bargaining ticket isn't worth a ride on a merry-go-round. They'd probably just as soon leave her on the farm than let her infect the rest of their society with her unusual interest in men."

"I'm afraid that's what I was thinking too," Julie said. "If we want our freedom, we're going to have to come up with something to offer them that they want but don't already have. The problem is, I have no idea what that could be."

Chapter 11

Brianne knocked lightly on Parisia's bedroom door. "Mother? It's four o'clock. Parliament will be convening in two hours. Are you awake?"

"Yes, dear," Parisia replied. "Come in."

Brianne entered, expecting to see her mother resting on her bed, but instead found her sitting at the window.

"I have such a lovely view of the city from this tower. Sometimes I get too busy to appreciate it."

Brianne heard a touch of melancholy in her mother's voice. Taking a seat beside her, Brianne touched her mother's hand. "Are you feeling all right? Did you get any sleep?"

Parisia blinked at her as if she only now realized she had company. Giving her daughter a soft smile, she said, "I'm well, and I may have gotten something better than sleep—an idea."

"Oh? For which problem?"

That made Parisia laugh. "It might be a way of solving two at once. Or create an even bigger one. I'm afraid I was sitting here brooding about how much I would miss the little extras I've come to take for granted if I was no longer prefect."

"That's a particularly odd thing to say considering the fact that your greatest opponent will probably never have the chance to hinder you again."

Parisia shifted toward Brianne. "You heard something?"

Brianne shook her head. "Nothing that was worth waking you for. Nadia's houseman confirmed that she has been missing since sometime last night. She has been paged throughout the imperial city, and no one has seen or heard from her. Iris is satisfied that the Earth woman has told the truth. They have captured Nadia. Who else would have had the nerve to give your name as hers and hers as the imperial prefect?"

"If we could prove what they said she did with that Earth man, I don't think anyone would find fault with me if I left her in the commune. Has the technician had any luck with the recording made by the sky monitor?"

"I don't believe so. The cloud cover was extremely thick last night."

"Last night, yes, but what about the night before? They said she was there the previous night." Brianne was already across the room calling Iris as Parisia completed her thought. "The only way I can permanently censure Nadia is with irrefutable, shocking proof. Otherwise, she's liable to concoct some story that will put doubts in certain minds, as she has in the past."

As Brianne completed her call to Iris, her broad smile lifted Parisia's spirits. "Iris was a step ahead of you this time, Mother. She just finished viewing a segment of the prior night's sky recording. She said the blow-up is very grainy, but there's no question about it being Nadia behaving most improperly with an Earth man. Apparently the techs were so busy watching the group in the transfer room, they missed the activity outside.

"To quote her, 'If you have the courage to show that film to Parliament, not only will Nadia lose every supporter she ever had, they will agree to anything you propose afterward.'"

Parisia's smile now matched her daughter's. "Then I'll just have to gather up my courage, because what I'm going to propose would be best presented to a Parliament that was already in a state of shock."

"Mother! Just what is this idea of yours?"

"First ask Delbert to bring me a snack and cup of tea while I bathe." As she headed for the bathroom and Brianne went to the door, she said, "Oh, yes, and a freshly pressed dress gown. The gold one, I think. I'll explain my plan while I get ready. I can't believe I was sitting there feeling sorry for myself. Remember this, Brianne. Every so often things need to be stirred up to keep everyone on their toes, no matter how frightening the change might look."

Brianne didn't care what the daring plan was; she would back it wholeheartedly if it meant seeing her mother happy. Just now Parisia looked as she had years ago—full of energy and spirit, anxious to do battle on the floor of Parliament.

She was halfway down three flights of winding stairs when she saw Delbert coming up, carrying a tray. On it was a silver tea service, two china cups, and a plate of sandwich triangles. "You've been reading Mother's mind again, Delbert." She smiled to let him know she was teasing as she walked back up the stairs with him. "She just asked me to have you bring her a snack and tea. She also requested—"

"A freshly pressed gown," Delbert finished for her. "Her gold one is hanging in her dressing room."

Brianne laughed. "You really do know what she wants before she does, don't you?"

Delbert lowered his eyes shyly. "We've been together a very long time, and Parisia has always been just a bit predictable. Do you require any assistance? Jason is helping the chef at the moment, but I'm sure he could be—"

"No, no. It's not necessary to interrupt him. I'm going to Parliament exactly as I am. No one will notice me with the show Mother and Iris have planned."

If he had suggested one of the other housemen, she might have accepted the offer, but she never felt completely comfortable about being served by her twin brother. Had they been born to anyone other than the imperial prefect, it would never have been a problem. When Jason turned twenty, he would have been put into service in another household. As the prefect's son, however, he was in the awkward position of being too exalted to work for a lesser family.

The imperial prefect had the exclusive option to terminate a pregnancy if she learned that a male had been conceived, and Parisia would have aborted if it had been a singular conception. With a female twin, however, her decision had not been so simple.

She had encountered a series of problems in her attempt to be impregnated, and the doctor had warned her that she might never conceive again. Knowing there would be difficulties in the years ahead for her son, she chose to bear the twins in order to have a daughter to carry on the family line.

Parisia was coming out of her bath wrapped in a warm robe as Brianne and Delbert reentered the suite. "He anticipated you, as usual," Brianne said as she and her mother both sat by the table where Delbert placed the tea tray.

"Would you like me to do your hair while you have your tea?" he asked Parisia while pouring her favorite brew.

She smiled up at him affectionately. "That would be very nice, thank you. Something to make me look very serious, I think."

Brianne wondered if she would ever find a houseman as perfect for her as Delbert was for Parisia. He was extremely bright and pleasant-looking for a man, and not at all clumsy like so many of them were, which were the reasons Parisia had chosen him to begin with, both as a servant and sire for her offspring.

Actually, Brianne thought she'd be happy just to find a servant that could style hair as well as Delbert. It was his exceptional skill and eye for beauty that had earned him the very rare privilege of touching Parisia and her daughter. Of course, it was only their hair he could touch, and he had to ask permission first. Otherwise, he always remembered to keep a respectable distance from them both.

It was somewhat unusual, but Delbert was the only man Brianne had ever had contact with, even as a child. Parisia had used his sperm to fertilize her egg, then kept him on as caretaker after the twins were born. Parisia never had reason to replace him in all the years since.

Though Brianne understood the reason, she still felt sad when she recalled the day she had become a woman and Delbert had no longer been permitted to treat her as a child. From that day forward, physical contact between them had been prohibited. It was upsetting at first, especially that day she fell and hurt her knee. She had cried for him to pick her up and give her a hug to make it feel better. He had been hurt that day too, but the law had to be obeyed—especially in the home of the imperial prefect.

The separation was much harder with Jason. She supposed it was because they were twins and bound in a different way than most brothers and sisters. They both had a difficult time remembering the no-touching rule, until finally Jason was threatened with banishment. Rather than be parted from his family entirely, he worked harder to adjust to the new rules. To help him along, his medication dosage was temporarily increased as well.

"Brianne?" Parisia said softly. "You look quite distressed. You mustn't be. I will admit that my proposal is radical, but with Nadia out of the way . . ."

As Parisia began to spell out her plan, Brianne shook off the confusion she always felt when she thought too long or too hard about Delbert or Jason. She was the daughter of the imperial prefect of Heart, which meant if there was no major opposition, she would be the next imperial prefect. It was not good to question traditions that formed the foundation of their society. Her role was to see that those traditions were carried on in order to insure domestic peace and tranquility throughout the world.

With part of her mind lagging in the past, she thought perhaps she had misunderstood what her mother was suggesting and asked her to repeat what she had just said. When she realized she hadn't misunderstood at all, she was filled with unease. It seemed extremely ironic that while she had been thinking of carrying on age-old traditions to insure world peace, the imperial prefect was planning on breaking a few—for the same reason.

Julie saw the rows of cots, the men with bandaged wounds, the IV bottles and bare lightbulbs. It's not real, she told herself. It's only a dream. You can make it go away if you really try.

She was sick to death of war, the senseless maiming and killing. How naive she had been to think that because she was a nurse, she could tolerate the sights and sounds in an army hospital unit. For each soldier she nursed back to health, another died. Soon one young man's face blended in with the next and the next, and there were times when she had to look at the chart to remember whether this was Bill or Troy or a new patient just arrived. Had he lost a leg or a hand? Or was this another drug overdose?

But there was one name she didn't forget. One face that stayed with her whether she wanted it to or not. She saw him there now, lying on his cot with his eyes closed, pretending to be asleep so she wouldn't bother him. But she was too smart for that ploy. He was going to talk to her today if she had to drag words out of his mouth.

As she did several times a day, she checked his pulse, took his temperature, and listened to his lungs, chatting to him all the while as if she expected him to respond. Suddenly he opened his eyes and looked at her, and he didn't need to speak aloud.

He adored her. He worshiped her. He needed her to love him and need him in return. She had never known a man whose loneliness matched her own, and yet, without a word, she knew he felt it too. "Logan," she whispered, and bent to kiss his lips. Somehow she was now beside him and beneath him, and they were on a bed of straw.

"I love you," he said. Then his hands and mouth aroused a hunger that had her trembling. She felt him against her, hard and ready to join their bodies together. But as she lay there, breathlessly awaiting the moment, Gianni and Higgs appeared, in their white gloves and MP helmets, and lifted him from her.

Julie watched them escort him away, his wrists

cuffed and his ankles shackled. "But he said he loves me," she cried. Gianni looked back at her and laughed.

The real sound of laughter pierced the dreamy veil and brought Julie abruptly awake. She immediately realized that the giggles were coming from Robin and Lee and had nothing to do with her, but her heart still pounded from imagined humiliation.

"Oops," Robin said when she noticed Julie sitting upright. "Sorry about that."

Julie waved away her apology. "It's okay. I'm surprised I fell asleep."

"We all did," Robin said with a shrug. "There's instant coffee if you need some."

Julie knew she needed something, but she wasn't sure exactly what. A flash of sensation from her dream came back to her, and she promptly swept it away. "You'd think they'd at least send us a message to let us know what's going on. This waiting without knowing how long it's been is driving me crazy."

"Now that you're up, do you mind if we watch another program?" Robin asked.

"No, but how about the news first?"

Robin turned on the entertainment center and selected the news. The weather report was followed by the same sports news they'd heard before. Julie was about to tell Robin to switch it when the pictured changed to the imperial prefect and her chief adviser exiting a room and being surrounded by reporters.

"Why did you call an emergency session of Parliament, Madam Prefect?" one reporter called out.

"What took all night to decide?" asked another.

"Why was the media excluded?"

Iris raised a hand and the crowd held their breath. "We apologize for any inconveniences or hurt feelings. A situation of utmost delicacy has occurred, and until all the parties involved have agreed on the actions to be taken, it will have to remain confidential."

"Until when?"

"Your constituents have a right to know what this *delicate* situation is!"

Parisia spoke in Iris's ear. She was clearly insisting her adviser make another statement, much to that woman's disapproval. After another exchange, Iris straightened her shoulders and stepped forward. "Parisia will answer all your questions at an open media conference at three o'clock this afternoon in the Grand Hall. She respectfully requests that you do not browbeat any other members of Parliament until then. They have had a long night also and have been sworn to confidentiality."

Robin said, "That's got to be about us, right?"

"Sh-shh," Julie sounded as the picture switched back to the commentator.

"That was just moments ago, and as you heard, we have to wait six more hours to find out what all the secrecy is about. For some educated guesses from women around the nation, we go now to our roving reporters . . ."

"Six more hours," Julie muttered. "Assuming they keep the same time as we do, that makes it about nine in the morning. Good heavens! We've already been gone more than a day."

"Can you imagine what everyone back on the farm is thinking?" Alicia asked. "They must be—"

Her words drifted off as the front door opened and Parisia and Iris entered. Robin turned off the center, and they all rose expectantly.

"We apologize for the delay," Parisia said. "It was quite complicated. Please sit down. We have several matters to discuss with you."

They all sat down, the Heart women on one side of the table, the Earth women on the other, but no one tried to pretend they were at ease. The tension in the room was too thick to cut with polite greetings and pleasant smiles, and neither faction bothered to make the effort.

Julie had once heard that in a bargaining situation, whoever talks first loses. She wondered if the person who said that had ever tried to sit quietly while his or her freedom was on the line. Thankfully, Iris didn't abide by that theory.

"Perhaps the best place to begin would be with introductions all around. You know that I am Iris of Mergany, chief adviser to the imperial prefect, Parisia of Acameir." She bowed her head briefly toward Parisia. "Please call us Iris and Parisia. We are aware that you were all involved in a violent confrontation—a war—before you came here. We would like to hear something of that. We'd also be interested in knowing what your fields of expertise are."

"I'm Julie Evans, a nurse. I was a captain in the

Army, which makes me the senior ranking officer of the women stranded here."

"Robin Pascal, mechanic. I can repair anything with an engine in it."

"Alicia Samples, helicopter pilot. But I'm licensed to fly single-engine jets."

"Lee Tang. I was in the infantry during the war, but back home I own a martial arts school."

Parisia wrinkled her brow. "That phrase is not familiar. What sort of art is taught at your school?"

"Strong mind, strong body. Self-defense."

Parisia's eyes widened. "Were you one of the women who fought with the men the first night?"

Lee grinned and pointed at Alicia. "She was the other one."

"Amazing," Parisia whispered, shaking her head. "We realize you must be quite anxious to begin negotiations, and I assure you we have a proposition that should interest you. However, it will be much easier to work out details if we each understand a little more about the other's background."

For quite a while she and Iris asked questions which mainly focused on the war, what the women's duties were, how it began, and how it ended. Julie supplied most of the general answers, with the other women offering personal details when requested.

When Iris and Parisia were satisfied with what they'd learned about Earth and its war, they took turns describing their culture and how it had taken a different direction from Earth's. Though Julie and her friends had gleaned a good deal of information from the fictionvision programs, they listened attentively, particularly when Iris related the legend of the Velids' attack on Heart and subsequent transfer of power from men to women.

"No one is certain about what actually happened or whether men were ever really in control. All recorded history begins centuries after the women enslaved the remaining men. The legend has survived primarily as a reminder of why men must not be allowed to exercise their natural urges. Based on what you've told us about this last war on Earth, we have acted wisely."

Julie felt as though she should come to the defense of her planet but the facts were against her. "Nevertheless, Earth is our home. We wish to return to our families and friends."

Robin sat forward. "And our men may have some terrible characteristics, but we prefer them that way rather than what your 'medicine' turns them into. Obviously, at least one of your women thought the same way."

Parisia blushed and cleared her throat. "With regard to your captive, we have confirmed everything you've said, except that she is Nadia, not Parisia. What she did was not sanctioned by Parliament, nor would it ever be. It has been decided that her punishment will be to remain in the commune for five years, at which time her case will be reviewed. Thus we have no wish to bargain for her release."

Julie's heart stopped and started again with a lurch. It was exactly what they had feared. She made herself keep breathing while she waited to hear what sort of decision had been made about them.

"However," Parisia said after she was certain her words had sunk in, "we wish to bargain for your services instead."

The four Earth women shared surprised glances. They had thought the game was over when it had barely begun.

"Iris related the positive aspects of our society. We are quite proud to boast of thousands of years of peaceful, nonviolent existence. But one of the reasons this has been possible is because we have no enemies in our solar system. No one has forced us to defend our world.

"Recently it has come to our attention that faster-than-light travel has been developed on other planets, that it is now possible for beings from distant galaxies to visit us one day. We would like to believe they would come in peace, to exchange ideas or establish trade. But that would be dangerously naive of us."

Iris picked up the narrative from there. "Parisia has just spent most of the night convincing Parliament that we can no longer assume that we are safe in our peaceful system, and that we need to be prepared in the event of an alien attack."

"That sounds reasonable," Julie said.

"To you perhaps," Parisia replied. "But this is a radical idea here. You see, we have no army, no defense system, no weapons of any kind. It will take vast sums of money to implement a plan of any sort, and there is no budget allocation for such. Without being able to see an immediate threat, several members of Parliament argued against diverting funds from ongoing projects."

"This is where we have you to thank," Iris interjected. "The loudest opponents to Parisia's defense proposal—as we anticipated—were Nadia's supporters. Once they were shown proof of what she had done, they were only too happy to withdraw their support of her and back Parisia."

Julie thought she heard an opening to start bargaining, but she couldn't be sure. It seemed too easy. "I'm glad to hear that our efforts weren't completely wasted."

Iris's wrinkled face relaxed into a near smile. "And now you are wondering if it was enough to trade for your freedom."

Julie was relieved to hear that they were finally getting to the crux of this discussion.

"Very simply, the answer is no," Parisia stated before Julie could confirm Iris's deduction. "However, I told you that we have a proposition, and in a moment you will understand why we took such a circuitous route to get to it. Our lack of a defense system and weaponry is only part of our problem. Even with Parliament approving the funds needed, we still lack something vital to our defense—the attitude necessary to commit violence.

"Our people abhor physical aggression. There's not a single person on this planet who has ever purposely harmed another living creature. Of course, there is the possibility that the proper attitude could be attained by certain select individuals . . . in time. Unfortunately, we may not have that time."

"I thought you said there was no immediate threat," Julie said when Parisia paused for more than a moment.

Parisia and Iris shared an apprehensive glance. It was becoming quite clear to Julie that the adviser was the more cautious of the two, and though they seemed to be in accord most of the time, Parisia occasionally ignored Iris's advice to play it safe.

This time Parisia hedged. "There is no impending danger that we are certain of. Just an unsubstantiated rumor. If it turns out to be true, we must be prepared. If it is false, it would still be wise to have a defense system in place against a possible threat at some later date.

"As I was saying, none of the citizens of Heart have the necessary attitude to implement a viable defense plan in the near future. You, on the other hand, have lived with violence all your life and have very recent experience with a deadly confrontation on a planetary scale. Thus you have an ability that we wish to utilize.

"In summary, we are asking you to create a defense system which would encompass everything from plans and strategy to weaponry and implementation. It is our hope that while you are doing that, we will find volunteers within our society willing to carry out your plans. Training those women for their new duties would also fall under your jurisdiction."

If Julie had been given a hundred chances to guess what Parisia had been leading to, she would never have come up with that. "As much as we would like to make a deal here, I'm afraid you've overestimated our capabilities. We're not experts at waging war; we've merely learned how to survive in a violent world."

"Which is more than we have," Parisia countered. "Our technology has advanced far beyond yours, but with instruction we believe you could comprehend it. You would simply have to determine ways to redirect the use of that technology for our defense. The four of you have most of the basic expertise needed: leadership, mechanical and navigational ability, and the proper attitude for defense. I assume the other six women have worthy skills that could be contributed as well."

Julie sighed. "It's not—"

"Wait," Iris said, holding up her hand to stop Julie's protest. "First hear what we are offering. In exchange for creating and implementing a defense system, your women will be given complete freedom in our society. After your work for us is done, we will allow any of your people—women and men—to return to Earth if you still wish to do so at that time."

"So you do know how to do it!" Julie exclaimed. "Nadia said the magnetic pull went only one way."

Parisia arched an eyebrow. "Nadia also told you her name was Parisia."

"Will you give us a moment, please?" Julie asked, then stood and motioned for Robin, Lee, and Alicia to follow her to the kitchenette for a whispered conference. She was hoping one of the others had some alternative ideas, but they were as bewildered as she was by the unexpected proposition.

None of them really believed they were capable of doing what was being asked of them. It was possible that Parisia could stretch out their duties indefinitely just by saying the defense system was not yet finished to their satisfaction. They had no reason to trust Parisia or Iris about anything.

But they had offered to send them home to Earth.

With nothing better to offer, they seemed to have no choice but to accept and negotiate for the best terms possible.

Julie waited several tense seconds after they were seated to present their counter-offer. "We will *attempt* to create a defense system, but you must free all the Earth people on the farm immediately. No more medication for women or men. And finally, we wish to set a specific time period for our return to Earth—upon completion of the defense system or six months from today, whichever comes sooner."

Parisia and Iris reflected little surprise at the demands. In fact, they didn't even need a private conversation for Parisia to give their reply. "Six months is unreasonable. Remember, we will need you to train our volunteers after the system is in place. One year, and you put in at least six full days every week during that time. Next, we will agree not to medicate your women. But under no circumstances will we release the Earth men from the commune, with or without medication."

"That's understandable," Julie said with a nod,

having been certain that was what they would say about the men. "Considering the structure of your society and the personalities of some of the men in our group, I can see how it could present a number of difficulties if they were all released at one time. On the other hand, there are men in the commune whose expertise far outweighs ours. It would be foolish not to take advantage of their talents and skills. Allow half the men to leave the farm, drug-free, and you'll have a better defense system than anything we could create alone, and it will be in place in half the time."

This time Parisia and Iris did need a private conference, and it took several minutes before they agreed on the next concession.

After they returned to the group, Parisia said, "Releasing even one unmedicated Earth male among Heart women is an incredible risk that we would prefer not to take. And yet we understand that committing violence and waging war are deeds more suited to men. Therefore we have a final compromise to offer, but it will have to be a completely confidential one. If you do not agree, you will be returned to the commune, and we will not have further discussions with any of you."

Julie frowned, but nodded her understanding.

"We propose that you choose ten men, and only ten, whose skills would be most helpful in completing this project. Each of the ten women may keep one of those men with her in the residence we will provide. She will be held responsible for his behavior. To outsiders it must appear that the men are your servants and that you are all abiding by our laws governing contact between the genders. Also, the men must act as if they are taking the required medication.

"If anyone suspects that the law is being broken, our deal will be automatically negated. Naturally, Iris will review everything you need to know in advance of your integration. Do you accept these terms?"

Julie summarized the deal as it now stood, then asked, Robin, Lee, and Alicia if they had questions or were ready to decide. All four voted to accept.

"It's better than returning to the farm and vegetating for a century or two," Robin said.

"We'll do it," Julie told Parisia in a much more confident tone than she felt. The problems they would have to overcome were mind-boggling—not the least of which was selecting the ten men to be freed and pairing them up with the women.

Chapter 12

By keeping her soft underbelly flat on the floor and all fifty of her legs curled tightly against the hard black shell of her back, Yeoman Ugmish assumed the most proper pose of respect as she slithered quietly into her superior's niche. She waited until he twisted the top half of his segmented body toward her and rubbed his antennae together.

"Was the mission a sssuccesss?" Commander Xytoc hissed through the narrow space between his two front fangs.

She twitched her antennae once in response, careful not to raise her head until he gave her permission to do so.

"You may rise and ssspeak."

Ugmish unfurled her legs and lifted her body off the ground. He was still half a length higher than she stood at full elevation. His hooded black eyes dared her to give him bad news, causing all three of her stomachs to churn even though her report was positive.

"Special Envoy TM7 has returned from Faxona. The mission was a success. The plans for the FTL transport have already been delivered to research for analysis."

"Excccellent. Tell them I will expect a preliminary timetable by firssst sssunrise."

"Yes, sir," Ugmish replied, knowing she would bear the brunt of the analysts' tantrums when they heard that deadline. The commander might have used the word *preliminary*, but he would hold them to whatever estimate they gave, and unfortunately, he always demanded answers in half the time needed to supply realistic ones.

"Return to me after you've delivered that message, I may have need of you."

With an obedient bow she slithered back out of the niche as quickly as possible.

Not for the first time, Xytoc congratulated himself on having found a yeoman who was as efficient at her duties as she was accommodating to his personal needs.

He stretched and scratched his lower belly with a pair of his hind legs. FTL travel! He had been skeptical when he first heard of its development. It was almost too fortuitous to be believed.

He should not have doubted the predictions of Master Astrologer Po, who had told him that he was the one who would lead the Velids into the final battle against their deadliest enemies.

The portion of his brain that housed the memories of his ancestors seemed to burn a bit brighter as he contemplated the glorious victory awaiting him. The fires of vengeance had been kept alive through the many generations passed by preserving those old memories.

Xytoc called them forth now to inflame his purpose and fortify his commitment.

It had begun as a mission, to seek out other life forms and study them to increase their understanding of the universe. This mission was to be ongoing, generation after generation, as the Velid ship made its way through myriad galaxies, exchanging information. Reports were transmitted back to their home planet after each encounter.

The first disaster had occurred in the Templar System, when they landed on a small, unnamed planet inhabited by a primitive life form. They were frighteningly ugly specimens of the humanoid race who utilized only the rear two of their four legs for movement. They lacked even the barest skills needed for universal communication. The creatures were terrified by the visitors and went into hiding. Two Velids tracked them down to try to make them understand that they had come in peace. For their efforts they were captured and stoned to death.

Many generations later, the Velid expedition found another, more advanced humanoid planet known as Heart. Recalling the Templar beings' negative reaction to the Velids' natural appearance, they changed their shape to match the natives', thinking it would put the Heartlings at ease. That time the entire landing crew was killed, without provocation, and the shuttle destroyed.

It was clear that the grotesque species had an innate, lethal hatred of the Velid race. They had to be stopped before their civilization progressed to space travel and threatened the Velids in their own galaxy. Prior to the remaining Velids departing from Heart's solar system, the mother ship repaid the humans with total extermination.

At least they thought they had.

From that point on, the purpose of the expedition had altered from academic studies to searching for and annihilating all humanoids. Most recently the battalion of exterminators had returned to the Templar System and eradicated every hint of civilization on the small planet where the first vicious attack had occurred.

Because of the development of FTL transport, information was suddenly being traded on an intergalactic scale in incredibly short periods of time. The Velids now knew that there had been a sufficient number of survivors on Heart to repopulate the planet and that those beings had since mastered space travel. Believing that it was only a matter of time before their enemies successfully launched an attack against the Velids, Xytoc was convinced that they had to strike first in order to survive.

The only way to do that, however, was with the latest technology. Thus he had sent Envoy TM7 to steal the plans for the FTL transport from the Faxons. Using the Velid ability to change shape and appearance to duplicate any living organism, the envoy's mission had been hardly a challenge.

Xytoc considered Po's exact prediction. He had said it would be the final battle. That had to mean it would mark the end of the humanoid race, because the Velids would not give up until there were no more humans to exterminate. "Their deadliest enemies" could only refer to the humans of Heart.

The facts gleaned about Heart also included that it was ruled by females who were completely peaceful, had no military, and no protection from outside invasion. Though Xytoc trusted the information to be accurate, it did not change his mind about the necessity to eradicate the race. The females currently in power may be unaggressive, but they were capable of bearing offspring who were genocidal.

Despite Po's prediction and the indication that Heart had no defenses, Xytoc still wanted to do everything possible to insure an overwhelming victory. He intended to recall every battalion immediately. When he departed for Heart, it would be with a massive show of strength. Every ship would be converted to FTL, every able-bodied Velid would be drafted to increase the size of the attack force to a hundred times what it was.

He would make certain that the name Xytoc went down in history as the most brilliant, forceful commander of all time—the Velid who exterminated the last human being in the universe!

Chapter 13

Simone's brain was clicking away faster than she could assimilate all the gossip. The entire imperial city buzzed with suppositions, rumors, and facts. The problem was in deciding which tidbit fell into which category.

The general consensus was that Nadia must have suffered a mental collapse: A small pocket of women believed she never had been a hundred percent normal, and an even smaller number, like Simone, found it very hard to believe that Nadia with her eyes focused on the imperial throne, would do something so blatantly risky, to say nothing of illegal.

This group privately whispered their doubts to one another. They were of the mind that Parisia might have orchestrated the entire fiasco, including fabricating the supposed recorded evidence, in order to get Nadia out of the way.

Had Nadia been present at the special Parliament meeting, Simone was positive Parisia never would have convinced them to go along with the radical changes she proposed. Nor would Parliament have been convinced to approve a revised budget so that billions of dollars could be diverted to something as useless as a defense system.

Heart had no enemies to defend itself from. More than likely the funds would be secretly redirected into some personal account of Parisia's or her daughter, Brianne's. And what better way to hide the misdirection than to use women from Earth, who wouldn't know what was being done and couldn't care?

Simone could not stand by and do nothing for five years until Nadia *might* be allowed to reenter society. She had to come up with a plan that would accomplish three objectives. One, speak to Nadia to confirm that she had been unjustly incarcerated. Two, free her and prove to Parliament that Parisia had lied. This, of course, would result in Nadia's position being elevated, possibly even to imperial prefect. And third, make sure Nadia felt eternally indebted to Simone.

She knew the third goal might automatically be achieved by the first two, but she would probably have to share the credit with other helpful supporters. Another idea formed that would bind herself to Nadia in a more personal way.

It took a few calls and promised favors, but she pulled it off with a minimum of difficulty. Nadia's relatives were tremendously relieved to so easily settle several potential legal complications. Simone's generous offer was accepted before the gossip died down and heads cleared.

By the end of the day Simone would move out of her mother's home and into Nadia's to keep it maintained in good condition until the owner returned. She also accepted responsibility for Fulton's employment contract and temporary guardianship of the child, Chloe. It was thought to be a very kindhearted gesture from Nadia's former best friend, especially since her family was so anxious to disassociate themselves from their relative and her criminal behavior.

Simone didn't tell anyone, not even the other women who were committed to helping Nadia get reinstated, but there was another reason why she was intent on carrying out the first step of the plan. She had an important, *private* question for Nadia.

If Parisia did not lie, and the visual recording Simone heard about truly existed, then Nadia had knowledge of something no one else did—what it was like to be touched by an unmedicated man.

Had Simone not witnessed the episode in the transfer room between the Earth man and woman and seen the woman's blissful expression, she would not have had a single question about Nadia's innocence. She had always been told no woman in her right mind would welcome a man's touch, and Nadia was not insane, so she wouldn't have "acted improperly" with an Earth male.

Unless she had seen what Simone had and couldn't erase the images from her mind.

Unless she also wondered if an enormous lie had been perpetrated for centuries to maintain the power of one family.

Satisfied that she had set her plan in motion, and that the details would work out along the way, she placed a call to Fulton to let him know that she would be moving in and reassure him and Chloe that they needn't worry about being taken care of.

"I promise you, everything will be fine," she told him sweetly. "And you mustn't concern yourself with learning new routines or duties to please me. Whatever you normally did for Nadia will be perfectly acceptable to me."

Julie hadn't expected to see anyone when they left the tack room. After all, a little over two days had passed since they'd gone in to request an audience with their caretakers. So it was quite a surprise when they opened the bolted door and saw Willy jumping to his feet.

He shook each woman's hand and happily welcomed them back. "Everybody's been so worried!"

"I hope you haven't been in here waiting for us all this time," Robin said.

"Actually, we've been taking shifts. Parisia tried to escape through here twice. Someone's guarding the outside door too."

"She's not Parisia," Julie said. "But that's the least important thing we've learned."

"I hope that means you were allowed to remember where you've been and what happened to you."

"Yes," Julie said, nodding. "And we have good news and bad news. But we'd better give it to Major Cookson first."

They found Geoffrey in the big house helping with lunch preparations. Julie instantly noticed how his handsome face was creased with worry and fatigue and that his usually neat blond hair looked as though he hadn't combed it all day. Geoffrey was so relieved at seeing the women and hearing that they had returned with a proposition that he kissed each one on both cheeks and returned Robin's exuberant hug.

"Thank heavens you're back!" he exclaimed with a very un-British burst of emotion. "I thought we were going to have to shoot Logan to put him out of his misery."

Julie's surprised expression made him laugh. "Don't tell him I said that. He's spent the last two days denying that he was concerned. As eager as I am to hear what happened, I'm going to ask you to hold off for a few more minutes so that Logan can hear it at the same time. Everyone should be coming in for lunch any moment."

Julie agreed, though she was anxious to get started. "If I might make a suggestion, we should go somewhere private for this debriefing. A lot of people aren't going to like it."

Geoffrey's smile faded. "That sounds rather ominous."

Before Julie could give him any reassurance, the first group of laborers came in from the field. Everyone was excited about the women's safe return, but no matter how much pleading or cajoling they did, Julie wouldn't reveal any details yet.

As soon as Logan arrived, a lunch tray was shoved into his hand, and Geoffrey and the women whisked him off to a shaded spot some distance from the big house.

Julie considered what Geoffrey had said about Logan's being worried. Either he had been grossly exaggerating or Logan was extremely good at hiding his feelings. He barely reacted to their reappearance.

Though Julie delivered most of their report, Robin, Lee, and Alicia, supplied some details and independent opinions throughout.

"I wish it was a better deal for more of the men," Julie said in an apologetic tone when she'd covered everything.

Geoffrey shook his head. "You did better than we expected." He glanced at Logan for affirmation. "When you were gone so long, we weren't at all certain you would be returned. Or if you were, that you would have any memory of what had happened."

"We were waiting one more day," Logan said. "Then we were going to march through the barrier."

"Does that mean you figured out how to use that little box?" Robin asked Geoffrey.

"Yes. It was really quite simple. But we didn't want to cause a disturbance if you were making positive progress, which, apparently, you were."

Julie felt obliged to be modest about their accomplishment, but he stopped her.

"None of that. You've negotiated an agreement that will result in everyone's being returned home. What we need to concentrate on now is selecting the ten men. Any suggestions?"

Julie was ready for that question. "We discussed this, and decided there's no way to be fair about it, like a random drawing. The most logical plan would be to make a list of every man's expertise and former career and choose by skills and qualifications."

Robin continued, "Once the ten men are chosen, they should be paired up with women who have experience in the same field if possible. Men don't have the freedom of movement women do over there, so it would be unseemly for a man to be servant to one woman but spend time with another."

"However," Alicia said, "we request one consideration that has nothing to do with skills. We may have to live with these men for as long as a year. We'd appreciate the opportunity to reject someone as a roommate if we are completely incompatible."

Geoffrey thought their selection plan was reasonable. He said, "If you get the other women to help, you should be able to interview every man before they return to their chores."

"What about the others?" Logan asked. "Some of the men who were here before us might have a useful talent. Hans told me he was a scientist. That could help."

"True," Julie said. "But only if the effects of taking the drug over a long period of time can be reversed. We don't know that, so I'd hate to risk it when we can only bring ten men with us."

"Agreed," Geoffrey stated. "Let's get to it."

The other six women were quickly gathered and given a brief overview of the situation. There would be plenty of time for in-depth explanations later. The individual interviews took less time than the selection process. A few men were immediately chosen as "definites." A lot more were noted as "possibles."

When the list of candidates was narrowed down to twenty-two, Geoffrey and Logan excused themselves to let the women make the final selections by compatibility. Both their names were on the definite list since Geoffrey was a strategist, as well as an engineer, and Logan was a weapons expert on top of his leadership capabilities.

Once the men left, the women felt free to eliminate a few qualified men, such as Wilkes, because of personality or personal habits.

To no one's great surprise, Ray Higgs turned out to be a computer hacker besides being an expert on science fiction and alien worlds, both of which made him a definite also. There was a brief dispute as to whether Alicia or Lee would claim him, and finally he was paired with Kara, who had majored in computer science before changing to nursing.

Robin's argument that a mechanic and an engineer were perfectly matched earned her the right to choose Geoffrey.

Though all the nurses had been required to take extensive math and science courses, Sunny and Trish had excelled in those subjects. They were paired with Edward Smith, the flight navigator and Jeremy Fleischer, the copilot, who had been working on his master's degree in nuclear physics prior to being drafted.

Darcy, who had been the office manager for a successful group of doctors, prided herself on her efficiency and organizational ability. It seemed appropriate for her to team up with Hal Becket, whose background was business and accounting, since a budget had to be adhered to.

From the balance of the list, they selected three other men: Thomas Jefferson (T.J.) Jones, Greg Oliver, and Kevin Atchinson. Like Logan, they were career soldiers, trained in weapons, experienced at fighting enemies, both seen and unseen, and familiar with bloodshed. The last qualification was about all they had in common with the four remaining nurses, but they were needed to complete the group of experts.

Julie didn't need to be psychic to see what was coming. One by one the women rejected Logan as a roommate and chose one of the others. Though he had done nothing negative the last few days, his criminal record and dangerous aura were simply too frightening to overcome. T.J. was another hard case, a young black man with a cocky attitude, but Lee felt she could handle him. Then Mandy and Charlene opted for Greg and Kevin.

That left Logan McKay.

And Julie Evans.

At dinner, the ten men were asked to join the women for a meeting in the barn. Julie repeated everything previously told to Geoffrey and Logan before announcing how everyone was to be paired off. Throughout her speech and the subsequent questions and answers, Logan's eyes were on her. Without looking at him, she felt him watching her and knew that somehow he had already guessed who he would be living with for the next year.

"How did you know?" Julie asked after the pairs were named and she caught the smirk on his face.

"Simple deduction. Being such a nice girl, you would have let everyone else pick first, and none of them would want to live with me. You don't either, but you had no choice."

"It isn't that—"

"Don't bother," he murmured, cutting off her attempt to deny the truth of his words. "I'm like the fat kid in the neighborhood. Always the last one to get picked in a game, but at least I still get to play. Don't worry. You're perfectly safe with me. I only assault and murder men . . . not women. And as long as no one's pumping me full of drugs, I can promise to keep my hands off you. I assume you can make the same guarantee to me."

Julie had a smart retort in mind, but she didn't get the chance to deliver it.

"Now comes the hard part," Geoffrey declared after each pair had shared a few words. "We have to tell everyone else what's going on and convince them to be patient while we fulfill our part of the bargain. I'm placing Gianni in charge of keeping the peace. He can choose whoever he wants to help him."

"What about Nadia?" Julie asked. "Willy said she tried to escape while we were gone."

"That's right," Geoffrey replied. "But she's no longer our hostage; she's a prisoner on this farm. It's up to her people to keep her here now, not us. But I'll take the control box with me just to make sure she can't leave too easily."

As predicted, there were a lot of unhappy men after they heard the details of the agreement. Naturally, Wilkes and his pals were the loudest and nastiest. But even they didn't match the fury that erupted from Nadia when she read the formal decree from Parisia that sentenced her to five years in the commune. It was decided to keep her restrained until she calmed down, or at least until the group of twenty left the farm.

Gianni understood that he had quite a job ahead of him, but he believed he and a few others could manage, especially since the major was leaving Nadia's paralyzer in his possession. Nevertheless, he considered forcing everyone to go back to drinking the water again.

Parisia and Iris had set the rendezvous for midnight and had given Julie a brooch with a timepiece in it. They thought it would be best to get the Earth people settled in when the least number of residents would take notice.

By the last hour of the day, most of the hostilities and envy died down, and farewells were said. The couples took nothing into the tack room with them but the clothes they were wearing, since they had been told everything would be provided. Moments after they all filed into the tack room, the back wall opened.

"Welcome back," Parisia said to Julie with a pleasant smile. On her right stood Iris with her fixed expression of worry; on her left was a younger, slightly taller version of herself. Behind them was a long, empty hallway. "Let's go to a more spacious area for our introductions." The three Heart women turned and led the group down the hallway to a vacant room that Julie thought was the one they had awakened in before.

The first thing Julie noticed after they entered the room was that Parisia and Iris kept their gazes away from the men, but the other young woman kept sneaking peeks at them. She appeared to be both curious and fearful.

Parisia introduced herself and Iris first. "And this is my first aide, Brianne, who also happens to be my daughter. She has volunteered to act as liaison and adviser for your group so that your integration will be as smooth as possible. Julie, if you'd be so kind as to provide each person's field of expertise with your introductions, it would be appreciated."

Julie ran through the roster, embellishing the men's capabilities to justify their questionable presence. From the relieved looks on the Heart women's faces, her additional effort had been sorely needed.

"Thank you, Julie," Parisia said. "We're pleased you have agreed to help us. But first we must see to getting you settled in your new accommodations. Brianne located a residential complex with a number of vacancies in the heart of the city that should be ideal. It's not far from the Imperial Palace or Parliament. Normally it is filled with visiting dignitaries, but, as luck would have it, an entire delegation returned to their home province yesterday. They vacated six one-bedroom and two two-bedroom apartments, and Brianne immediately leased them for all of you. To make it even better, there is a large conference room on the top floor that has been converted into a work area for you."

Logan whispered into Julie's ear: "Six plus four

equals ten bedrooms. Where are the servants' quarters?"

Iris's nostrils flared as she inhaled sharply. Looking only at Julie, she said, "Your houseman will be forgiven this time, but be certain that he and the others are aware of our laws in the future. A man never speaks unless spoken to first by a woman, nor does he look directly at any part of her. A man *never* makes physical contact with a woman, no matter how slight. There should always be a minimum of one arm's length between a man and a woman unless he is in the process of performing a requested service."

"Do we have to walk two steps behind them too?" T.J. asked sarcastically.

Lee swiftly pinched a muscle at the base of his neck, making him wince in pain. "Not so funny anymore, is it, wise-ass? Get this through your thick macho heads, boys. This is no joke. You ever want to see blue sky again, you play along the way we've been told. If that means you bite your tongue and walk two steps behind us, you do it. Got it?" She waited for a jerky nod from T.J. before she released him. To Parisia and Iris, she said, "I apologize for the impertinence of my stupid houseman. He'll improve quickly, I'm sure."

Julie thought Brianne's eyes were going to pop out of her head for a moment, but she got her shock under control when her mother started to speak again.

"With regard to the apartments, even though you may be somewhat crowded, we felt that it was better to have you all in one building rather than scattered throughout the city. As it is, people will be watching you every chance they get for a while. It would be best not to give them too many opportunities to find fault.

"There's a shuttle waiting to take you to the residence. Brianne will escort you and fill you in on the essentials along the way. We wish you good luck and good night." Parisia and Iris left the room and headed in one direction, as Brianne led the group in another.

Julie sensed the woman's anxiety. Moving up beside Brianne, she murmured, "There's nothing to worry about. We train easily and hardly ever bite our teachers."

Brianne's eyes opened wide again, then she realized Julie was teasing her. "This is not the sort of thing I'm usually required to do," she said in a confidential tone. "I'm a little nervous."

"Then you must be able to imagine how we feel."

Those were apparently the right words, for Brianne cleared her throat and found the confidence to begin her task a moment later. "As Parisia said, I will be your liaison for the duration. We prefer that you limit your contact with the other residents of the city as much as possible."

She stopped the group at the foot of a wide escalator that spiraled upward. "Please watch your balance. These stairs are moving rather swiftly." Brianne stepped on and turned to face the others. When the last man had boarded, she continued, "Your apartments have been stocked with some food and other supplies. Accounts will be established for each woman to purchase goods as needed, including clothing. Each apartment comes equipped with a manager, which is similar to the entertainment center some of you have already seen, but it does much more. For instance, it accesses a purchasing channel that allows you to order whatever you require and have it delivered."

"It is our custom to have our housemen go to the market to personally select fresh food every few days, but I understand that Earth men are not always skilled in the culinary arts. If that is the case, prepackaged meals can be ordered for delivery as well."

By the time they reached the top of the escalator, Julie estimated they'd gone up at least forty floors. From the last stair they stepped onto a moving walkway. This carried them outside onto a rooftop which could have been a parking lot, though none of the objects sitting between the parallel lines looked like vehicles she was familiar with.

These things made her think of a child's bubble pipe with the stem and bowl sitting on the pavement and a big bubble emerging from the bowl. There was a range of sizes and colors, and the bubbles seemed to have been blown in a variety of formations, including an enormous oblong one that was probably the shuttle Parisia had mentioned.

Glowing lights from the city lured Julie and most of the others to the railing at the edge of the building. Between the artificial illumination and the clear, star-filled sky, she got her first peek at the futuristic city. The rooftop view made it possible to see that a network of narrow silver ribbons wound between and over skyscrapers, which were formed like pyramids, cylinders, spheres, and corkscrews. Most of them appeared to be constructed of reflective metal, colored in a rainbow of pastel shades.

A closer look revealed that a few of the bubble pipe objects were speeding along the ribbons. "How do they move?" Julie asked Brianne with open fascination.

"A system of magnets. It's quiet and completely energy-efficient." Brianne pointed to her right. "You see the building over there, with the golden dome and towers at each corner? That's the Imperial Palace."

"Wow! It looks like the Taj Mahal," Robin said.

Brianne directed their gazes to the aqua cylinder next to the palace, which was nearly as high as the structure they were on. "That's Parliament. Your residence is in the section of smaller buildings behind that."

Julie scanned the faces around her and knew the others were stricken with the same awe she was. Even Logan was unable to maintain his bored expression as he took in the alien panorama.

"Shall we go?" Brianne asked, clearly pleased that they were impressed by her home.

Julie's guess about which object was the shuttle proved accurate. As they boarded, Brianne reminded the men that they were required to sit in the rear of the vehicle with at least one row of vacant seats between them and the women in the front.

For the trip down the side of the building, the forward portion of the shuttle lifted so the passengers seats remained level. Brianne had the conductor take them on a tour of the vicinity surrounding their residence, so they would have an idea of how to get around. She pointed out the marketplace, shuttle stops, grooming and fitness salons, and so on. The swift, silent ride didn't last nearly long enough for Julie, but she reasoned that she'd have plenty of time in the coming months to explore every inch of the beautiful city.

The residence was a salmon five-story pentagon with a garden courtyard in the center. For expediency—it was getting close to dawn—Brianne took the entire group into one apartment to demonstrate anything they might not be familiar with, such as the manager and how to arrange the pieces in the main room to form a couch large enough for the men to use as a bed. She then pointed out where the available apartments were located and let the women choose.

Kara and Darcy, and Trish and Mandy, solved part of the problem by offering to occupy the two two-bedroom apartments on the ground floor. Julie and Robin both selected units on the top floor, and the others took the ones in between.

Brianne handed them each the appropriate access card and said, "I believe it would be wisest for everyone to get some rest and take this first day to get acquainted with your new home. Tomor-

row I will come by and show you the workroom
we've prepared for you."

They bid one another good night and broke off
to do exactly as she suggested.

Julie had avoided thinking too deeply about the
new arrangements, but once the door to her apartment closed and she and Logan were alone in a
relatively confined space, she could no longer
avoid it.

While she stood in the middle of the main room
trying to decide how to begin, Logan went about
rearranging the furnishings to create a bed for
himself.

"We should probably talk about this," she said
as he moved around her.

"Are you giving me permission to speak?" he
asked without looking at her.

"Don't you pull an attitude with me, Logan
McKay. I didn't make the rules here."

"No, you didn't make them, but you have to
abide by them, same as me. The way I figure it,
our best bet is to follow their laws to the letter,
even when we're in here alone. That way it becomes habit, and we're less apt to make a mistake
in public. I intend to give that order to all the
men."

"*You* intend to give the order?" she asked with
a challenging air. "The first habit you'd better adopt
is that *you* don't give orders to anyone anymore."

He glared at her for several seconds, then turned
away. "You're absolutely right. From here on,
you're the chief of this operation."

She clucked her tongue and rolled her eyes. As

he walked past her to get another foam cube, she touched his arm to stop him. "Logan, please—"

"No touching," he said, jerking away. "It's against the law."

Despite the fact that the excuse for his attitude sounded logical, Julie thought he was being a horse's ass. She was positive he resented the role reversal and planned to take his bad mood out on her, even though he knew it wasn't her fault. Well, two could play that game.

"Fine," she said, sticking her nose up in the air. "As of right now we're no longer Julie Evans and Logan McKay of Earth. *I* am supreme commander of the Armed Forces of Heart, and *you* are my houseman." She snapped her fingers at him. "Run me a bath, turn down my bed, and make me a cup of herbal tea to help me sleep."

Logan gnashed his teeth, but he nodded and headed for the bathroom. Insisting that they obey Heart's laws when they were alone had been the only thing he could think of to keep a rein on his sanity. The mere thought of her taking a bath and going to bed a few feet away from him made his skin itch.

As long as she abided by the arm's-length rule and remained annoyed with him, he figured he could hold the ache in his chest to a dull throbbing. If she insisted on touching him and being *nice*, there was no telling how long it would be before he was making a fool of himself again.

Julie frowned as she followed him into the bedroom. The fact that the only access to the bathroom was through there would present problems between any two people who were less than lovers. She and Logan were going to have to sit down and work things out very soon, but she was probably going to have to tweak his nose a few more times before he'd start being reasonable.

The bathroom was only one obstacle. They were facing as much as a year of cohabitation, and it would go a lot easier if they didn't try to do it as enemies. She was willing to block out his criminal background and the previous incidents of intimacy if he would try to behave like a gentleman. They didn't need to become best friends, but they did need to be able to get along with each other.

While he was in the bathroom, she inspected the contents of the clothes closet and bureau drawers. Brianne had said the apartments would be stocked with a few items. The key word had been *few*. There were four plain caftans hanging on the rack—two aqua and two pink. The pink were considerably longer. She took out a smaller one and laid it on the bed. Most of the drawers were empty, but one had two pairs of large pink boxer shorts in it, and another had two sets of aqua chemises and tap pants. Obviously, the first order of business upon awakening was going to be a shopping spree with the manager.

The scowl on Logan's face when he came out of the bathroom and she showed him the clothing selection was more explicit than a thousand curse words, but he still managed to hold his tongue.

"I'll have my tea while I bathe," she said in a regal tone, then went to keep an eye on the water level in the tub while he marched off to the kitchen. She was pleasantly surprised to discover that he had added perfumed bubbles to the water, set out a fluffy towel and washcloth, and formed a head rest with another towel rolled like a log. Perhaps having him as a personal servant wasn't going to be so hard to get used to.

When he brought in her tea and set it on the ledge of the tub, she was firmly set in her queenly mode. "That will be all for now. But I'm sure I'll be famished when I wake up, so plan on preparing a full meal."

On his way out, he mumbled, "You sure you don't want me to scrub your back, *madam*?"

Julie smiled. He couldn't possibly keep up the subservient act for long. She estimated that he'd either explode or be ready to negotiate a truce within twenty-four hours.

Chapter 14

A quarter of the time Julie had set for Logan to detonate flew by while she slept more soundly than she had in a very long time. The unmistakable smell of sautéing onions and garlic seduced her out of a pleasant dream that dissolved without a trace of recollection.

She slipped out of bed, made a quick visit to the bathroom, and put on the aqua caftan. Thinking Logan might need to use the bathroom while she was asleep, she had tried sleeping in the caftan, for modesty's sake, but her legs had immediately gotten twisted in the yards of material. The satiny chemise and tap pants were not as prudish, but they were much more comfortable.

Following her nose, she found Logan at the stove, with his back to her, stirring something in a frying pan. He was wearing only the loose-fitting slacks from the farm, obviously having decided against the pink caftan. The pants were hanging dangerously low on his hips, and she had the most wicked urge to give them a yank the rest of the way. She remembered the vision she had had of him wearing an apron and wondered if she could find one to cover him with. There was probably some law in this place against a man going shirtless, especially a man built like Logan. She thought it best not to mention it, though, lest he think she was bothered by his display of muscles.

"Something smells wonderful," she said, mainly to alert him to her presence. When he didn't turn around, she tried again. "I see you didn't waste any time learning your way around the kitchen." Still no response. "Logan! Do I have to order you to talk to me?"

He turned to get a jar out of the cabinet and was momentarily surprised to see her standing in the doorway, looking annoyed. Removing two plugs from his ears, he asked, "Did you say something?"

She came closer to look at the tiny plastic disks he had set on the counter. "What are these for?"

He went back to stirring a strange-looking green concoction in the pan. "They're sound remotes for the manager. I was listening to the news."

"How did you figure that out?" She peered into the pan on the stove. "And what are you making?" She couldn't help but notice that each time she came near, he took a step away. He really was carrying this too far!

"I'm making breakfast. You requested a full meal, but you weren't specific. I hope this will do. I think it's supposed to be like an omelet."

"You think?"

He almost smiled. "They don't eat eggs here, or animal meat either. They're vegetarians."

"How do you know that?"

"I just did what any new kid on the block would do. I went next door and met our neighbor."

"Logan! We were told to limit our contact with the natives."

He shrugged. "It was a choice between asking one of those natives for help or starving to death. Don't worry. Vance, the houseman, was the only one home, and he took pity on me. Showed me how to dig recipes out of the manager and gave me some basic instructions. You'd like him . . . Oh, I almost forgot. No fraternizing between sexes." He spooned the cooked mixture onto two plates and placed one on the table, where there was already a glass of juice, napkin, and flatware.

She sat down and waited for him to bring the other plate to the table. Instead he began eating at the counter. That's when she realized he had set only one place at the table. "This is ridiculous. Come over here and sit down."

"A man is not supposed to sit at the same table with—"

"Stop it!"

"—a woman." He ate another forkful of food.

"All right. But a houseman has to obey his mistress's orders, and I order you to sit here and eat with me . . . at every meal."

With exaggerated slowness he carried his breakfast to the opposite side of the table from where she was sitting.

"Now what are you doing?" she demanded.

"Practicing. Remember, we men are supposed to look medicated. That was the other reason I wanted to make friends with Vance. I'm studying him."

At least that made sense, she thought. "That reminds me. You don't have to worry about what you eat or drink here. Men are given their medication in a concentrated dosage once a week." She took a taste of her food. "This is very good . . . whatever it is. Sort of a quiche-omelet-souffle. It's hard to believe there are no eggs in it."

As they both ate, she tried to keep her eyes downcast as he was doing, but her gaze kept creeping across the table. Again she was brutally aware of how her familiarity with the male physique as a nurse did not immunize her against the effect Logan's body had on her senses. "Did you, uh, spill something on your shirt?"

He glanced down at his chest, as if he'd forgotten it was bare. "No. I just hand-washed it, and it hasn't dried yet."

"You could have put on the pink robe. I bet you'd be darling in it." She was satisfied to get a sneering glance from him. At least he'd looked her in the eye for a second. "We both need clothing. Let's go see what the purchasing channel has to offer."

When she tried to clear her place, he growled at her, so she left him alone to clean up the kitchen. Surely by the end of the day he'd stop being so unreasonable about strictly obeying the laws. She would simply have to push a little harder to make him see the silliness of it when they were alone.

While she waited for him to join her in the main

room, she decided to let some sunlight in. As Brianne had shown them, she brought up the manager's utility-control index, stroked Shutter, then Open. Instantly what had appeared to be a solid wall folded back, accordion-style, to reveal the outside world. Julie had to touch the wall of clear glass to assure herself that a barrier was actually there. One side of the floor-to-ceiling window opened on to a balcony that ran the entire length of the apartment.

"Logan! Come here, quick!"

He was at her side on the balcony in a flash, the urgency in her voice overriding his intentions to keep his movements slow.

"In your wildest imagination, did you ever think you'd see something like this?"

Relief that she was all right rushed through him. He grinned at the delight in her voice despite his vow not to react to anything she did. Fortunately, she was too intent on the view to notice him.

"I thought it looked incredible at night, but now it's . . . it's . . . I can't even think of a good word. I wonder what the buildings are made of. I once saw some titanium jewelry that shimmered with those same metallic pastels. Depending on how the light hit, it turned aqua, pink, or lilac. I wonder if Robin and the others have taken a look outside yet."

He didn't think she needed a response. Besides, all his concentration was focused on remaining at arm's length from her, when what he was dying to do was wrap her in his arms and absorb every last drop of excitement she was experiencing.

"I know we probably should stay inside, but I can't do it. We've got to take a walk after we do our shopping. Okay?" She turned her eyes to his in question.

With tremendous effort he made himself look at the view. "It isn't right to ask my permission to do something. Remember that."

His icy voice cooled her enthusiasm. "I was *not* asking your permission. I was asking you if you'd— Oh, never mind." For a moment she had forgotten that they weren't two friends who could take a walk and enjoy the sights together. "Let's just go get our purchase order in before it's too late to have it delivered."

It took only a few minutes on the manager's purchasing channel to learn that men had the option of wearing simply styled caftans or the two-piece outfits that they'd worn on the farm. There was a choice of colors, probably more to be pleasing to the mistress's eye, and weight of material for warmth. The women's wardrobe selection was expanded to include a variety of embellishments. However, the basic item was still a caftan, which Julie found to be unwieldy. She wondered if she could get away with wearing a small-sized man's pants outfit. Perhaps later, after they were no longer a curiosity to Heart's natives, she could afford to be a little eccentric.

Though Logan had done a fine job making breakfast from ingredients on hand, they agreed that they should stock some prepacked meals. A trip to the public marketplace would also be best put off for a later date.

Delivery of their purchases was scheduled for early that evening.

Julie barely had a chance to think about her next diversion when her door chime sounded. She started to get up, but Logan barked at her.

"Sit!"

She bristled at his using a one-word command as if she were his trained dog. As he opened the door, however, Julie could see how right he was to insist on playing butler, for two unknown women were standing in the doorway. Their shocked gasps and expressions of dismay when they noticed his naked, hairy chest had Julie up and improvising in a heartbeat. "You foolish man!" she scolded Logan, mimicking the mistress from the *Mother Knows Best* show. "When I told you one of your duties was to answer the door, I didn't mean you should stop in the middle of dressing to do it! Don't you have any common sense at all? Now go in the other room and put your robe on before I'm forced to punish you."

Logan's head had remained bowed through her tirade, but as he slowly moved away from her, he let her see his gritted teeth. She knew she'd gone a bit overboard, but he deserved that for snarling at her.

"Please excuse him," Julie said to the women. "He's very new to his position."

The embarrassed flush on their faces began to fade as the younger of the two said, "Yes, of course. We understand. In fact, that is why we're here. We heard quite a few new people moved in during the night, and we wanted to be the first to welcome you and offer any assistance you might need."

Beneath the gracious words Julie clearly heard the voice of a very snoopy female who wanted to be first on the block with fresh gossip. "Please, come in," she said just as graciously and waved them into the room. "I'm Julie."

Again the younger visitor spoke. "And I'm Reva. This is my mother, Syracuse. We live on the first floor."

Julie observed the rather elegant way they seated themselves and arranged their caftans, and attempted to imitate them. "May I offer you a cup of tea?"

"That would be very nice," Reva replied.

"Logan!" Julie called toward the bedroom. "Come here."

As he sluggishly dragged himself into the room wearing the pink caftan, Julie had to cover her mouth and pretend to be coughing to smother the giggles. He looked positively hilarious!

"My, my," Syracuse said. "That cough is an unhealthy symptom. You must make a visit to the sanatorium as soon as possible."

"I could show you the way," Reva offered brightly.

Julie cleared her throat and avoided looking at Logan again. "Thank you. I don't think it's anything serious, but I'll let you know if it gets worse. Logan, my guests and I would like some tea. Let's see if you can manage that without burning yourself or breaking anything."

She could practically feel the frustration spew-

ing from him, but the satisfied expressions on her
visitors' faces confirmed that they were both behaving in an acceptable manner. She had no
doubt, however, that Logan's shirtless debut would
be talked about for days.

"How ever will you manage with only the one
bed and bath?" Reva asked. "This size unit is usually leased out to women visiting without a
servant."

Julie sighed as if she was terribly put out by the
arrangement. "It was the only thing available on
such short notice, and as you can imagine, it's
going to be difficult enough *training* him without
having to deal with a lack of privacy." She sighed
loudly again. "But we'll all manage somehow."

Reva and Syracuse were as practiced at posing
veiled questions as a top-notch detective, but Julie
felt fairly certain that she wasn't saying or doing
anything that might jeopardize their situation.
Thankfully, Logan remained out of sight most of
the time, for she couldn't look at him in that pink
granny gown and keep a straight face.

Also, very thankfully, the interrogation session
was interrupted by more visitors.

"Logan!" Julie called again. "Don't pretend you
didn't hear the door, you lazy man."

Logan shuffled from the bedroom to the door.
The only thing he did swiftly was put his finger
to his lips as soon as he saw that it was Robin
and Geoffrey.

As required, Geoffrey entered several feet behind Robin. His head was obediently bowed, and
he was wearing the same pink caftan as Logan.

For some reason, though, Julie didn't think he looked nearly as funny as Logan.

Julie introduced everyone and was vastly relieved when Reva and her mother said they had to leave—probably to spread the tale of having seen the barbarians at close range.

"Whew!" Robin sighed, flopping down on a cushion. "We came over here to escape the two that decided to visit us. I guess we really are going to have to be on our toes every minute."

Logan smirked at Julie without saying "I told you so" aloud.

She was humble enough to admit that his assertion hadn't been entirely ridiculous. "Logan suggested we practice acceptable behavior by never acting as we normally do, even in private."

"I agree," Geoffrey said so quickly that he had to have been thinking the same thing.

"You do?" Robin asked with a pout. How was she ever going to break through his resistance if he never looked at her and they never made physical contact? Could it be that he really didn't want her to break through? She had never known a man to be so disinterested in her. Between that and how comfortable he seemed in a dress . . .

"Yes, I do," he said. "Consider how those women who came to visit us reacted to your being in pants."

Robin made a face and explained to Julie and Logan, "I didn't think I was committing a crime, but apparently the hospital scrubs we wore on the farm are only appropriate for men in the city. We're supposed to stick with these tents." She pulled the aqua caftan away from her body to demonstrate her point. "It was strongly recommended that our men be instructed to wear their robes when they go outdoors, however. The pants are only for inside, private wear to make doing their chores easier. They don't approve of any clothing that might reveal the shape of the body for either men or women."

"Geez!" Julie said, shaking her head. "What an upside-down, inside-out place."

"I don't wish to belittle your sense of frustration, Julie," Geoffrey said with a frown. "But *we* are the ones being forced to wear pink nightgowns."

The giggle Julie had previously suppressed threatened to bubble out again, until she caught a glimpse of the thunderclouds in Logan's eyes. Robin also managed to hold her amusement to a muffled snicker.

"I'm sorry," Julie said. "It's not funny. Maybe we should pay a visit to all of our people this afternoon and reinforce the seriousness of our situation."

Logan had been quietly brooding, but he thought of a better way to handle it. "More than likely everyone else has also been visited, or will be soon, by nosy neighbors. Call them to come here so we can all share anything new we've picked up. Make sure you remind them what to wear and how to behave on the way. There's no telling how many busybodies are peeking through their windows."

Julie noted that he wasn't having any trouble being his usual bossy self in front of Geoffrey. She wasn't sure which way he annoyed her more—domineering or subservient. Following the instructions Brianne had given, she called the other apartments and summoned the group together.

As Logan had guessed, almost everyone had been officially welcomed to the city by a "friendly" neighbor, then pumped for information. Occasionally they had learned a tidbit in return. Logan was the only one who had dared to make contact with another houseman, but the others agreed that it might be useful to establish a friendship with another servant if the opportunity arose.

"Just remember one thing," Julie warned sternly. "Under no circumstances can you risk revealing that you are not medicated or that you're performing any services different from theirs. The way the women checked us out, I think we should assume they'd try to get their servants to pass on anything they see or hear as well. Some of them may just be curious. But others may be opponents to Parisia's defense plan, looking for a reason for Parliament to reverse its decision. Without that plan we all go back to the farm indefinitely."

When the delivery woman arrived with Julie's order, the group returned to their individual apartments to collect their deliveries as well. Geoffrey and Robin returned a short while later to share dinner with Julie and Logan.

Much to both women's irritation, the men insisted on practicing their servant roles despite Julie and Robin begging them to put it off for another hour.

By the time they'd finished eating, and Logan

and Geoffrey had everything cleaned up, Julie retaliated.

"I want to take a walk around the block before it gets dark," she said to Robin. "Would you like to come?"

Robin shrugged. It didn't look like she was going to be making any progress with Geoffrey anytime soon. "Sure. Why not?"

Julie turned to Logan and put on her most regal air. "You will accompany us . . . at the proper distance of course."

She saw Logan's jaw clench and waited for him to balk at having to parade outside in a dress. Then she'd have him! He couldn't play the servant only when it was his preference. Unfortunately, he deduced the same thing. Taking a deep breath, he went to the door and held it open for her.

Robin couldn't resist. With a smirk and a crook of her finger, she ordered, "You too, Geoffrey."

Logan's continued stubbornness pushed Julie into dragging out the walk much longer than she had originally intended, in spite of the fact that curious eyes observed their progress every step of the way. It was Robin who eventually took pity on Geoffrey and brought the walk to an end.

The moment Julie and Logan were alone in the apartment, she knew she'd made a serious mistake. He was absolutely fuming! Her stomach squeezed into a knot of anxiety. How could she have forgotten how dangerous he was? He wasn't a kitten that she could tease with a piece of yarn; he was a full-grown panther.

And he was stalking her.

"Now, Logan," she said, trying to conceal her fear as she backed away from him, "it's your own fault. I mean, I probably went too far—"

"Too far?" he growled. "You paraded us halfway back to Earth!"

She kept walking backward around the room, occasionally bumping into furniture, but he continued to track her. She had only wanted to push him into a compromise, but now she could see she'd pushed him way beyond that.

"If you would just be reasonable about this servant business when we're alone, I'd be reasonable about acting the mistress when we're in public. It makes me extremely uncomfortable to have you waiting on me. I understand the need for caution, but we also have to find a way to live together in this apartment without driving each other crazy."

"That's not possible. You've already driven me there. You think you're uncomfortable? Look at me! This is uncomfortable!"

She obeyed his order to look at him without thinking of the consequences. A giggle escaped before she clamped her hand over her mouth.

"Go ahead, *mistress*, let it out. You've been strangling on it all day."

She sucked in her cheeks to hold back the smile. "I'm sorry, Logan, really—"

"Too late for sorry. I want to hear you laugh. I want you to get every last giggle out of your system, before you wreck this whole operation by cracking up in public . . . or before I go completely nuts and turn you over my knee!"

She thought the predatory gleam in his eye

seemed to glow a little brighter with the thought of spanking her. "Logan, please, you're scaring me. I said, I'm sorry—"

"And I said, I want you to laugh. If you can't do it yourself, maybe I need to help you." He took a large step toward her, but she escaped his grasp.

"Stop it!" Julie ordered and sped up her retreat.

"I'll stop it when I hear you laughing," he countered, then picked up his own pace.

She evaded him for almost a whole minute as she circled the room and dodged between furniture. Suddenly his hands latched onto her waist, bringing her to an abrupt halt. As she tried to get free again, his fingers wiggled in her sides. "Laugh, Julie," he said, tickling her without mercy.

She squealed from the unexpected tickle and saw a victorious grin spread across his face, instantly erasing any trace of meanness. It was such a relief to realize he had intended to tickle rather than hurt her, she almost gave him the laughter he'd demanded. But her own stubborn streak kept her from giving in that easily. "You can't make me!" she declared.

He found an extremely vulnerable spot below her ribs that caused her to squeal again, but she still managed to hold back a real laugh.

The more she squirmed in an attempt to escape, the more effort he put into tickling her. The struggle tilted them both off balance, and they went tumbling down over a row of foam cubes and onto the floor in a tangle of legs and arms and yards of pink and aqua fabric.

That did it for Julie! She burst out laughing and Logan joined her the next second.

"You broke the couch," she teased between chuckles and gasps for air.

"I can fix the couch. What are you going to do about my broken back?" He returned, managing to reduce his laughter to a crooked smile.

"No problem," she said as seriously as possible. "I'm a nurse. I'll fix your back for you." With him sprawled half on top of her, she reached around to his back and scraped her fingernail down his spine, giving him a taste of his own medicine. His reflexive jerk gave her such satisfaction, she tried to extract a bit more revenge by tickling his sides as he had done with her. But that only caused him to pay her back again. As each tried to get the better of the other, they rolled across the floor, laughing too hard to really administer a good tickle.

"I give up! You win," Julie finally said, fighting more for a deep breath of air than for her freedom. His body had hers pinned to the floor, and though he looked much too pleased with himself, she didn't have the strength to continue the mock battle.

"If I win, that means you lose, and you know what happens to losers?"

She cocked one eyebrow suspiciously.

"They have to pay off the winner," Logan informed her. "Now, what payment should I demand?"

Chapter 15

Logan looked as though he was giving a great deal of thought to choosing her payoff.

"I won't make you go on any more walks," she offered quickly, before he could think of anything more difficult for her to forfeit.

He shook his head. "Not enough."

"Umm, I won't talk to you like you're a complete idiot in front of guests." Now that she was no longer laughing or engaged in a tickling match, she began noticing other things—like how his hard body felt covering hers and how she could feel the coarseness of the hair on his legs because their caftans were twisted above their knees. How he shifted to find a more comfortable position, how his lower body was changing shape where it was pressed to hers . . .

"Still not enough," he murmured as the expression on his face turned serious and his eyes darkened with desire.

Without conscious thought her gaze lowered from his seductive eyes to his mouth. She couldn't verbalize her third concession to the winner, but her eyes closed and her lips parted in preparation of giving him the prize he wanted.

His sigh sounded more like one of resigned defeat than glorious victory, but before she could question it, his mouth came down hard on hers. Rather than the tender consideration he had shown her before, this kiss was filled with greedy passion. Without being granted the time to weigh rights and wrongs, her instincts claimed full control of her response. She angled her head beneath his and drew his tongue deep into her mouth. There was no battle for superiority here, nor concerns about the past or future. There was only the present and the explosive sensations he ignited within her.

It took only a slight maneuver to push the caftans above their waists, leaving only his cotton boxers and her satin pants as obstacles to their suddenly raging need. Instinctively she parted her thighs and wrapped her legs around him, cradling his hips so that he was perfectly centered on her.

His mouth continued to devour hers, and she returned his hunger in full. Their tongues stroked and licked, moving in and out to match the rhythm set by their lower bodies as they rubbed against each other, harder, faster, wanting more, but unable to stop the pleasure they were taking long enough to make it even better.

Moaning in frustration, she tightened her legs, bracing him hard against where she needed him most and was unexpectedly flung over the edge. Between her sharp movement and cry of relief, it was more than he could handle, and he too felt the uncontrollable burst of sexual release.

He rolled them both onto their sides and held her close while they caught their breath.

Julie's mind was enveloped in a sensual fog while chords of pleasure continued to thrum through her body. A worrisome thought strained to surface, but she suppressed it. Whatever it was that needed to be considered could wait a few more minutes. Then it was forgotten altogether, for Logan's lips returned to hers, gentler now, the way she remembered his kisses from before.

She felt herself floating and knew he had picked her up in his arms and was carrying her, but all her attention was focused on his incredible mouth and the way he could make a simple kiss say so much.

His lips barely left hers for more than a heart-beat or two, and yet he managed to remove their caftans and underwear, pull back the bed covers, and lie down with her still nestled in his embrace.

Logan would have loved to simply stand beside the bed and memorize how his angel looked from head to toe, with no part of her concealed from him. Her eyes were closed, her face flushed with passion, her body writhing against his. He was afraid that if he ended the kiss to do as he wished, the sensual spell she was under would be broken. She'd awaken and realize who she was with and what she was doing. Her common sense would return and end his chance to live out one of his fantasies.

So he gave up one pleasure for another and determined to keep her in her current state of mind-less lust as long as possible. If he was very, very good, perhaps she could be tempted to repeat the experience occasionally. After one day he knew his sanity could never stand a whole year of either a mistress-servant relationship or the casual roommate arrangement she was pushing for.

He had no delusions of convincing her that he loved her or receiving her love in return. He was simply hoping for a cease-fire and whatever concessions he could seduce from her.

Though climaxing without being inside her had never been one of his fantasies—it had never even occurred to him that that could happen to him at his age—the release did give him the patience he needed to carry out his new plan.

Straddling her closed thighs, his lips paid homage to every feature on her face, his teeth nibbled on her ears, his hands leisurely stroked her neck, shoulders, and arms, while at the same time, as if entirely by accident, he moved his chest so that his hair brushed lightly back and forth over her breasts. Only when she arched upward to increase the contact did he take her breasts in his hands and knead them gently.

Her groan told him that was almost but not quite what she had in mind. He smiled against her mouth, then kissed his way down her neck, across one shoulder and down to the nipple that had hardened for him. Her abrupt intake of breath was his reward for closing his mouth and teeth around the peak and stroking it with his tongue. As his hands continued to massage the fullness of both breasts, he moved his mouth to her other nipple, until her attempts to gyrate her hips beneath his weight reminded him that she still had more peaks and valleys impatiently waiting to be explored.

Planting a trail of kisses over her abdomen, with a brief pause to lick at her navel, he led her to believe he would soon arrive at his ultimate destination. However, he had a detour in mind. As long as she remained willing to bear his lovemaking, he intended to taste every beautiful inch of her.

But he thought it best to give her a preview of coming attractions to entice her to tolerate the delay. Easing his way upward so his shaft was once again full and heavy against her stomach, he eased his way down her body again until he was knocking at her door. She was so bewitched by his touch that the slightest move on his part to change his position had her spreading her legs to accommodate him.

With his hands beneath her thighs he bent her legs toward her chest to expose her even more. The sight of her femininity glistening with the moisture of wanting him practically unmanned him, but he pulled himself together and carried on. "So beautiful," he whispered, unable to hold back all of what he was feeling.

He allowed her to hold him for the moment it took to guide him to her entrance; then he moved her hands away and held them. As he slipped into her depths, he reclaimed her mouth for another long, deep kiss. With little more than the skillful rotation of his hips, he drove her to the brink once more.

Then he withdrew from her body.

Her breath caught in her throat and her eyes

flew open. She didn't understand, and she was too dazed to ask. Scraping his callused thumb over the tiny bud of nerves he had teased, he felt her shiver and murmured, "Patience, angel."

It was the mantra he had been saying over and over in his own mind, for it was becoming more difficult by the second to do what he intended. Leaving her body after finally learning the feel of it just took the number one spot on his list of hardest things he ever had to do. But keeping his plan in mind helped him accomplish it.

He crawled back far enough to be able to kiss her toes. When he'd caressed every part of one foot, he alternately kissed and licked a path up that leg, then repeated the slow procedure on the other. This time, however, he didn't stop at the top of her thigh.

He gave her warning of his next sweet torment by cupping his hand between her legs and lightly stroking the soft curls.

"Logan, please."

He had not thought it possible for her to make his name sound like a prayer, yet she did, and he could not help but comply.

Her womanhood was wet and open as he slid two fingers slowly up and down, bringing her back to the point where he had left her before. He watched her clutch the pillow beneath her head and listened to her kitten cries grow stronger with each breath. When she began tilting her hips to meet his strokes, he quickened his efforts for several seconds, then pinched her sensitive, extended flesh between his fingers.

She whimpered and trembled and sighed with immense satisfaction, but he wasn't finished with her. While the aftershocks of pleasure continued to hold her in thrall, those same two fingers; that had so exquisitely released her tension, delved deep inside her and pushed against the upper wall.

The shock of sensation jolted her so intensely that only the press of his mouth kept her hips on the bed. As his tongue rekindled her smoldering fire, his fingers scissored rapidly back and forth inside her. Within seconds she cried out again, and her body went limp.

"Please," she gasped. "No more. I'll die."

Logan's heart swelled. He'd done it—satisfiied her until she begged him to stop. Another part of his anatomy was uncomfortably swollen in the real sense of the word. But that was something he was used to around Julie.

He moved up alongside her, pulled her into his arms, and covered them both with the sheet. Though he wasn't trying to be obvious, she couldn't help but feel his hard length against her thigh.

She reached down and stroked him, but he quickly brought her hand back up and kissed the palm.

"Thank you," he whispered. "But no."

She turned her face to him and frowned. "No? But you're . . . you haven't—"

He cut her off with a soft kiss. "It doesn't matter. This time was just for you. Do you feel good?"

"Mm-hmm," she murmured contentedly and snuggled into a comfy position.

"Good. That's what I wanted most. Now go to sleep. We start work tomorrow." Above all else, he had not wanted her to think he had seduced her for his own satisfaction. The only way he could think to avoid that was by acting as he had. Next time would be different.

She was quiet for a minute or so, and he thought she'd already dozed off when she spoke again.

"Logan?"

"Hmm?"

"Does this mean I won the argument about your playing servant when we're alone?"

He chuckled and gave her a squeeze. "I guess so."

"Then you're the loser this time."

He smiled and kissed her head. "I don't know about that. If this is what losing feels like, I can hardly wait to find out what sort of payoff you're going to demand."

"I want an explanation!" Robin demanded, staring down at Geoffrey with her fists planted on her hips.

Geoffrey blinked the sleep out of his eyes and strained to focus on the woman standing over him. Even half asleep and in the dim light, he could tell she was furious with him. "I beg your pardon?"

"No, I will not pardon you. Not unless your explanation is completely believable."

Geoffrey pulled himself to a sitting position, careful to keep the sheet over his lower parts. When he'd opted to sleep in the nude, as he regularly did, he hadn't expected Robin to accost him in the middle of the night. "I will be most happy to explain whatever you'd like, but couldn't it wait until we've both had a bit more sleep?"

Robin huffed. "That's easy for you to say. *You* weren't laying here wide awake wondering whether you had bad breath or body odor!"

Geoffrey pinched the bridge of his nose and shook his head. He was fully awake now, but she still made no sense. "I'm afraid you have me at a disadvantage, Robin. Perhaps if we begin again, and you explain what you want *me* to explain, we can solve your insomnia."

Robin huffed again and paced back and forth a few times before she could get it out. Even when she began to speak, however, she faced away, rather than have to look at him when he answered. "Are you homosexual? I mean, if you are, I'm fine with that, as long as I know it up front."

Geoffrey couldn't have been more stunned. He couldn't imagine what he'd done to cause her to question his sexual preference other than wearing a pink dress, and he hadn't been given a choice about that. However, he figured if he ever wanted to go back to sleep he'd best answer her question. "No, I am not homosexual."

"Then what is it about me that you find so unattractive?" she asked before she lost her nerve.

Her second question proved he could be more stunned after all. "I—I don't find anything about you unattractive, Robin. You're—you're a beautiful woman." The most beautiful he'd ever encountered, he added to himself.

She whirled around at him and crossed her arms defensively. "Then why do you step away when I come near? Why do you avoid looking me in the eye? Why haven't you picked up on a single one of my obvious flirtations? And don't tell me it's because you're trying to fit in around here. You were doing your best to ignore me from the first minute we saw each other. I will admit that it's very egotistical of me, but I am not accustomed to being ignored by men. Usually it's the other way around. On the rare occasion when I choose *not* to ignore the man, I expect him to be receptive."

Geoffrey was finally following her train of thought, convoluted though it was. He had unintentionally bruised her feminine ego. By *not* drooling over her the way he was tempted to do, he'd become a challenge to her. Though he'd wished her attraction to him was real, he hadn't counted on it. That would have been no less than a miracle. Now it was up to him to say something that would salve her pride and spare him embarrassment at the same time.

He cleared his throat and chose a lead-in sentence. "I have a confession to make." Although he avoided looking at her, he sensed her coming to his side.

"A confession?" she asked, her tone of voice revealing her eagerness for an acceptable excuse.

He nodded. "I'm . . . I'm rather shy with women. Especially very beautiful women like you. I never know quite what to say or how to behave."

She shifted from one foot to the other and considered his words. As she recalled the different times that she'd thought he'd been ignoring her, she decided that shyness could have accounted for it. Julie had even said something about her coming on too strong for a man like Geoffrey. Julie, with her greater ability to analyze people, had hit the problem on the head in one try, but Robin hadn't taken her advice. Now that she understood the situation, she was certain she could fix it.

She sat next to him and smiled at the way he quickly scooted away and pulled the sheet more protectively around him. It was the first time she'd seen him without a shirt, and she liked what she saw. He was lean but firm, with just enough muscle development for definition. She had to curl her fingers into the palms of her hands to keep from touching him.

"I really do make you nervous, don't I?" she asked sweetly. "I don't mean to. I just go after what I want."

He closed his eyes. How he wished she truly wanted him and not simply another man's heart for her trophy shelf, to be won, then forgotten. But he knew beautiful women and how they thought. He had learned from experience that the only way not to end up on that shelf was never to play the game at all.

A light touch on his cheek made him open his eyes again.

"There's no reason to be nervous," Robin assured him. "Unless you're a virgin. You're not, are you?"

Geoffrey was able to laugh at that. "No, I am not a virgin either."

"Good. Then there really is nothing for you to be shy about. I have all the same parts as any other woman you've ever been with. And if there's anything you're not sure about, I'll help you."

He cleared his throat again and tried another tack. "My being shy is not the only thing holding me back from . . . from being intimate with you. I pride myself on being a gentleman, as old-fashioned as that may sound. A gentleman would never take advantage of a woman when her resistance was down, even if she thought she wanted him at the moment. To act on my attraction to you, while you are so vulnerable, would be akin to my seducing a grieving widow. Only a rogue would behave so unconscionably."

Robin narrowed her eyes at him. "Hold on one teeny second. Let me try to rephrase your explanation into plain English . . . I mean, American. You think this wacky situation we're in has made me a weak little girl whose mind is too mucked up to know the difference between being attracted to a man and needing a strong shoulder to lean on."

Geoffrey grimaced at her annoyed tone. "I merely said that you're vulnerable right now—"

"Exactly. But here's a news flash for you, smartass. I was attracted to you the first time I saw you, *before* we boarded the plane. Not only did I think you were an absolutely gorgeous man, there was something about you—your aura maybe, who knows?—that made me want to find out more about you. If all I needed was a man to protect me from the unknown, do you honestly believe I would have picked you rather than Logan or

Wilkes or any of the other muscle-bound young apes in our group?"

Geoffrey didn't know whether he'd just been flattered, insulted, or chastised, so he gave no reply whatsoever. It worried him that her arguments sounded logical. Despite his previous experience and knowing the inevitable outcome, he realized that Robin had the power to drag him into the game if she remained determined to do so.

It would be different if they weren't sentenced to spend a year together in a small apartment. On the farm he could have avoided her until her fleeting interest turned to another man. He let his thoughts drift ahead in time, imagining that he allowed himself to be seduced by her beauty. Undoubtedly he'd fall in love, as he had before. Then, as before, once conquered, he'd no longer be of interest to her. She'd switch her attentions to another man and forget Geoffrey existed.

Only this time they'd still be living together long after she turned away.

"Time's up, Geoffrey," Robin said, breaking into his imaginings. "You don't want to answer my question because you know I'm right and you're wrong, but you're not ready to admit it. So let's make a deal. You say you are attracted to me, but don't want to take advantage of me because I'm vulnerable right now. Okay. How much time do you think needs to go by before I stop being vulnerable and start knowing my own mind?"

He could see where this was headed and tried to derail her. "A year."

"Bzzt! Wrong answer. Try a week. One has gone

by already. More than enough time to get over a shock."

"Six months."

"One."

"Three," he said, combing his fingers through his hair in frustration. "Damn it, woman! I don't even know what I'm negotiating about."

"Two months," she said firmly. "I won't insist you give up this foolish chivalry for two months. But if I still want us to be more than roommates after that, you're mine to do whatever I want with."

Geoffrey shook his head and sighed. Since he was certain her interest in him could never last as long as two months, he agreed to her ultimatum.

"Good. Now there's just one more thing." Before he could avoid her, she twined her arms around his neck and pressed her mouth to his. He resisted for a moment, but she held tight until he was kissing her back.

She had wanted to make sure, and now she knew. This was definitely more than an ordinary attraction between a man and a woman. *This* was the magic she'd been looking for!

For a few more seconds she savored his kiss and the feel of his hands roaming up and down her back. Then she eased away. "I just thought you should have a taste of what you'd be enjoying tonight if you weren't such a gentleman." She left him in the confused condition she'd intended and returned to her own bed, alone. She didn't feel badly that he'd negotiated her into a two-month period of neutrality. After that kiss he'd never be able to hold out that long.

*   *   *

Nadia shoved her breakfast aside. How could they expect her to eat this slop every day for the next five years? The least Parisia could have done was to send Fulton over to prepare her meals and take care of her laundry!

Losing Fulton after putting so much time into his unique training made her punishment that much worse. She wondered who would hire him now, and whether his new employer would figure out how to bribe him for gossip about his previous mistress.

If others learned of the services she had required of him, she might have difficulty hiring any houseman in the future. Even if she managed to acquire someone suitable, she knew she would never again be able to take the risks she had before—not if she ever wanted to climb back up the political ladder.

And the only thing that was going to keep her spirits up for five years was the belief that it was possible for her to recapture lost ground one day.

She was no longer under guard and the restraints on her wrists and ankles had been removed, but what good did it do? She was still a prisoner in a primitive commune while the Earth women now had freedom in her world. Ray Higgs, the scarred man, and the blond man were gone too. By eavesdropping she'd learned of the outrageous defense plan Parisia had pushed through Parliament. If only she had been there—

But she hadn't been, and there was no use fretting over past mistakes. What she had to do now was figure out how to improve her present circumstances.

Escaping was not an option at the moment. The controller had gone with the blond man, and her earlier plan to get Simone to help her was no longer feasible. Not that anyone would stop her from going into the transfer room and pleading for assistance while Simone was on duty. It was just logical to assume that Simone would never jeopardize her own future by aiding an exile.

Actually, the only option she did have was which communal task she would perform in exchange for sustenance. As if it wasn't demeaning enough to have to manage without a servant, the Earth cretins kept insisting she would have to do manual labor or she would not be permitted to eat. And it wasn't even decent food!

The mere thought of dealing with smelly four-legged beasts, or dirtying her hands in the fields, was completely repulsive to her. It was beyond her imagination to envision herself serving or cleaning up after men. The only chore she thought she might learn to tolerate was the preparation of food. At least that work was done indoors and required clean hands.

"Mornin'. Nadia, ain't it?"

Nadia looked up . . . and up. The man who had dared to approach appeared to be taller and broader across the shoulders than she was. His hair was blond, but cut so close to his scalp that he looked nearly bald.

"I'm Guy Wilkes," he said, as if she should be

impressed, then sat next to her without asking permission.

She glared at him, but it didn't seem to faze him in the least.

"Thought you might be needin' a friend about now." With a bold look on his face, he placed his hand over her knee.

Shocked at his impertinence, she bolted up from her seat. "How dare you touch me without permission?" she hissed.

Wilkes laughed out loud and slapped his thigh. "I'll be goddamned! You really do think you're some sort of queen bee, don't you?"

She turned her back on him to walk away, but he grabbed her robe and brought her up short. Sneering at him over her shoulder, she ordered, "Release me this instant, or I'll—"

"Or you'll what?" he challenged her right back. Standing up, he exchanged his hold on her robe for a fistful of black hair, tugging hard enough to make her eyes water. "If you think you can scare me like you did that wimp Higgs, you'd better think again. In my world—which happens to be this here farm at the moment—men do the orderin', not broads. And that includes when and where they screw."

Nadia's heart pounded with fear. It was quite clear that this man was capable of hurting her very badly, but she had no idea why he would or what he wanted from her. She had no experience with physical force, other than the few times she had caused Fulton minor pain to keep him obedient. Not knowing what else to do, her gaze darted from side to side in search of someone to come to her rescue. However, the elderly men working in the kitchen seemed completely oblivious to her plight.

"Don't bother lookin' to them for help. These old geezers can't move fast enough to get out of their own way, and everyone else is out doin' their chores already. But don't get the idea that the others would help even if they were still around. Let me tell you the score, plain and simple. There's a whole bunch of men on this farm who were both angry about bein' left behind and bored with havin' only five-fingered Mary for company. It don't matter how important you were where you come from. Here, you're just a horny broad who's already spread her legs for one of our kind, so you oughta be just as obligin' for everybody else."

She inhaled sharply. Though some of his expressions were unknown to her, his hand gestures were adequately explicit. "I was conducting an experiment."

Wilkes smirked. "Yeah, right, babe. You just stick to that story if it makes you feel better. As a matter of fact, I have a little experiment you can help *me* with."

"I have no intention of helping you with anything!" She tried to pull out of his grasp, but he only held on tighter.

"Listen up, bitch. Every man here heard how you ordered Higgs to give it to you, and I'm not the only one who thinks you should try a real man on for size. Now, before this situation gets messy, I figger somebody oughta take control of it."

She angled her head at him. The word *control*

caught her attention. "And I suppose that some-body is you?"

"None other," he answered with a cocky grin. "I have a business proposition for you, but I don't want anyone to overhear it. Let's go to my tent."

A business proposition, like control, was some-thing she could understand, even if his methods and other terminology were unfamiliar. Thinking she had a chance of coming out ahead in this en-counter after all, her self-confidence returned. Straightening her shoulders and lifting her chin, she demanded, "Remove your hand from my per-son, then I will allow you to accompany me to your tent for a discussion." He released her hair, but she could see he didn't like giving her even that slight advantage.

Wilkes had been right about everyone being gone. There wasn't a man in sight between the big house and his tent. At the last moment something warned Nadia not to go inside with him. "No one can hear you now," she said, stopping in front of the tent. "What is your proposition?"

He motioned for her to enter. "Inside first. I don't want to take the chance of anyone seein' us talkin' either."

That seemed somewhat extreme, but Nadia de-cided she was better off doing as he suggested rather than risk angering him again. Since the tent wasn't high enough for her to stand erect, she sat on one of the cots while he closed the tent flap and lit a lamp. Her patience and confidence were both fading quickly, but her curiosity kept her from walking out on him.

Without warning Wilkes turned and backhanded her cheek. She cried out more from shock than pain. When she tried to get up and away, he hit her again, this time so hard that she fell back onto the cot. A scream welled up in her throat, but before it erupted, his hand closed over her mouth.

"Not a sound," he growled and viciously squeezed her cheeks while he straddled her body. "Rule number one: you keep your goddamned mouth shut 'cept when I tell you otherwise. I'm the boss here, and the sooner you understand that, the faster we can get down to business. What you just felt were nothin' but love pats compared to what you'll feel if you don't behave. Got it?"

With her cheeks throbbing and his greater weight pinning her down, she did the only logical thing she could—she nodded in understanding.

"Good girl. Rule number two: you don't go nowhere or do nothin' without me. From now on we're Siamese twins. Got it?"

She nodded again. All the stories she'd ever heard about men came back to her, and with a sinking sensation she now realized just how accurate they were.

But Ray Higgs hadn't been cruel, or even aggressive. And the blond man had seemed fairly rational. Perhaps one of the men left behind— She tossed that thought out. None of the others she'd seen looked as strong or mean as Guy Wilkes. She had to accept the fact that she was completely at his mercy—at the moment.

Wilkes released her cheeks and stared down at her, as if daring her to speak without his permission. After a few seconds he seemed satisfied with her obedience and said, "Here's the deal. You gotta work to eat around here. Now I figger, you bein' the only woman oughta be worth a hell of a lot. 'Specially one who likes gettin' stuck as much as you do. If you keep givin' it away, though, it ain't gonna be worth nothin'."

She thought she comprehended what he was saying, but his speech was so peculiar, she couldn't be certain. Rather than question him, however, she held her tongue and hoped she'd catch on as he continued.

"Instead of you doin' chores like the men, you'll provide them with your personal, one-of-a-kind service, and they'll make sure you get all your needs taken care of. 'Course, you gotta have somebody plenty smart and strong to manage your business for you, and I just happen to be sick of wastin' my talents pickin' fruit and milkin' cows. You got the picture, babe?"

She could hardly believe her ears. She had been fretting over what chore she could tolerate in exchange for food, and though she found Guy Wilkes to be as repugnant as a man could be, he had come up with an option she hadn't thought of. Thinking of how enjoyable her experiences with Ray Higgs had been, she smiled up at the man who thought he was so smart.

He grinned back at her. "Rule number three: no lyin' here like a dead fish. No matter who you're with, you act like you're lovin' every minute of it, just like you did with Higgs. And just to be sure

you do, I'll be right here watchin' you every minute
you're workin'. Got it?"

She gave him another nod as she felt a twinge
of anticipation in her lower abdomen. The thought
of him observing while another man pleasured her
was strangely exciting. Even better than watching
herself with Fulton in the bathroom mirror. She
wondered if the image had a similar effect on Guy
Wilkes. The answer to that came the next instant.

"Time to show your boss what a good little
worker you're gonna be," he said, and tore open
the front of her robe. Letting out a soft whistle of
appreciation at the sight of her breasts, he groped
and kneaded them in his big, meaty hands. "The
boys are gonna love these tits, babe."

Feeling a surge of power at his male weakness,
she made the mistake of letting him see it in her
eyes. He immediately repaid her by giving her nipples a harsh, twisting pinch. *"Ouch,"* she whimpered before recalling his order not to speak, and
he quickly pinched her again.

"That was just a taste of how it can be between
us. You obey the rules . . ." He bent down and
sucked one of her nipples into his mouth, teasing
her with his tongue and teeth until she moaned
for him. Then he abruptly bit into her flesh. "Or
you can fight me and get hurt. It's your choice,
babe."

She massaged her bruised breast with one hand
while wiping the moisture from her eyes with the
other. When he rose to his knees and shoved his
pants down below his partially swollen manpiece,

she was no longer certain this was going to be better than dealing with smelly four-legged beasts.

"Now you can open your mouth," he told her with an ugly sneer on his face.

She obeyed his command, but what followed wasn't anything like it had been with Ray Higgs, or even Fulton. Obviously the ultimate pleasure could only be achieved when *she* was the one giving the orders.

Simone stretched luxuriantly and moved her arms and legs over the satin sheets on Nadia's big bed. She mentally congratulated herself once again on having made such an excellent move.

Nadia's unusual tastes had proven to be an unexpected bonus. Simone knew that she was supposed to disapprove of the lavish bathroom with its mirrored wall, the rich foods Fulton served, and the satin sheets. But the truth was, she found it all very stimulating to her senses, as well as her thought processes.

There was only one thing that truly shocked her, and even that had turned out to be delightful. When Fulton had offered to prepare a bath for her, she certainly hadn't expected to find him waiting to attend her in the nude. Nor could she possibly have guessed at the extent of his assistance. When he had asked her about her wishes, she had simply told him to do whatever he normally did for Nadia. Once she got over the initial embarrassment of being disrobed by him, she quickly overcame the shock of being touched as well. Wanting to learn everything there was to know about Nadia and recalling the scene she had witnessed in the transfer room, Simone decided to allow Fulton total freedom and soon made some amazing discoveries!

She stretched again and ran her hands over her body, touching and stroking places where she had never lingered before. That sort of contact was considered sinful and ultimately harmful to one's mental health. Perhaps there was a good deal of truth to that. Giving in to the physical pleasure that could be derived from such touches had certainly caused problems for Nadia.

But Simone now knew there were also lies mixed in with the truth. And Nadia had been exiled rather than be allowed to reveal the real truth about what it was like to be stroked by a man.

The more Simone thought about it, the more convinced she was that Nadia had had a valid reason for trespassing into the Earth commune. It made sense to Simone that before Nadia could challenge age-old laws and traditions, she would need to do more research. Unable to conduct that research among her own people, she must have decided it was worth the risk to use Earth men.

Simone had not been able to learn all the details, but apparently the Earth women had been instrumental in exposing Nadia's misdeeds. She wondered if they were also responsible for convincing Parisia that Heart needed their assistance in developing a defense system.

There was clearly something very strange going on about that too, but Simone wasn't well enough connected with Parisia's advisers to get to the bottom of it. Nadia had had plenty of strong allies, but without her to speak for them, they had all backed off rather than defy Parisia and chance the same future as Nadia.

As much as Simone would have liked to be the courageous woman to oppose Parisia's defense plan and challenge Heart's traditional laws, she knew she didn't have the strength of character or charisma that Nadia had. Besides, she had been playing both sides for so long, it would be hard to convince some people that she had finally made a choice.

For many years she hadn't been sure which side would provide her with the best future. More recently she had been leaning toward Nadia for a number of reasons. For one, Nadia's political opinions suited her better than Parisia's. More important, however, Parisia and Brianne's inner circle was firmly fixed and nearly impenetrable. Nadia's court was still flexible. Though Simone didn't think she had leadership qualities, she did believe she'd enjoy being the leader's chief adviser. The mere thought of possessing the same power now held by Iris gave Simone a shiver of excitement.

She continued to mull over what facts she had with those she had to guess at. Considering every possibility along with her personal goals, she eventually came to a conclusion.

She had to come up with a plan to help Nadia escape. Then, together, they would challenge Parisia for the imperial throne.

Chapter 16

Julie awoke to the sound of running water. She blinked several times before she recognized her surroundings and identified what she was hearing as the bathroom shower. Once total awareness set in, she closed her eyes again.

For a few heartbeats she considered hiding under the covers or hurriedly leaving the apartment, but neither action would be terribly mature. Not that what she had done last night was all that responsible; it was just that two wrongs never make a right.

How had it happened? What excuse did she have for abandoning all her common sense, forgetting everything Logan had ever done, and thinking of nothing but the moment? That wasn't like her at all. And yet she wasn't drunk or drugged, as she had been when they were in the barn. Nor was she blinded by dreams of a beautiful future as she had been when Logan was her patient.

What she *was,* however, was tired. Tired of the war, the maiming and killing, tired of anticipating the worst and still not being prepared when it happened, tired of being the one responsible for every decision. She was just plain tired. Too tired to hold her self-protective barriers in place against a man that she continued to want in spite of everything she knew about him.

She heard the shower turn off and thought she should at least get out of bed for the conversation they needed to have. As soon as she sat up, though, she saw that her caftan was on the floor near the bathroom door. Rather than take the chance of Logan catching her undressed and thinking she was coming to join him, she remained in bed with the covers pulled up to her shoulders.

The bathroom door opened and, through the steam, Julie saw Logan toweling dry his hair. Her breath quickened at the sight of his incredible body. She forgave herself for that reaction, acknowledging that she wouldn't be much of a woman if she didn't appreciate the beauty of his masculine form. That didn't mean she was in love with the man.

She tried not to think about what that body had felt like pressed against hers. Her hands still remembered the texture of his skin, his hair, the hardness of his muscles. Her lips were still tender from his kisses.

Logan stepped out of the bathroom with the same sort of feeling he had often had upon approaching enemy territory—tense, anxious, uncertain, and hopeful. That hope rose as he noted the way Julie was watching him, but it immediately plummeted again as she turned away with an embarrassed flush on her cheeks.

She didn't need to say it aloud. He could see

that she regretted making love with him, wished she could go back to last night and prevent it. Wrapping the towel around his waist for the sake of her modesty, he chided himself. What had he expected? A miracle?

As he sorted through the boxes of clothing that had been delivered yesterday, he recalled his naive idea that if he serviced her well enough, she'd be anxious to share her bed with him again. He would have been satisfied if that was the only part of her life she had been willing to share.

For a few hours he had purposely forgotten that she wasn't the kind of woman who could set aside who and what a man was and think only of her own pleasure.

He supposed that the gentlemanly thing to do under the circumstances would be to say a few words to let her off the hook, but with his heart clenched painfully in his chest, he didn't have it in him to play the gentleman. On the other hand, he could make a gentlemanly, silent promise not to seduce her again. The only way he would touch her in the future was if she begged him to.

Knowing that would never happen, he had no other option but to get back into his servant role. As he picked out one of the pants outfits, he spoke in a flat voice. "I'll be in the kitchen making breakfast. Is there anything in particular you'd like?" He glanced toward her only long enough to see the negative shake of her head, then left the room.

Julie cursed herself for being such a coward. She should have said something right away, but instead she had hesitated. Deep down inside, she had been hoping he would speak first, that he would say some magical words that would make everything work out just wonderfully.

But he hadn't, and like most men, he probably didn't think there was anything to talk about—what happened, happened, and might or might not happen again, depending on his mood, and didn't bear much relevance to the rest of his life.

Unfortunately, she couldn't dismiss it so easily. Not counting the incident in the barn, last night was the first time in her life she had made love with a man she wasn't having a serious relationship with. Even if she could set aside her own moral standards, there was something of greater importance here.

Pregnancy. Never before had she been so distracted that she forgot about the possible consequences of her actions. Though he had not climaxed inside her, he had penetrated her body, and sometimes that was all it took.

Good Lord! She must have been completely out of her mind. Considering the current circumstances, the last problem she needed to add was a baby. Suddenly she had a vision of herself with a dark-haired little boy on her lap.

"Mommy, do I have a daddy like the other kids?"

"Of course, dear, but he lives on a planet in another universe. He didn't come back to Earth with me because he was a convicted murderer and traitor to his country. If he came back, he'd have to go to prison for the rest of his life. So you wouldn't get to see him anyway."

Julie shook the silly daydream out of her brain and headed for the shower.

There was one thought she couldn't shake off as lightly. Why had Logan held back last night? What was it he had said to her? She was certain he hadn't used the excuse of not wanting to get her pregnant, but she couldn't recall exactly what his excuse had been. Why would he go to such lengths to please her and go unsatisfied himself?

That question was still hovering around her head when she joined Logan in the kitchen. "Why?" she asked from the doorway.

Without looking at her, he placed two plates of fluffy omelets on the table. "I didn't know what else you'd like." He pulled out a chair and waited for her to be seated.

She started to speak again, then decided the conversation might move along better if they were both stationary. "You know that isn't what I was asking," she said, sitting down. "Logan, please. I realize you may not feel the need to talk about what happened, but I do."

Logan continued to keep his gaze averted as he sat across from her and replied, "Fine. I apologize for taking advantage of you. It won't happen again."

That wasn't even close to what she expected to hear. "There is certainly no need for you to apologize. If anything, I took advantage of you." She took a deep breath and gathered her courage for what she knew had to be said aloud. "But you're right about it not happening again. It *can't*. For

one thing, I can't risk the chance of getting
pregnant.

"For another, in spite of how I behaved last
night, I don't feel comfortable engaging in, um,
casual sex. I think our situation is complicated
enough without our being . . . intimately involved."
She decided mentioning his criminal record on top
of all that would be overkill. "What I would like
to know is why you . . . why you didn't . . ."

"Forget it, okay?" he snapped at her. "We were
both over-stressed. I can't explain what I did any
better than you can." He looked into her eyes for a
moment, then turned his attention to his breakfast.

Julie should have been satisfied with his response, perhaps even pleased that he seemed to
have returned to his usual indifferent, nearly rude
attitude. Instead she had the oddest feeling of disappointment, though she couldn't quite identify
the cause. "Right. Um, one last thing. Are you
planning to go back to playing my servant all the
time again?"

"That would be best."

She felt another stab of disappointment, but he
was right. It was best if they maintained as much
distance between them as possible. Especially considering the fact that despite his obvious lack of
interest, she had the strongest urge to go cuddle
on his lap. And despite all her good, commonsense
reasoning, she was afraid that if he spoke to her
the way he had last night, she might fall apart and
ask him to make love to her again.

Right after they finished breakfast, Iris called
Julie to request that she gather her people in the

top-floor conference room that had been prepared
for them.

The group barely had a few minutes to exchange
greetings before Parisia, Brianne, and Iris arrived.

"I hope you are all comfortably settled into your
apartments," Parisia said pleasantly. "Because we
are most anxious to begin. I thought we should
take this morning to orient you, commencing with
a history lesson so that you might understand our
sudden need for a defense system. However, I
must first ask you each to take an oath of confidentiality. We believe it would be extremely detrimental to our cause if certain people learned any
detail of what we are doing here."

As soon as the Earthlings agreed to maintain
total secrecy, Parisia launched into the legend
about the early days of Heart and led up to the
recent rumors about the Velids once again being
on the warpath.

Iris delivered the second speech. "From our previous conversations, it is clear that Heart's technology has progressed beyond Earth's, but is not as
advanced as some other civilizations we have encountered. For instance, we are able to travel
through space, but not at faster-than-light speed;
nor are our ships equipped with weaponry of any
kind. Our scientists have learned to harness the
energy of the sun and the power of laserlight, and
have discovered how to utilize magnetic energy in
a variety of ways, such as transportation and health
care. The barrier around the commune is maintained with magnetism as well."

Julie raised her hand and waited for Iris's acknowledgment. "Could you tell us more about the health care?"

Parisia answered, "I will do better than that. I would be pleased to take the women on a tour of the sanatorium this afternoon. I'm afraid the men will not be able to accompany us, however. While we're at the sanatorium, my son, Jason, will be taking the men on a trip to the market and other places they should become familiar with."

Iris explained that the specifics about their technology and that of other cultures could be accessed through the computers in the room. Brianne would remain with them at all times to guide them through the data systems and supply any other assistance they might need.

Julie got the distinct impression that Brianne would also be staying with them in the role of watchdog.

Iris concluded her segment with a statement that everyone was relieved to hear. "We do not expect you to singlehandedly build weapons or convert our spacecraft into vehicles of war. If you formulate a viable plan based on the technology available, we will provide you with the means and staff to create it."

Julie felt Logan staring at her and, with little more than a glance in his direction, guessed at what he was thinking. Again she politely raised her hand before speaking. "As you are aware, our men are more familiar with waging war than we women are. With all due respect to your laws and traditions, it would be much more efficient if you would allow the men to address questions to you directly."

Parisia and Iris glanced at each other, then Parisia said, "Of course. That would be reasonable under the circumstances. As long as they remember to resume a submissive nature outside of this room."

For several hours, both the men and women of Earth posed questions, and Parisia and Iris took turns answering as well as they could. Regarding information they didn't know, Brianne made notes to help them research it later.

One thing was very clear. The Heart men couldn't, and the Heart women wouldn't, perform any violent or aggressive act, even in defense of their homes. If an enemy was coming, it would have to be dealt with before it had a chance to land on the planet, and in such a way that a woman would not be expected to do much more than push a button to activate an automated system.

Around midday, Parisia's son, Jason, arrived with a cold lunch for everyone. As custom dictated, he was introduced to the men but not the women.

Robin whispered in Julie's ear. "Now, *that* is a crime against nature!"

She didn't need to say more for Julie to understand. Jason was in his early twenties, and so attractive he could be called beautiful. His long black hair was tied back, showing off strong cheekbones and jade green eyes. Unfortunately, the vivid color failed to mask the blank expression in those eyes. Though he seemed to be built tall and extremely thin, he kept his head bowed and his shoulders sloped, giving himself a shorter, more rounded appearance. How could a mother do that to her own son?

Julie's gaze moved toward Parisia, but it was Brianne who caught her attention. That young woman's eyes were filled with compassion as she watched her brother unpack the lunches he had brought. Was it possible that not every Heart woman thought men should be drugged into passivity?

After lunch, the group split to go on their separate tours, with plans to return to the workroom in two hours. Though Robin, Alicia, and Lee weren't nurses, they were still highly impressed with the sanatorium.

While they walked through the facility, Parisia told them about the advancements their medical experts had made over the years. "Our doctors perfected the laserlight to repair broken bones or torn tissues centuries ago, but it wasn't until they began experimenting with magnetia—a fusion of magnetic and crystal energy—that they dicovered how to speed up the healing process. The human body may be mostly water, but it contains metallic substances as well. When the body is injured, those elements are thrown out of balance. With magnetia they can be properly readjusted."

"One of our men was brought here with a migraine headache," Julie said. "How was his pain relieved?"

Parisia smiled. "That was a combination of magnetia and medication. A headache is caused by an imbalance of the chemical makeup of the brain, which in turn disturbs the metallic properties."

Julie knew that some healers on Earth used magnets and crystals in their treatments, but it was not a widely accepted practice. Up to that moment she had been concerned only with getting home. Suddenly she realized how their strange adventure could have enormously beneficial results.

"Would it be possible for us to observe and study some of these procedures?" she asked. "If we could take this information back to Earth, it could revolutionize health care overnight."

Parisia and Iris exchanged another of their visual communications before Parisia answered. When she did, Julie had the feeling she was saying something very different from what she was thinking.

"Of course," Parisia replied. "As long as it doesn't take away from time you should be spending on our plan."

Julie was more than satisfied with that. Not only would she be doing something constructive in her leisure time, it would provide her with an excuse to avoid being alone with Logan every evening in their apartment.

Logan's muscles were beginning to feel the strain of purposely restricted movement as he and the other men imitated Jason's slow progress through the marketplace. He vowed to begin doing calisthenics every night in the privacy of the apartment just to burn off all the energy being trapped inside his body. It might even help him deal with the pent-up frustration Julie caused, he thought, though he didn't really believe anything could accomplish that feat.

Jason was quietly and boringly explaining how to select the best potatoes for mashing when Logan lost control of his patience. A quick glance at the others in his group let him know he wasn't the only one being driven over the edge. As soon as they moved out of earshot of the female vegetable merchant, he said, "We've seen more than enough, Jason. Let's go back."

It was somewhat easier to pretend to be drugged once they knew they would soon be able to act normally again. The moment they were inside the workroom, the men groaned and stretched and teased one another on their performances. Their joking was a natural outlet for the tension of the last hour in public and continued for several minutes.

Then, at the same instant, Logan and Geoffrey noted Jason's wide-eyed, bewildered stare, and realized the enormity of the mistake they had just made. They had completely forgotten that the act had to be kept up at all times.

Geoffrey loudly cleared his throat and moved his eyes to remind the others that Jason was watching them. But it was already too late. "I hope you will pardon that display, Jason," he said. "I'm afraid we still have a ways to go to be perfectly behaved Heart men like you."

Jason's brow wrinkled slightly. "I remember . . . laughing . . . with Brianne." The thoughtful frown relaxed into a complacent smile again. "Brianne and I are twins. We were permitted to socialize with each other when we were children."

"How lucky for you," Logan muttered sarcastically.

"Yes, it was," Jason replied with absolute sincerity. "No other imperial prefect has ever had a male child. I have caused difficulties."

T.J. snorted. "Somebody 'round here oughta 'cause—"

"*T.J.!*" Geoffrey said, cutting him off. The young man rolled his eyes and slumped into a chair with his arms crossed. Geoffrey made himself a mental note to have Julie or Robin speak to Lee about loosening the reins on her roommate a bit before he exploded.

"What kind of difficulties?" Logan asked, not certain why he wanted to know but sensing it could be important. Jason blinked and angled his head at him, and Logan realized his train of thought had been derailed by T.J.'s aggressive behavior. "You said that your being a male has caused difficulties."

Jason nodded. "Yes, it has."

Logan reminded himself to practice patience and spoke to Jason as if he were a little child. "What are those difficulties?"

"Employment. As the imperial prefect's son, I cannot work in a lesser household. I try to assist in the palace kitchen, but I do not seem to be of much help. I could be Brianne's personal servant, but she insists my waiting on her makes her uncomfortable."

Logan recalled Julie's similar claim, but as a

Heart-born woman, Brianne shouldn't have been bothered by her brother serving her. "You said you used to socialize with your sister. When did that stop?"

Jason frowned and squinted with the effort it took to remember. "When she became a woman. Then it was no longer proper for us to play children's games."

Geoffrey was looking at Logan curiously, and Logan gave him a brief hand signal to let him continue. "Are you given some kind of medication once a month?"

"Of course. All men must take their medication on schedule."

"Do you remember when you got your first dose?" Logan prodded.

Jason rubbed his temples, as if all this thinking was making his head hurt. "It was . . . I think it was . . . also after Brianne became a woman."

Logan turned to Geoffrey. "You know, we could probably use a young man to help around here, running the household errands we won't have time for, fixing lunches, that sort of thing."

"And *you* know we aren't supposed to fraternize with the natives," Geoffrey countered. "What's on your mind?"

Logan shrugged. "I'm not sure yet. An experiment maybe. Or a little insurance." Or a soft spot for the underdog, he added to himself. "I'll figure it out as we go along."

"All right, but have Julie put in the request so you don't ruffle feathers more than necessary."

"I would very much like to work here with you," Jason said somewhat shyly.

"We'll see what we can do, kid," Logan said with a wink. "Before we're finished, we might even find a way to solve your difficulties permanently."

At the end of the sanatorium tour, Parisia requested a few minutes alone with Julie.

"I have something to give you," Parisia said after taking Julie into an empty office. "But I do not wish for either Iris or Brianne to hear of it."

Julie agreed to keep her secret, and Parisia extracted a small wooden box out of her caftan pocket. She carefully raised the hinged lid and handed it to Julie.

Inside the little box was a quantity of what appeared to be vitamin E capsules, only smaller and more golden in color. She picked one out and rolled it between her fingers. It also had the soft, gel-like quality of vitamin E pills. She gave Parisia a questioning look and noted that the woman's usually ivory face and throat were flushed with color.

"I hope you do not think it too indelicate of me, but I don't know of a better way to handle this. Since your men are unmedicated and circumstances require that you reside in pairs as woman and servant, it has occurred to me that you may not be able to control their, uh, biological urges indefinitely. If one of the men should force his, uh, attentions on a woman, and that mating resulted in her becoming pregnant, it would be most difficult to explain.

"Rather than risk such a problem, I would appreciate it if you would divide these pills up among your women. If they take one on the first day of each menstrual cycle, they will be rendered infertile for the remainder of the month."

"Birth-control pills?" Julie asked in amazement. "Why on Earth would you— I thought your men couldn't—"

Parisia held up a hand to stop her. "They can't. These are given to our female house pets to prevent accidental conception." She smiled at the disbelieving look Julie gave her. "Don't worry. I assure you they are completely safe and effective for human females as well."

After what had happened so spontaneously between her and Logan last night, she certainly couldn't promise that none of the couples in her group would engage in sex for the next year, so she pocketed the box and assured Parisia that she would take care of it.

An irritating little voice whispered through Julie's mind: one of her excuses for avoiding Logan had just been taken away.

The remainder of the day was spent with Brianne demonstrating how to extract information from the data systems and interpret the universal and planetary maps.

At the first opportunity, Logan had Julie request Jason's assistance. Though Julie agreed to make the request, she doubted that Brianne would allow it.

Thus it was quite a surprise when she went

along with the idea after no more than momentary consideration. In fact, it was Brianne who came up with an acceptable justification for his presence. As her personal servant it would not be unusual for Jason to accompany her back and forth between the palace and the workroom, then stay with her throughout the day in case she had need of him.

Before Brianne and Jason departed, Logan managed to get Jason off to the side for a private conversation.

"Your sister seems happy about you spending time with us," Logan said.

"Yes. I am also, and I promise to serve well."

Logan saw Jason's expression change to thoughtfulness and asked, "Do you have a question?"

Jason nodded slowly. "I do not understand who I am to serve."

Logan considered his answer before he spoke it. He was treading on dangerous ground, yet he was convinced the risk was worth it. "As of this minute, I'm your employer."

Massaging his temples, the younger man said, "But you are a man. Men are servants, not employers."

"That's right," Logan assured him. "But this is an unusual situation. We're helping your sister and mother with a very big difficulty, so the usual rules can be broken."

Jason's frown vanished.

"Now, the first order I'm going to give you has to be a secret between us. You can't even tell Brianne. Do you understand?" He waited for Jason to give him another slow nod. "When are you due to take your medication again?"

Jason closed his eyes for a second, then said, "Soon, I think."

"Okay. I don't want you to take it while you're working for me."

Jason's eyes grew wide, and he whispered, "But that's against the law."

Logan patted his shoulder. "Remember what I said. In order to help Brianne and Parisia, we have to break some of the rules. The question is, can you avoid taking the medication without anyone finding out except me? Maybe pretend to take it, then throw it out?"

"I suppose," Jason said reluctantly.

But will you remember this conversation ten minutes from now? Logan wondered. He figured he'd have to remind the kid at the end of every day until he found out what date his medication was regularly administered.

Both Geoffrey and Julie had asked what he had in mind, and he had hedged. The truth was, he wasn't all that sure of the answer to that himself. He just couldn't stop thinking about Duncan and Hans and all the rest of the men who had been fermenting on the farm for decades.

Through Jason he hoped to discover whether or not the effects of the medication would wear off in time. If so, it might be possible for those men to resume normal lives and return to Earth with everyone else.

Besides that, he couldn't help but hurt for that poor kid who had never even had the chance to feel what it was like to be a man. Maybe when the time came, he'd give Jason his seat on the plane for the return trip to Earth, and he'd stay here as Brianne's houseman. Compared to the sentence awaiting him at Leavenworth, the Imperial Palace was looking pretty good.

Logan let out a resigned sigh. Don Quixote was back in the saddle again.

Chapter 17

A delay?" Commander Xytoc shouted at the quivering scientist. "I will not tolerate any delays. You will complete your work according to ssschedule, or you will be sssquashed!"

The senior scientist crept a bit closer to the exit before attempting to explain again. "It is not our fault, sir. The plans for the FTL unit call for an element that we do not have on this planet. It is impossible to complete production without it."

"Where *can* thisss element be found?"

The scientist's antennae twitched nervously. "The closest planet is in the Aries System."

"Aries!" Xytoc roared. "It would take nearly a thousand sssunrises to get there and back. No! I will not wait that much longer when we are ssso clossse to total victory. You are a ssscientist! Jussstify your position. Find a sssubsssstitute for the element. Sssynthesssize it. I do not care how you do it, but our troops *will* be taking off in shipsss capable of FTL no later than ninety sssunrises from today. Disssmisssed!"

The scientist slithered away as quickly as possible, content that he had gained an additional thirty sunrises to complete his task. He was already working on a synthetic for the missing element. It had a slightly unstable quality to it, but it should work well enough to satisfy the commander and keep himself and his team from being squashed.

He was just glad that he didn't have to be on any of those ships when they departed for Heart!

Chapter 18

Gianni noted that the line in front of Nadia's tent that night was a lot shorter than it had been the first week she went into business. When he first had realized what was going on, he'd felt obligated to have a talk with both Wilkes and Nadia, mainly to verify that the woman was a willing participant. Based on her responses and previous behavior with Higgs, he was convinced that the arrangement was acceptable to her.

Now, three weeks later, Gianni wondered what he would have done to keep the peace if Wilkes hadn't become her pimp. It kept two potential troublemakers busy, while pacifying an entire troop of restless men. Capitalizing on Nadia's sexual appetite was working so well, Gianni had taken advantage of her services himself a few times, but lately he just hadn't felt the need.

The first few days after the advance team had gone beyond the wall, griping and speculating could be heard from sunup to sundown. Hardly anyone mentioned it anymore. For the most part the men had settled into a routine of working all day, playing cards with a deck they'd made up or visiting Nadia in the evening, then sleeping until it was time to go back to work.

Most of the men, Gianni included, found that having a glass of the sparkling water with dinner was the equivalent of a cold beer. It was relaxing without scrambling their brains, and it helped to make the long, boring days a little easier to get through, knowing there was something pleasant waiting for them back in the big house.

"That's it, then," Geoffrey declared. "Everyone agrees this is the plan we're going to suggest." He received a chorus of endorsements, then addressed Julie. "Are you prepared to present it as is?"

"Absolutely," she said without hesitation. "It's not complicated. I shouldn't have any problem answering any questions about it."

"Shall I call my mother and Iris?" Brianne asked her.

Julie glanced at Geoffrey and Logan and noted their nods. "Yes. We're ready."

As Brianne made the call, Julie pondered over the progress made during the past month. Though the team was made up of a wide range of talented men and women, they had all had plenty of doubts that any of those talents would be of use in performing the task they'd been given. Fortunately, their doubts had been groundless.

Kara's and Ray Higgs's computer expertise smoothed the way through the research stage, and Ray had a bottomless reserve of science fiction stories from which to draw ideas.

Jeremy's, Trish's, and Sunny's backgrounds in

math, general science, and physics came in handy for translating Heart's technology into language the others could understand, while Geoffrey and Robin used their engineering and mechanical skills to come up with ways to apply it.

Alicia, Nathan, and Edward applied their navigational knowledge to interpreting the maps.

As expected, Logan, T.J., Greg, Kevin, and Lee concentrated on defense strategies and ideas for weapons.

Hal's and Darcy's business acumen was temporarily on hold, but they knew they would be needed as soon as the plan was approved and set into motion.

Julie, Mandy, and Charlene had little to contribute to the war effort other than acting as sounding boards for everyone else. Therefore they used the bulk of their time studying the medical data banks in hopes of returning to Earth with a wealth of valuable information.

Generally progress had also been made in personal areas, each couple gradually drifting into relationships of one kind or another.

After a rough start, T.J. eventually had accepted Lee Tang in a maternal role. Alicia, Darcy, and Sunny had settled into comfortable friendships with their roommates, while Trish's, Mandy's, and Charlene's partnerships had clearly progressed beyond that. Shy little Kara had Ray acting like an adolescent with his first attack of puppy love, much to everyone's amusement.

Robin and Geoffrey were spending so much time brainstorming together, they often finished each other's sentences. Geoffrey had not yet given in to Robin's urging that he share her bed, but Julie could tell that he didn't have much resistance left in him.

Robin had told her what his main excuse was, and though it was quite admirable, Julie had the feeling there was more to it than he was admitting. If Robin could find out what his real excuse was, Julie was certain there could be a happily ever after in their future.

Only she and Logan had failed to find a workable solution to the dilemma of living together. She let her gaze land on him for a moment, but as soon as he noticed, she looked away, just as he did when she caught him watching her. Their tasks didn't require that they work side by side like Geoffrey and Robin, so it was not difficult to avoid each other all day.

Every evening one of them managed to have a reason to stay out of the apartment until it was late enough to go to sleep. Julie often went to the sanatorium, and they spent many evenings separately visiting others in their group. Recently some of the less tactful of her friends had been ordering her to go home.

Robin, of course, honed right in on the problem and told her to lock herself and Logan in the bedroom and stay there until they either had sex or killed each other.

They had gotten so good at avoiding contact with one another, they were able to get ready for work every morning in the small apartment without spending more than a few seconds in the same room together. Julie had been convinced that, in time, she wouldn't have to *think* about ignoring him; it was bound to become routine sooner or later.

So why, a whole month since they'd made love, did her heart still flutter when he walked by? And why did she feel so disappointed that he never made any attempt to break the stalemate, when she knew nothing positive could come out of a relationship between them?

And why, since she absolutely, positively, did not want an intimate relationship with Logan McKay, had she taken the birth-control pill on the first day of her menstrual cycle, just in case?

To further complicate her mind, with each passing day she saw more about him to admire and less to fear. He was intelligent and reasonable, a strong leader when he had to be and a gentle persuader at other times. Everyone in the group looked up to him with respect and trust. No one seemed to remember the court-martial or his chains. Julie couldn't help but wonder if she remembered only because she kept reminding herself.

Once she allowed herself to consider him in a less negative light, other things became apparent, such as the possibility that he *was* attracted to her but respected her decision that they keep their distance. Though she had tried not to think about it, she had to acknowledge that on the two occasions they had been intimate, his primary concern had been satisfying her. That was not the way a self-centered, heartless man would behave.

The most confusing thing of all was that she had begun to suspect that his indifference and rudeness were an act, and that the sensitivity she had gotten brief glimpses of was more natural.

Which was the real Logan McKay? The hard-as-nails criminal or the considerate, responsible man? And did it really matter so much anymore?

She forced herself to think of someone else— Brianne and Jason. It had taken most of the month, but Brianne had finally stopped being flustered when one of the men forgot the rules and addressed her directly or accidentally made physical contact.

Jason had literally become Logan's shadow. He was always ready to perform any service requested of him, but he would look to Logan before going ahead. The most interesting thing about Jason was that lately he seemed to be standing a little taller than he had at first. Julie thought perhaps he was watching Logan so closely that he was beginning to mimic him.

Parisia's and Iris's arrival ended Julie's ponderings. The time had come for the Earthlings to prove their worth.

"The plan itself is fairly simple," Julie began as soon as everyone was situated. "And from what we've researched, all the technology required to implement it exists already. Since Heart has no ground forces willing to combat an enemy face to face, and we assume that it would be difficult to find enough volunteers to pilot a large force of armed aircraft, there is only one solution.

"Using the same principles that went into constructing the invisible wall around the farm, a shield could be created to envelop the entire planet. Instead of simply being a barrier, however, the magnetic energy would be strengthened to the point that it would repel anything attempting to penetrate it. In other words, if a ship tried to break through, it would rebound and possibly self-destruct in the process. If they tried to fire a projectory, it would boomerang back at the ship that launched it. Thus an enemy invasion could destroy its own fleet without anyone from Heart having to do a thing."

"That sounds quite logical, but what about a friendly visitor?" Parisia asked.

Julie gave Geoffrey a glance. He had said that would be the first question. "Any approaching ship would be picked up on monitors in a continuously staffed space traffic control tower. Visitors would have to identify themselves and their purpose, and deactivate any weapons systems before being granted entrance. To enforce that, a squadron of ships assigned to constantly patrol the air space inside the shield would be equipped with several devices:

"One, a controller, similar to the one you use to create an opening or repair a weakness in the barrier wall, only on a larger scale. Second, a weapons-detection system to scan the visiting ship to make sure they are unarmed or at least deactivated.

"And third, a laser cannon capable of destroying a large ship if it becomes necessary. The main reason for this is, we have to assume that an enemy could develop a controller like you have and be able to create an opening in the barrier themselves, in which case it would be the patrol ships's responsibility to stop them before they reached the planet's surface."

Parisia and Iris murmured to each other for a few seconds, then Iris responded for them both. "What you have proposed is so simple, it is somewhat embarrassing that we had not thought of it ourselves, but as we have explained, defense has never been a priority on Heart. There is only one part of the plan that we can immediately foresee as a problem, and you pinpointed it in your opening statement. It could be nearly impossible to recruit pilots for the squadron of patrol ships who would not only have to be trained but be willing to perform a lethal act."

Julie nodded in understanding. "Yes, we took that into consideration, and came up with a suggestion. We have already agreed to stay and work for you for as long as a year, although the system we've proposed shouldn't take half that time to install.

"All of these men, and most of our women, are willing to take on the task of patrolling the barrier while you search for trainees to replace them. The rest of the women would supervise the space traffic control tower. We strongly recommend that you release the remaining men from the commune and allow them to serve as pilots as well. That would give you over a hundred patrol pilots in all, enough to provide uninterrupted surveillance of the entire planet."

Parisia and Iris were clearly disturbed by the idea of having more free, unmedicated Earth men to deal with. After a little more whispering, Parisia said, "We will consider it, but only if we fail to find enough volunteers ourselves."

Julie had anticipated their reaction. "Then we have another suggestion we'd like you to consider. If you fail to recruit a hundred women to be trained as pilots, perhaps you need to adjust your laws so that some of your men—"

"Stars above!" Iris exclaimed. "Don't even say it aloud. We have pushed Parliament to the very limits of their tolerance with this defense plan. They would never agree to something that would erode the very foundation of our society."

Julie had anticipated that as well. "Then we strongly recommend you begin the search among your women as soon as possible. Our agreement was for no longer than a year. When that time is up, we expect you to hold to your part of the bargain and send us back to Earth, whether your defense system is firmly in place or not."

For some time Parisia and Iris asked more specific questions which, in several cases, had to be answered by others in the group. It was eventually agreed that the Earth women should be on hand when Parisia presented the plan to Parliament the next afternoon, in the event she might have difficulty with a question.

Between the concern that the plan would not be approved and the anxiety attached to the women's having to appear before Parliament, the next twenty-four hours dragged by under a cloud of nervous tension. When it was time for them to go, the men decided to wait together in Logan's apartment.

The men's companionship was strained as the first hour melted into a second and a third. By the time they'd finished dinner, they were behaving like trapped animals.

"I gotta get outta here!" T.J. declared and headed for the door. "I'm goin' for a walk."

"Hold it," Logan said, moving quickly to block his path. "You can't go storming out of here to burn off energy. Somebody could see you acting very *un*servantlike, and this is definitely not the time to rouse suspicions. Do some push-ups instead. Besides, Lee would be very disappointed if you weren't around to hear their news when she gets back."

"Screw her," T.J. said, not really meaning it. In a huff he marched across the room and out onto the balcony, but his outburst had served to release some of the tension in the apartment.

The moon and stars were shining in a black sky when the women finally returned. The men held their collective breath as the women filed solemnly into the apartment and closed the door behind them.

"The plan was approved with an enormous budget," Julie announced quietly, and pandemonium erupted the next instant. Squeals, laughter, and congratulations were accompanied by hugs and kisses all around. In the midst of the celebrating crowd, Julie found herself facing Logan, the only one she hadn't hugged. They stood there, staring at each other for several seconds before Logan made a move to walk away.

On impulse Julie reached out and caught his arm to stop him. "This is ridiculous," she said and held up her arms to give him a hug too. He responded so slowly that she wondered if time had been somehow slowed down. But then his arms circled her waist and hers went around his neck, and their bodies eased together.

Julie's eyes drifted shut as they each tightened their hold on the other. "Dear Lord, this feels good," she whispered with complete honesty, not caring about the repercussion of such an admission. She felt him exhale heavily against her ear and held him even closer. She had no idea how long they were like that before she realized that the room had become silent.

"It sure is getting late," Robin said in a louder than normal voice. "We'd better get to bed so we'll be ready to start on phase two tomorrow."

From the expressions on all their faces, Julie could see that no one was thinking about sleep, but they understood that it was time to leave Logan and Julie alone. As she was walking to the door, Robin pointed at the bedroom and hand-gestured as if she were locking a door. Julie wrinkled her nose at her and shooed her out of the apartment.

There is a large gap between knowing something is going to happen and taking the first step toward it, but Julie managed to take that step. Placing her hand in Logan's, she led him into the bedroom, closed the door, and locked it.

"What's that for?" he asked, his eyes filled with apprehension.

"I'm locking you in with me."

Arching one eyebrow, he spoke sarcastically. "You may not have noticed, but the latch is on this side. I could walk out whenever I want."

"It's symbolic," she said, then watched his other eyebrow rise to match the first. "Robin ordered me to lock us in here until we either had sex or killed each other." She let that explanation sink in before adding, "I'd rather stay alive."

Instead of accepting her subtle invitation to sweep her onto the bed for a few hours of unbridled passion, Logan backed away and crossed his arms defensively. "And what if I'd rather not?"

Her heart stopped and started again. Had she misread him again?

"Death might be preferable to what you've put me through the last few weeks," he told her bluntly.

Now she was really confused. Did he want her or not?

"*If* we get on that bed together again, it's not going to be just for you, and it's not going to be for only one night."

She swallowed hard. "I know."

"No regrets in the morning?"

She kept her eyes on his and shook her head. "None. I promise."

"What about pregnancy?"

She gave him a half smile. "I took one of Parisia's birth-control pills."

He bit his cheek to keep from smiling back. "I thought you didn't appove of casual sex."

That erased her smile. "I have always believed that I should have a serious relationship with a man before having sex with him. I finally realized the problem with us is that we can't break through the sexual tension long enough to develop a relationship of any kind. Maybe if we get the sex out of the way, we can become friends."

"Are you saying, you think once we have sex a few times, it won't be such a big deal and we can settle down to being buddies?"

She shrugged. "Maybe."

Logan couldn't help but grin over such a foolish idea. He had other questions nagging at him, but he didn't want to destroy what progress he'd made by saying them out loud.

What about my past?

What about the future?

How many nights will you give me before we go our separate ways?

Instead he said, "No matter how much I've wanted this, I swore I wasn't going to try to seduce you after that one night. I promised myself not to make another move unless you asked me to. Actually, I think my exact oath was, you'd have to beg me to touch you again."

Julie wasn't terribly surprised that he felt that way after how she had behaved the morning after he'd made such beautiful love to her. Though she believed she'd had good reasons for insisting on an

arm's-length relationship, she now knew what he
must have known all along—it had been a complete waste of time. The physical attraction between them was much too strong to ignore. Once
she admitted that to herself, the rest, even submit-
ting to his terms, was going to be easy.

He was still waiting for her to make the next
move, but it looked like his patience was wearing
thin. Smashing down her obstructive moral code,
she stepped toward him, then knelt at his feet. "I
was wrong. If you really want me to beg—"

She never got to finish her sentence, for he was
suddenly on his knees with her, claiming her
mouth as he would soon claim her body. Julie gave
herself three seconds to regret the past month of
futile abstinence, then let go of any thought that
might interfere with how Logan made her feel.

Now that she had stopped denying the attraction
between them, she was free to acknowledge that
no other man's kiss had ever transported her beyond awareness. But Logan's mouth, the taste of
him, the way his tongue made love to hers, this
was all the reality she needed at the moment.

Until his hands began their magic. With a touch
as light as a summer breeze, he awakened every
nerve in her body. She felt his fingers gliding over
her face, her back, her hips, as if she were a fragile
piece of crystal that he was afraid to handle yet
couldn't resist.

Only with the greatest effort did she refrain from
giving in to the temptation to lose herself one more
time in the pleasure he was so willing to give. The
first two times they had come together had been

entirely for her. This time she wanted to be the giving one.

Gently parting from him, she rose to her feet, then urged him up as well. Immediately he dipped his head to recapture her mouth, but she leaned away. "No," she whispered. "Your kisses make me selfish. I don't want to forget that I locked you in here so that *I* could make love to *you* for a change."

He brushed his thumb over her lips and smiled. "I want you to be selfish. Just watching you unravel makes me feel good."

"Not good enough," she murmured and slipped her hands beneath his shirt and up his chest. Her fingers found his nipples and toyed with them until they puckered. "I promise to be selfish again . . . next time." Raising his shirt out of the way, her fingers combed through the hair on his chest as she kissed and nibbled one aroused little peak, then the other.

Uttering a low groan, Logan pulled the shirt off completely and tossed it away. Though she wanted to do all the giving, she didn't stop him from using his hands to show how appreciative he was of her gift. Before she let him take control again, though, she loosened the waistband of his pants and eased them and his shorts down his legs.

The strength of his erection was visible proof of how she made him feel, but she wanted more. She wanted him in the same state of mindlessness he had put her in before.

Kissing her way down his abdomen, she knelt to help him out of the rest of his clothing. In that position her fingers explored the hard muscles of his calves and thighs, then moved up to learn the feel of his well-formed buttocks and the tautness of his stomach. She softly blew her warm breath along his arousal, making him twitch in response before she touched him with her hands.

Though she had felt this part of him before, she hadn't been lucid enough to fully realize his size. For a brief moment she worried that she would be too small for him, but the mere thought of what was coming caused a rush of damp heat between her legs, and she knew there would be no problem.

Wanting to bring him as close to the edge as possible, she teased him with her tongue and teeth until his fingers tangled in her hair to still her head. She knew what he wanted and gave it to him—for a few seconds. But as soon as he began moving rhythmically within her mouth, she backed away and stood up.

He swayed a little after her untimely departure and tried to bring her closer, but she stepped farther from his reach.

With a seductive smile she slowly opened the closures on her caftan. "Now, Logan, you know I'm not going to make it that easy. Not after how crazy you made me last time." She let her robe and chemise slide off her shoulders and down to her waist, baring her breasts to his gaze. It would take all her nerve to do what she was planning, but when she noted his sharp intake of breath, she knew setting aside her usual modesty would be worth it.

"I believe you said you liked watching me unravel. Maybe you'd also like to watch me do other things." Her hands cupped her breasts, lifting and kneading them as she watched his rigid control slip away. When he took a step toward her, she held up a hand to stop him. "Uh-uh. I'm not ready for you yet. You see, I'm going to save you the trouble of preparing me to make love to you."

Her hands returned to her breasts and massaged them into readiness. "I must tell you, though, I like this better when you do it." Lowering her arms, she let the caftan drop to the floor, then shimmied out of her chemise and underpants.

"No matter what I said afterward, you know I enjoyed your touching me. Especially when you did this." Her fingers grazed over her belly to the nest of curls below. Closing her eyes, she made herself follow through with what she'd started, knowing she was driving him insane with her actions as well as her words. She parted her legs so that he could see where she stroked herself and how damp she was already.

After a few seconds she stopped and opened her eyes. "It's not the same as when you touch me, Logan." She closed the distance between them, put her arms around his neck, and begged, "Please make love to me."

In one swift movement he lifted her up to his height and answered her with an eating kiss that left no doubt that he planned to take as much as she was about to give. Wrapping her legs around his hips, she felt the tip of his shaft pressed against her core and moaned her need into his mouth. Even before they made it onto the bed, he was inside her body, feeding that need and stirring a deeper, hungrier one.

As much as she wanted to make the pleasure last, it was impossible to hold off the rampaging flood of sensation that took possession of both her body and her mind. She felt and heard Logan succumb to his climax within seconds of her own, and yet he didn't seem at all relieved.

Barely giving her a moment to catch her breath, his body was again arousing hers, demanding she stay with him in that other world where nothing mattered but giving and taking pleasure. Without another thought she turned herself over to his tender, loving care.

"Good God!" Robin muttered as soon as she saw Julie in the workroom the next morning. "You're positively glowing."

Julie smiled and winked at her. "I took your advice."

"Oo-o-o," Robin sounded, wiggling her eyebrows. "Just tell me two things: did you get any sleep at all last night, and is he as hard as he looks?"

"No and yes. Now hush before he realizes we're talking about him."

Robin smirked. "He's a man! His automatic assumption would be that we were talking about him. The only question he'd have is how you rated him."

Julie glanced over at him and blushed when his gaze snared hers. "I think he knows the answer to that too."

"Well, that tears it!" Robin said. "I've given Geoffrey more time than I should have to be reasonable. I'm just going to have to rape him, that's all there is to it."

Julie laughed aloud at the impossibility of Robin forcing herself on Geoffrey. "I have another idea. It's obvious to everyone that you're mad about each other, even if he keeps denying it. The two of you have gotten very close in impersonal ways. Why not get him talking about his background, you know, family, childhood, old girlfriends? You could start it by talking about your own experiences. Somewhere along the line you might dig out the real reason he's putting you off."

"You mean, play psychiatrist instead of seductress?" She considered it for an instant, then stated, "If you and Logan solved your problems with my advice, maybe yours will work for me."

Chapter 19

Despite Robin's best efforts to follow Julie's advice, Geoffrey thwarted her at every turn. She suspected that he saw right through her attempts to steer their relationship on to more personal ground, but then subtlety never had been one of her strong traits. As the days of their second month together turned into weeks, she accepted the fact that he was going to hold out until the last minute of the postponement he had agreed to.

But the morning of that day had finally dawned. Anticipation had Robin bouncing out of bed with more energy than usual, but she was determined not to say a word to Geoffrey until they were alone in their apartment that night. There was no sense warning him in advance and giving him all day to think up another excuse to put her off.

Seeing how happy Julie was hadn't improved Robin's frustration level during her waiting time. The glow she had noticed in Julie's eyes after she and Logan finally solved their problems had actually gotten brighter. Although, when Robin said something to her about the benefits of being in love, Julie insisted it was only lust and refused to

discuss it further. Robin didn't understand what
Julie's problem was any better than she understood Geoffrey's.

Another mysterious thing she didn't understand
was what was going on between Logan and Jason.
Being a connoisseur of handsome men, Robin
couldn't help but be aware of the changes in the
young man regardless of how innocuous he was
most of the time.

When he had first shown up, he had been very
much like the old men on the farm. Now, two
months later, his eyes seemed more focused. He
was able to follow conversations even when several
people were talking at once. She even thought he
appeared more confident, though that could be because Logan kept reminding him to stand up
straight and raise his chin and look him in the eye
when they spoke to each other.

These things could have been her imagination,
but the change in his physical appearance was
definitely real. He'd put on enough pounds that it
was noticeable. Rather than the extra weight making him soft and pudgy like other Heart men
though, it seemed to be having the opposite effect
on Jason, almost as if he were working out. Over-
all, he just looked more masculine.

Robin had asked Julie about the numerous private conversations she saw Logan and Jason having, but she said that other than saying that he
liked the kid, Logan was being very secretive
about it.

Fortunately, their project was keeping everyone
too busy to fret over anything for long. With the

backing of Parliament and the extravagant budget, Parisia had been able to assign sufficient technical staff to carry out the details of the plan. A factory was turned over to them and prepared for the new work that would be accomplished there—making weapons and converting passenger craft to patrol ships.

Once the actual labor began, the team of Earthlings was able to concentrate on learning how to fly the aircraft and developing the operating systems for the space traffic control tower. Mastering the lessons needed to pilot the ships turned out to be easier than driving a car. Nevertheless, Julie, Kara, Mandy, and Charlene elected to remain closer to the ground in tower supervision assignments.

The only real obstacle they had encountered so far was Parisia's hedging about bringing the rest of the men over from the farm. She kept insisting that the search for volunteers among their women was proceeding, and that they might not need to do anything that could upset parliament when they were being so cooperative.

As Geoffrey served Robin her breakfast, she had to bite her tongue half a dozen times so as not to alert him about what day it was. Once they got to work at the factory, she actually managed to forget about it herself for several minutes at a time. She even forced herself to sit still through an unusually long dinner with Kara and Ray without revealing how anxious she was to go home.

However, when Kara yawned without trying to

hide it, Robin could have kissed her for finally giving them an excuse to leave.

"Oh, Kara, I'm sorry. We're keeping you up," she said, looking as if she had just realized the time. "Come on, Geoff. Time to toddle off, mate."

She was mentally congratulating herself on being an Academy Award—class actress as they entered their apartment. Certain he still wasn't aware of what day it was, she was vacillating between saying a few words to convince him that she hadn't changed her mind in the past two months or simply tackling him to the floor.

She was about to go for the tackle when he practically ran to the bathroom. Thinking he was ill, she went to the closed door and knocked. "Geoff? Are you all right?"

"I'm fine. Just thought I'd take a shower before bed."

Robin smiled. He usually took his shower in the morning. Maybe he knew what day it was after all and was planning to surprise her. Quickly she retrieved the gold bow and ribbon she had put away for this moment, then stripped off her clothes. After tying the bow around her neck, she checked her image in the mirror and decided against greeting him so blatantly. On second thought, she remained naked with the gold bow, but got on the bed with the sheet covering her from the waist down.

With thoughts of the night ahead filling her mind, she was ready to go back to the idea of tackling him by the time he finally emerged from the bathroom. She expected him to laugh, or be surprised, or at least join her on the bed. She did not expect him to take one brief look at her, groan, and cover his eyes as if he couldn't bear the sight of her.

"Oh, my God," she whispered as reality crashed in on her. Julie had been right about him not giving her his true reason for not wanting to consummate their relationship. She just had never considered the possibility that the truth was that he found her unappealing. She yanked off the silly bow and buried her face in the pillow so she wouldn't have to watch him walk out of the room. Before she could stop it, a sob welled up in her throat, and she burst into tears.

She felt his hand on her shoulder and cried harder. The last thing she wanted was his pity.

"Aah, Robin, please don't cry," he murmured, stroking her hair.

"I c-c-can't help it," she stuttered into the pillow. "I f-f-feel like such an idiot!" She felt his weight on the mattress beside her.

"If there's an idiot in this room, it's me, not you."

She shook her head. "Don't try to be nice. That's been the problem all along. If you had just come right out and said you didn't want me—"

"Not want you?" He turned her onto her back and made her look up at him. "I'm on fire day and night from wanting you."

She sniffled and swiped at a tear trickling down her cheek. "I don't understand."

He caught another tear with his finger and wiped it away. "No, I wouldn't expect you to. As you once said, you go after what you want. You'd never let something pass you by for fear that it might cause more pain than pleasure."

"Will you please speak American?"

He gave her a shy smile. "My experience with beautiful women has taught me that they are fickle creatures. You being the most beautiful woman I have ever seen, I was certain your interest in me was fleeting at best. Though I couldn't avoid you completely, I thought if we at least didn't go to bed together, I could stop myself from falling in love with you, thus preventing a broken heart."

"That is one of the dumbest things I have ever heard," she said with a grimace.

"Dumb and utterly futile. I fell in love with you anyway."

Robin's eyes filled with moisture once again as he took her into his arms. "Well, it's about time, you wretched man, because I've been in love with you forever."

As his lips met hers in the kiss that would mark the beginning of their life together, she regetted only that she hadn't tried bursting into tears two months ago.

Fulton massaged his temples to ease the discomfort in his head. He didn't want to think about what he had just heard, but it wouldn't go away. He liked working for Simone. She never scolded him or made him hurt inside the way Nadia had. She never threatened to stop him from seeing Chloe. He had felt good since Nadia left and Simone came to stay.

But what he had just heard could change that. Simone and four other women who had visited before were making plans to bring Nadia home. The mere thought of having to go back to serving her made Fulton's head hurt worse.

He had heard Nadia had done something bad and that the imperial prefect had punished her. Though he didn't know what Nadia had done, he did understand that she was supposed to stay away and that Simone and her friends did not agree with the punishment. They were also very upset about something called Parisia's defense plan and thought they could stop it by freeing Nadia.

Simone was now his employer, but the imperial prefect was hers. It was bad to do something against one's employer's wishes. So, Simone must be planning something bad. If she succeeded, Nadia would be back, and he knew that was bad.

He felt as though he should do something about it, but what? The law forbade him from approaching any woman other than his employer.

Certain the thoughts that were making his head hurt would soon go away by themselves, Fulton distracted himself by washing the dishes from Simone's meeting.

He realized how important this matter was when he hadn't forgotten about it by the next morning. Fulton's head felt a little better when he awoke, but upsetting dreams had kept him from getting a good night's sleep. *Nadia had come back.* Tormenting. Scolding. Frightening and petting him. There had to be a way to stop the dream from coming true.

Later that day, while he was at the marketplace, he saw Jason, the imperial prefect's son, and an idea occurred to him. Nadia had always hated it when he tried to make a decision on his own, but Simone had praised him when he had something ready for her before she asked for it. Good or bad, he had to tell somebody what he had heard, and if Jason would listen, he could possibly pass it on to his sister. And then Fulton's head would stop hurting completely.

He barely got his information out when Jason grasped his arm and started pulling him away from the marketplace.

"Can't you move a little faster?" Jason asked in the impatient tone that Nadia usually used.

Fulton pushed himself, but he was already feeling a little dizzy from trying to keep up. There was something curious about Jason's behavior, but confusion over their destination took precedence in his brain. He obediently followed Jason to a big room on the top floor of a residence. There, four men and two women were seated around a table with Brianne of Acameir. They had papers in front of them, as if they were having a meeting. *But men were not permitted to sit at the same table with women.*

Jason left Fulton by the door while he went over and whispered something to a man with dark hair. Fulton's confusion turned to shock when that man looked directly at Brianne and suggested she hear what their visitor had to say. He tensed, waiting to see what horrible punishment she would deliver to that man, but all she did was rise and walk beside him and Jason.

Jason introduced Fulton to Logan, then Brianne put him at ease again by addressing him. "You have permission to speak in front of me."

Fulton kept his head bowed as he related what information he had retained. "My employer, Simone, has met with four other women in her residence many times." He paused to glance at Jason for reassurance.

"Tell them what you told me," Jason said. "What do they talk about when they meet?"

"I do not usually listen," he said for Brianne's benefit. "But sometimes they speak loudly. About the imperial prefect and Brianne. And . . . and Nadia."

Jason gave him a prompt to continue. "You heard them talking last night . . ."

Fulton looked at him curiously. There was definitely something different about him, but he could not tell what it was. His gaze moved to the man called Logan. There was also something very unusual about him.

"*Fulton*," Jason prodded. "Last night."

"Yes. Last night they were making plans to bring Nadia back home."

Brianne gasped. "That's ludicrous. They wouldn't dare."

Logan frowned at her and said, "Is it possible for this man to lie?"

Fulton felt Brianne staring at him and tried to make himself disappear.

"No," she replied. "It must be true. Did you hear now they planned to do this?"

Fulton nodded. "One of the women, Olympia, had a box she called a controller."

After a few seconds Jason had to give him another push. "Now tell them what you heard them say they will do after they bring Nadia back."

Fulton swallowed nervously. This was the part that had made Jason grab his arm. He prepared himself for another strange reaction. "They are going to go to the Imperial Palace while Parisia, Brianne, and Iris are asleep. Then they will take the three of them away, and Nadia will be made the imperial prefect."

"They speak treason!" Brianne exclaimed. "I must warn my mother and Iris immediately."

"Call and have them come here," Logan said. "Maybe we can help." He turned back to Fulton. "Did they say when they were planning to act?"

Fulton frowned. "I—I don't know. But I think it was soon." They made him promise not to repeat any of what he had told them, or let Simone know he had revealed her plans. Then, much to his relief, they allowed him to leave before the imperial prefect and her chief adviser arrived.

"How did Parisia and Iris take the news?" Julie asked Logan as they cleaned up the dinner dishes together.

"They were shocked right out of their perfect manners. Apparently Nadia's been a pain in the ass for years, but no one ever attempted to overthrow the government before."

"So, is Parisia going to take these women into custody, or what?"

Logan drained the soapy water from the sink. "She can't. Fulton isn't permitted to testify against a woman. Besides that, Iris thought Nadia and her friends needed to be caught in the act to prove to everyone that they really are traitors."

That word hung in the air between them, but neither voiced their thoughts. Julie had successfully put Logan's criminal record out of her mind for the past month, and she was content to let it stay away awhile longer. "How does she intend to do that?" she asked. "Or should I say, what plan did *you* come up with?"

Logan gave her a modest smile. "Fulton is supposed to let Jason know if he hears anything else, but we can't depend on him. Because a few doubts keep popping up about the validity of the video of Nadia and Higgs, Iris doesn't want to simply rely on recordings made by a camera. She's decided they need human witnesses to put a stop to the gossip once and for all. Parisia is assigning a group of women to secretly watch the barrier around the clock. She told them she heard a rumor that some Earth men are planning an escape.

"The instant anyone from the farm is seen coming through, the message will be passed along a string of observers, all the way to the palace. These women will be instructed not to interfere with the escapees' progress and also to prevent anyone else in the area from getting in the way.

"Our ten men, Alicia, and Lee will be waiting for them inside the palace, where Iris is going to make sure there is a reliable witness to whatever happens."

"But how will you know when to expect them?"

"We won't, unfortunately. We'll just have to set it up and wait."

Julie narrowed her brows. "Beginning . . ."

"In two hours," he finished for her.

"Until . . ."

He met her worried gaze, and warmth seeped into his heart. "Until it's over."

"But that could be days, or weeks." She took a step closer and let her eyes tell him what she was thinking.

With a sexy smile he eased her into his embrace. "True. It's impossible to tell how long I'll have to stay at the palace."

Wrapping her arms around his neck, she murmured, "Then I'd say we'd better make the most of the next two hours."

"My thought exactly," he whispered as he picked her up in his arms and carried her to the bedroom.

Three days later, Julie could barely concentrate on her work. Excuses for visiting the palace kept disrupting her sensible thoughts. She hadn't expected to miss Logan so much in such a short time.

Being in the apartment without him was more nerve-wracking than when she and Logan had been trying to avoid each other. She missed seeing him across the kitchen table, watching him shave, sharing the shower with him, waking up in his arms. Somehow in the hours since they'd called a truce, she'd become addicted to his presence. When he was near, she felt secure, protected, cherished, and desired, all at the same time. When he wasn't, she felt . . . *alone*.

She only hoped this strange addiction could be overcome when their time together ended.

At one o'clock in the morning, Simone and her small band of daring rescuers donned their black hooded capes. They had purposely chosen a cloudy, moonless night, and didn't want to take any chances of being spotted or identified ahead of time.

Olympia carried the controller that would get them through the barrier, and they each had a canister of paralyzer spray in case they should encounter any of the savage Earth men along the way.

As Simone had assumed, the Earth men had retired by the time the women entered the commune. Since she had studied the recordings made by the sky monitor, she had little difficulty locating Nadia's tent.

Also from the recordings she knew that there was usually a man in the tent with her, so she thought it best to get Nadia to come outside to talk. "Nadia," Simone whispered into the dark tent. "Are you in there? It's Simone." When she heard no response, she poked her head inside.

Suddenly she was grabbed and held immobile by a powerful arm across her waist and a hand around her throat. All she could manage was a squeak of warning to the others, but they were too terrified to run.

Olympia was the only one who thought to use her spray. As she pointed the canister above Simone's head, however, Nadia exclaimed, "Stop! Guy, please let her go, she's a friend."

Simone felt the clamp on her throat loosen, but the monster bracing her against his huge body didn't release her as Nadia had ordered.

"First we find out why she's here," he said in a chilling voice. "Then I'll decide whether to let her go. Get your ass outside with the rest of them so I can see what's going on."

Simone could not believe her eyes as Nadia practically jumped to obey his command. Since when did anyone—let alone a man—order Nadia to do anything?

Once he'd hauled her outside as well, the big man gave another order. "Everybody give Nadia your weapons and anything else you brought with you. And let me see some faces." When they hesitated, his fingers circled Simone's throat again and tightened painfully enough to cause her to whimper. "Do as I say or I break this one's neck."

That threat got him what he wanted, and he ended his choke hold. Without letting her move away, he pulled back Simone's hood and gave her hair a hard tug to make her look around toward him. "Hmmm. I'm glad to see not all Heart's women are ugly cows like Nadia."

Simone's shock at his impertinence was surpassed by Nadia's failure to do anything but bow her head in shame.

"Now, explain," he said simply and gave Simone's hair another yank so she'd know he was speaking to her.

The slight pain didn't bother her nearly as much as the way he combed his fingers through her curls and stroked her neck when she began to speak. "We have come to bring Nadia back and put her on the throne." With the man scaring her half to death, the speech she had planned didn't come out as intelligently as she'd intended.

Simone told of how many women were suspicious of the recording Parisia had used against Nadia and how they disapproved of the new defense plan, but were afraid they would be exiled like Nadia if they spoke out against it. There were also serious concerns about the Earth women and men who had been freed among the more civilized Heart residents.

And finally, taking care that only Nadia would understand what she referred to, Simone said, "To protect your interests while you were gone, I moved into your home, took temporary custody of Chloe, and maintained Fulton's employment. He is quite a devoted and *well-trained* servant. I found his assistance with my personal toilette particularly . . . *stimulating*."

Nadia's eyebrows arched in comprehension. "Am I to understand that you approve of the way I trained him?"

"Absolutely. And I think there are other women who should be told—"

"Enough!" Guy growled. "I don't give a damn about how you train those sissies you call men. I want to hear how you figured on putting Nadia on the throne."

Simone had to fight the fear he instilled in her. "I . . . *we* thought that a direct takeover would be most effective. It would never be expected, and if we got Parisia, Brianne, and Iris out of the way entirely, we could fabricate a story about them fleeing the planet with the imperial treasury. At the same time Nadia could explain how she was unjustly accused, creating a mood of sympathy and support for her as the new prefect. We were hoping Nadia would have some ideas of her own to add once we got here."

Nadia's gaze scanned the expectant faces before speaking. "This is the best idea I can offer. Go home. Continue to talk privately to other women about your concerns until the number of our supporters grows. Then, in five years when I am released, the transition of power will occur as smoothly as the sun rises every morning."

"Five years?" Simone asked incredulously. "We were hoping you would come back with us now."

Nadia shook her head. "The risks are too great. You must be more patient."

"Hold it," Guy said, finally releasing his grip on Simone and turning her to face him. "Are we talking a real throne and palace and servants? Crown jewels? Stuff like that?"

"Of course," Simone replied, trying to smooth the wrinkles he'd made in her caftan. "The imperial prefect has enormous wealth."

"And power?" he asked.

She grimaced at his ignorance. "She rules the entire planet of Heart."

Guy rubbed his jaw thoughtfully and paced back and forth a few times. "Are the Earth people in the palace?"

"No, but they are housed in a residential complex a short distance away," Simone answered.

"What kind of resistance were you expecting between here and the palace?"

Simone frowned and shook her head. "I do not understand."

"Who might try to stop you? Police? Security?"

"We have no need for human security on Heart. Everything is monitored and recorded by computer. On a night such as this, however, it is too dark and cloudy for the sky monitors to pick up a clear picture. No one saw us coming here. It will be the same going back."

"Damn!" Guy exclaimed, slapping his thigh. "It's almost too easy. Okay. Here's what we're going to do. I got at least a dozen men who'll follow me if I tell 'em to. That should wipe out any risk. First we grab the three broads you talked about and stash 'em back here. Then we take out our own people to make sure they don't make waves neither. Sounds like we could all be sittin' pretty in about twenty-four hours!"

Nadia grasped his arm. "Guy, please listen to me. This is not wise."

Without a pause he backhanded her cheek. "Shut your mouth, bitch. I'm gonna make you a queen."

Chapter 20

Heads up," Logan said, shaking Geoffrey's shoulder. "We're about to have visitors." Between the two of them, they had their group awake and alert in a matter of seconds. Using the wrist communicator Iris had given him, he notified her next. According to plan, she took care of getting the witnesses, Parisia, Brianne, and herself into the specially constructed space off the enormous foyer, where they would be safe from danger while still able to observe the proceedings.

As Logan had instructed, dim lights remained on throughout the palace at all times so that an intruder would not be able to slip by unnoticed.

Logan counted heads to make sure every one of his people were present. "Okay. It looks like our waiting has finally paid off. About two hours ago, I got a report from observer three that five hooded figures disrupted the barrier and entered the commune. Just now those five came back out, but they brought a hell of a lot more than Nadia out with them. Apparently some of our men decided they'd had enough of farming."

"How many?" Geoffrey asked.

Before Logan could answer, his communicator beeped. "Go ahead," he said into the tiny speaker.

"Um, this is observer seven," a woman said in a clearly flustered tone. She and the others had been warned that a man might answer, but that didn't make it acceptable. "A large number of suspicious-looking people just walked by my post. Most of them were men, but I'm sure there were several women too."

"How many all together?"

"Um, they were moving too fast to count, but I would estimate fifteen to twenty."

"Good work. Out." Pressing the button to end the communication, he said, "That's about the same number the first observer guessed. Higgs, do those two locations help any?"

Higgs showed him the map he was holding. He had already marked the third and seventh posts.

Logan took a quick glance and with his finger drew a line down one street and across another to the palace. "Since they aren't expecting a reception, they probably won't bother to make any detours. The only question is which way they'll come in. They aren't carrying ladders, and we've made sure there's nothing on the grounds to help them scale the walls, so we can probably go with our original assumption."

There were twenty ground-floor entrances, all of which were securely locked except the kitchen. Brianne had told them everyone knew that door was often left unlocked for deliveries. Thus, unless Simone had managed to get hold of the palace keys, they would probably head for the kitchen entrance. To get to the tower where the imperial suites were located from the kitchen, the would-be revolutionaries had to pass through the foyer.

The furnishings had previously been arranged to provide hiding places for the Earthlings lying in wait, so that the intruders would not be aware of the trap until they were all within the foyer.

Logan received three more reports in quick succession which confirmed that Simone was indeed leading her group directly to the kitchen door.

"That's it," Logan said. "T.J. and Lee—go on to the kitchen, just like we planned. As soon as the last one's inside, you follow them at a distance and block any attempted retreat. Greg and Alicia—up the stairs to the first landing just in case someone makes it that far.

"Everybody remember what we promised. If at all possible, avoid physical violence. We're being watched and recorded, and it would help Parisia a lot if we appeared to be civilized. Make sure your laser pistols are set for extended stun. No higher, no lower. We've had plenty of practice with these new weapons, so I don't expect to see any of you getting caught in cross fire."

Geoffrey gave them their final instruction. "We still don't know for certain, but since it is possible that they are armed with paralyzer spray, put your masks on and keep them on until you are advised that the air is safe to breathe. Good luck."

They quickly shook hands with one another, donned their masks, and went to their assigned positions. Logan's communicator beeped one more time with a report from an observer just outside the kitchen door, then he turned off the sound. They had repeatedly timed the walk from the kitchen to the foyer so that they would know approximately when to expect the uninvited guests, but counting off the passing seconds only served to increase the anticipation.

Finally a short figure tiptoed into the room, followed by several taller ones. The men and women in hiding had been ordered not to reveal themselves until they heard T.J. whistle, which would mean the last rebel was inside the foyer.

Logan was beginning to wonder if the observers had been wrong about the number of people involved when T.J. gave the awaited signal.

Before Simone's group had a chance to analyze the sound, Logan's team opened fire. Streaks of silent light zapped one bewildered intruder after another, instantly stealing their consciousness. As they dropped to the floor, some of those who had been shielded attempted to use the paralyzer spray, but it was no match against the laser pistols.

The entire confrontation was finished in less than a minute.

By the time Julie awoke that morning, every household in the city was buzzing about the failed coup. As soon as she heard on the news that it had happened hours before—and yet Logan had not come home—she was seized by panic. Immediately she tried to reach Brianne, but no one at the palace was accepting calls. She then contacted the other seven women to make sure they'd heard also.

Thoughts of their men being injured sent them racing to the sanatorium.

A number of people had been confined there during the night, they were told, but none of them were the men specifically inquired after. At least they were able to confirm that the incident at the palace had not resulted in any fatalities.

Though the women had been advised not to go to the palace previously, they were too worried to care about protocol.

As it turned out, there was so much activity in and around that building, they had to work at getting attention. Eventually they were led up a long flight of stairs that ascended to Parisia's tower suite.

Julie's fear was replaced by annoyance the moment she entered the parlor. The group of men and women she'd been so worried about were enjoying a leisurely breakfast. The men rose to their feet as soon as they saw who their visitors were.

Robin's temper exploded the quickest, but the others were right behind her. "Why didn't you call to let us know you were all right?"

"Do you have any idea how upset we were?"

"We went to the sanatorium, thinking you could have been hurt!"

Parisia stood and held out her hands. "Ladies, please forgive me. Your friends are not at fault. I am. I promised them that I would require their attendance for only a short time, then they could retire. But another crisis arose as they were about to leave, and I detained them again. We did make an attempt to contact each of you, but you must have already left your apartments."

The women had to accept Parisia's gracious apology and explanation, though there was still a good deal of tension reverberating through the room.

Julie walked over to Logan with her heart pounding against her ribs. The sight of him standing there, unhurt, and looking like he missed her as much as she missed him, melted away any irritation. She knew Parisia and Iris would not approve, but she couldn't wait another second to touch him. Her need was mirrored in his eyes, but they both restrained it and limited the contact to holding each other's hand discreetly and sitting side by side on a sofa.

The others followed their lead, and Parisia and Iris pretended not to notice the forbidden behavior. On the other hand, Brianne had spent so much time with the Earthlings she was no longer shocked by all the touching that went on between the sexes.

"Ladies, please have some breakfast," Parisia said, "while we bring you up to date. Logan, perhaps it would be best if you related the events that led up to the capture of our dissidents."

Julie thought he sounded terribly tired while he stated the highlights of what had happened during the night. She squeezed his hand as if that might pass a little of her energy over to him, and he gave her a reassuring smile.

Logan brought his report to an end as quickly as he could. "Once they were all unconscious, we were able to identify them. It wasn't much of a surprise to see that the men were Wilkes and twelve of his pals. What *is* a surprise is, why so few? Why didn't more of the men break out if they had a chance?"

Geoffrey gave a possible answer. "We hope it was because Gianni was able to convince them not to cause trouble, but we're not so sure that makes sense. Parisia has given us permission to go into the commune when we leave here and check on the men who stayed behind."

"We were told at the sanatorium that a number of people had been confined there," Julie said to Parisia. "Have you decided what you're going to do about them?"

She nodded. "They are being heavily medicated at this time. In a week or so, once they are sufficiently reoriented, they will be exiled to the Earth commune for a period of no less than twenty years. Our people are working on a new means of administering future doses of the medication that will not be avoidable, as the water was."

Julie didn't like the sound of that, not as long as there were still innocent Earth men in that commune who could be affected as well. There had to be a way to protect them.

"I am not certain there is an adequate way to express our appreciation for what you did for my family," Parisia said. "Without your help I doubt that we could have prevented a disaster."

"Just make sure you include Fulton and Jason in that appreciation," Logan reminded her. "Without them you wouldn't have been warned ahead of time."

"Yes, of course," Parisia agreed. "We intend to reward them with some special privileges."

"Lucky them," Logan muttered under his breath, and Julie squeezed his hand again.

Parisia frowned but continued, "As I was saying, we are extremely grateful for everything you have done on our behalf, but I'm afraid we must ask you for even more." She paused and gave Iris a slight nod.

Though Iris's face remained passive, her nervousness showed as she cleared her throat, straightened her spine, rearranged her caftan, and clasped her hands together on her lap. After a few more seconds of hesitation she said, "Parisia mentioned another crisis that arose this morning. The news we received would have been horrendous at any time, but for it to come in the aftermath of the attempted takeover seems almost too much to bear."

It took her another moment to organize her thoughts. "We are a neutral planet, unaffiliated with any universal organization. However, the United Planetary Association sends us reports and advisories that might be of interest or import to us. Usually by the time we receive something, it is relatively old news. That was not the case this morning.

"A courier arrived an hour ago from UPA on a ship equipped with faster-than-light capability. His orders were to personally deliver a confidential letter from the president of UPA to Parisia. Allow me to preface what the letter stated by saying that sufficient proof and details were provided to remove any doubts as to the authenticity of the information gathered by UPA agents."

She paused again and shared a look of grave concern with Parisia. "This is the crux of the matter. The rumors about the Velids that we heard a few months ago have now been substantiated. They do exist, and they are intent on destroying the human race. It has also been confirmed that the humanoid population on at least four known planets was completely annihilated by the Velids. To make a catastrophic situation worse, there is evidence that they have acquired plans for an FTL transport, which means distance will no longer be an obstacle to their goals."

"How much time do we have?" Logan asked, jumping directly to the bottom line.

Parisia sighed. "As Logan has already concluded, the Velids may already be on their way to Heart. The UPA sources could not uncover any specific timetable; they were able only to warn us of impending danger."

"The good news," Geoffrey said, "is that we're almost ready for them. Weapons development and ship conversion is nearly completed. The barrier is ready for final testing, the space traffic control tower is operational, and strategies have been worked out to combat a wide range of eventualities."

Logan wasn't as confident. "There's still one big piece missing. We have yet to start training the additional pilots needed to patrol the barrier."

Parisia and Iris exchanged another one of their looks before Parisia responded. "We thought we had more time and didn't need to force the recruitment so soon."

"Have you found anyone willing to train?" asked Julie.

Parisia's cheeks flushed a little as she admitted, "No, not yet."

"Then I have a recommendation," Julie declared. "After discounting those involved in the attempted takeover, there are still eighty-four able-bodied men with wartime experience inside the commune. They could be trained in a matter of weeks, and with them you wouldn't be taking the chance that they might panic when the time came to act, the way some of your women might."

Brianne spoke up for the first time since the women had sat down. "I agree with Julie," she told her mother. "We have no other realistic choice. Parliament will endorse anything you suggest right now. But to keep the situation under control, perhaps the additional men could be housed in the flight center outside the city where they would be training."

Parisia murmured a few words to Iris, who then gave a reluctant nod and asked, "Julie, do you think those men would agree to remain isolated and stay away from the women in the city if we freed them?"

"The only men who could not be trusted to cooperate are the ones in your sanatorium right now. I believe the rest of them will agree to anything that would save their lives so that they could eventually get back home. Logan? Geoffrey? What do you think?"

"We definitely need them," Geoffrey said.

Logan added, "If anyone causes trouble after he's released, he'll be sent back to the farm. That should be threat enough to keep them in line."

As Brianne had pointed out, they had no other choice. Since time had suddenly become of great importance, Parisia had Brianne escort their twenty guests to the transfer room and into the commune immediately.

They did not have long to wait before all the men began gathering in the big house for lunch. Expecting something close to a surprise homecoming celebration, it was bewildering when their presence was barely noticed—until Julie caught sight of Gianni and several other of their men across the room, getting themselves water directly from the hand pump. "Logan, look over there, at Gianni."

"Oh, no," he groaned as soon as he spotted the man. "That's why so few men broke out with Wilkes. They've been drinking the water."

"What are we going to do now?"

"Exactly what we came to do—take them back with us."

Julie wrinkled her forehead. "But if they've been consuming the medication for any length of time, their aggressive natures have been neutralized, and their reflexes are probably shot."

Logan leaned closer and murmured, "The effect of the drug is reversible, even after years of taking it." He waited to see if she could figure out how he knew that.

Realization brightened her eyes. "This has something to do with Jason, doesn't it?"

"Right," he answered with some pride. "He was given regular doses for more than ten years, but in only two months without it—"

"He's starting to look and behave more like a normal man," Julie said, finishing his sentence. "So, that's what you've been up to with him! I should have guessed." She rose up on her tiptoes and kissed his cheek. "You're a good man, Logan McKay. Of course, Parisia would probably exile you if she found out."

"True, but so far Jason's been careful to behave the way she'd expect him to when he's around her. I'm only surprised that she hasn't noticed any change in his appearance."

Julie shrugged. "Maybe she has and doesn't disapprove as strongly as she's supposed to."

He arched an eyebrow at her. "Hmmm. Let's just deal with one problem at a time."

Much to everyone's relief, the men who had been left behind on the farm had not become total puppet people, because most of them had limited the amount of water drunk each day. They were clearheaded enough to understand that they were being freed, while sufficiently relaxed to follow any orders they were given.

With Brianne's help, the slightly dazed men were efficiently herded through the transfer room and onto shuttles that took them straight to the flight center. It was decided that someone had to stay and baby-sit the newcomers until their minds cleared enough for them to comprehend what was going on. Geoffrey, Robin, T.J., and Lee volunteered to take the first shift, while Brianne made arrangements for beds, food, and other necessary supplies to be delivered. Everyone else was free to go home and catch up on their sleep.

In spite of the many things they could have discussed on the way back to their residence, Julie and Logan made the trip in silence. She assumed that exhaustion had made him too tired to talk. For her, however, it was a matter of having too many things to say after such a long time of saying nothing of what she was really thinking. Before she spoke her mind, she wanted to have it all sorted out, and she wanted to make sure he was awake enough to hear her.

Her assumption about his state of fatigue was proven wrong the moment they were inside their apartment.

She was about to ask if he'd like something to eat when he abruptly pulled her against him and his mouth stole the words right out of hers. Any uncertainty she had had about whether he had missed her was erased in the next few seconds. His kiss was hard and greedy and told of long nights of unsatisfied need for her.

Unlike the gentle, beautiful way he usually made love to her, what he was doing to her now was closer to ravishment. He was completely out of control as his tongue stabbed at hers and his fingers tore at the closures on her caftan.

And she couldn't have loved it more.

She hadn't even known how desperate she had been to feel his hands on her breasts until they were there, molding her flesh and feeding the runaway fire his kisses had ignited. He was behaving like an uncivilized animal, and it was exactly what she needed to release her inhibitions.

Her fingers tangled in his hair to force him to hold still for a return attack on his mouth. She wanted him in a way she didn't understand and didn't care to. With no further preliminaries, she yanked open his pants and pushed them over his hips while his hands were just as hurriedly lifting her caftan and underslip and disposing of her panties.

She gasped once as his body roughly pinned hers up against the wall and made her feel the raw power of his desire. But she brought him inside and used him with a savagery that she hadn't known she was capable of.

She took everything he had to give her.

He took everything she had to give him.

And the explosive release of their pent-up emotions left them trembling in its wake.

Wordlessly Logan carried her to the bathroom, where they shared a shower that was much more arousing than cleansing. When they finally made it to the bed, they were again frantic to join their bodies in an attempt to put out the blazing fire. Their second frenzied coupling dampened the flames enough for them to fall asleep in each other's arms.

Julie awoke with the feeling that she'd left something undone. Careful not to awaken Logan, she quietly got out of bed and put on the blue satin slip she'd discarded so hastily a few hours before. She walked from room to room, hoping something would give her a clue as to what she had forgotten to complete, but it didn't help.

Not tired enough to go back to bed, she stepped out on the balcony for some fresh air. She loved the city at night. Somehow it was both visually stimulating and emotionally calming. It exuded a sense of security she had never felt back home in the United States.

From what they'd heard today, however, this was no longer a safe haven. Unless she and her people successfully performed the tasks requested of them, the entire planet could be decimated at any moment.

As terrifying as that possibility was, that wasn't what had awakened her. As she stood at the railing, gazing at the skyline without seeing it, she realized what was nagging at her.

When they had first moved in together, she and Logan had worked at physically avoiding each other. They had given that effort up as futile, but continued a different kind of avoidance—they never talked about themselves or anything remotely personal. As if by unspoken agreement, their time together back in the field hospital was never mentioned; nor did either of them ever bring up Logan's criminal record.

During his absence she had spent many long hours exploring her feelings and analyzing her reasoning. There were things she had decided they were going to talk about when he returned, whether he wanted to or not, but verbal communication had once again been shoved aside in the onslaught of passion.

She sensed a movement behind her a moment before Logan wrapped his arms around her and kissed her bare shoulder. Leaning back against his solid chest, she sighed with the contentment she always felt when he held her like this.

"I reached for you and you weren't there," he whispered into her ear.

She folded her arms over his. "Sorry. I couldn't sleep."

"Worried?"

"Yes, but that's not the reason." She took a deep breath and asked the question that had been on her mind for days. "Are you planning to go back to Earth?" She felt his heartbeat quicken as she waited for his answer.

"I'm not sure. It's not like I have a lot of choices. I go back and I end up serving a life sentence at Leavenworth. I stay here, and I could be turned into a house pet for somebody like Nadia."

"We could appeal the conviction."

Logan tensed. Had he heard her correctly? "What did you say?"

She turned around in his arms. "You heard me."

"Say it again, slowly."

"We . . . could . . . appeal—"

"You said 'we.' "

She nodded.

He still didn't want to leap to any conclusions. "For every crime I was accused of, there were at least two witnesses who swore I was guilty, and half of them were officers. You can't appeal that kind of case."

"You can when you're innocent," Julie declared.

Too stunned to do much else, he stared at her for several seconds, then murmured, "You think I'm innocent?"

She stroked his cheek. "I know that the man I've been living with and working beside could never commit the heartless, self-indulgent acts you were accused of. And there are at least another hundred people around you who would offer testimony to that fact."

"Oh, God," Logan whispered and hugged her tightly. The horror of the trumped-up court-martial came flooding back. Suddenly he couldn't hold it inside another minute. "Everything would have been just fine if I'd minded my own business, but I was never very good at that. Just about everyone in the company knew about the drug smuggling and suspected there was some spying going on too. It didn't take much for me to find out that my captain and a number of others were involved, but I needed some solid evidence before I could turn him in.

"One day I saw him taking a young Chinese boy into his tent and thought if I got close enough, I might hear something important. Instead I wound up stopping my illustrious captain from raping the kid at knife point."

Julie's sharp intake of breath caused him to pause before going on. "I didn't mean to kill him. When the boy ran out, the guy turned the knife on me. We fought; he lost. But he was still very much alive when I went for help. Somebody—I never figured out who—cut his throat before I got back."

"Could it have been the boy?" Julie asked.

He shrugged. "Maybe, or one of the man's partners who decided to take advantage of an opportunity to be rid of him. I might have been able to save myself from being brought up on a murder charge if I hadn't opened my mouth about my suspicions to the wrong major. I was locked up so tight after that, it was a week before I found out what I was being accused of. Apparently the whole network was about to be exposed and they needed a scapegoat, fast. I had conveniently offered myself up to them, and they didn't waste a second accepting."

"But I heard you pleaded guilty on all charges. Why didn't you defend yourself?"

He let out a dry laugh. "I tried. And got beaten nearly to death for it. I was informed in no uncertain terms that I could plead guilty and accept a prison sentence with a remote chance of parole someday . . . or die."

"How awful. I wish you had told me sooner."

"I didn't think you'd believe me," he said quietly.

"I suppose I wouldn't have, at first, but later, when things changed between us—"

"You never asked. I just figured you didn't want to talk about it."

Julie lowered her lashes. "You're right. I didn't But you're as guilty of not wanting to talk about certain things as I've been. If I ask you something now, will you answer me honestly?" His body went rigid again for a heartbeat or two, but then he agreed. "What was the real reason you changed your mind about us when you were in the field hospital?"

Grimacing, he said, "It's not important now."

"It is to me. I really cared for you and thought you cared for me too. Then you just shut me out."

He let out a sigh and looked away from her. "You cared for all your patients. I wanted more."

"So you pushed me away?" She gave him a little shove and stepped back to see his face better.

"It made sense at the time," he said with a shrug. "Since I didn't believe you could ever feel about me the way I felt about you, I thought I was better off without you."

Planting her fists on her hips, she shook her head in disbelief. "That is the least intelligent thing you have ever said. But I'll forgive you if you tell me what you felt for me that you didn't think I could feel for you."

"I already told you," he said, bringing her back into his arms. "That day in the barn. The drug may have been responsible for loosening my tongue, but it didn't make me lie."

Sliding her arms around his neck, she gazed up at him and smiled softly. "I think I've known that all along, but I wasn't letting myself believe it. We've both been the worst kind of fools, but I'm certain the condition is curable with a little more honesty."

She drew his head down to give him a tender kiss, then said, "I love you. I knew you were special from the first moment I saw you, but when I thought you'd lost interest, I was too hurt to ask you about it." He moved to kiss her again, but she touched her fingers to his lips. "Wait. I'm not finished. If you decide to go back to Earth, I won't let you push me away again. We'll get married, appeal your case, then have three children and live in a pretty house with a big yard in a small town."

He kissed her quickly, before she could stop him again. "If you're going to make all the decisions, we may as well stay here on Heart."

His grin assured her that he was teasing, so she said, "There's a tiny bit of room for negotiation in my demands, such as the number of children or precise location of the small town."

As their lips came together this time, it was with mutual consent, but Julie broke the kiss when he tried to deepen it. "I know you told me before, but I'd like to hear it again."

He ran his fingers through her hair as his eyes adored her. "I wouldn't want to overdo it and have you get tired of hearing it. We have a lot of years ahead of us."

"I'll let you know when I've heard it too often. Now, say it."

He chuckled at her attempt to sound bossy, then became very serious. "I love you, angel. And I promise to do my best never to let you forget it." After one more long kiss to seal their new commitment to each other, Logan said, "Now maybe I'll be able to concentrate on making sure our way home isn't destroyed before we get started on your list of demands."

She smiled and led him back into the apartment. "I think the Velids will wait another hour or so."

Closing the bedroom behind them, Logan turned the lock and agreed to put his worries off for just a little longer.

Chapter 21

Julie looked around the busy space traffic control room with a great deal of pride. She could hardly believe how quickly the last six weeks had flown by. Earth and Heart people alike sent up grateful prayers for every day that passed without any sign of an attack force.

The group of dissidents had been peacefully exiled to the commune after time-release capsules of medication were surgically implanted in their thighs. Even if they never touched the water, the drug would be periodically dumped into their systems for a full year. By that time the medics hoped to have perfected an inhalant form of the medication that could simply be blown into the air on the farm without affecting the people in the Imperial City nearby.

Gianni and the other men staying at the flight center were back to normal by their third week off the medication and had been flying practice missions ever since.

A few problems had shown up when the barrier was first formed, but the last series of tests had gone perfectly.

Though no one had thought it could be done in such a short time span, Heart's new defense system had been fully functional for two weeks now. A few Heart women had even volunteered for control tower assignments once they were assured their jobs would be nonviolent.

"Julie?" Charlene called from her monitor station. "Could you come take a look at this?"

Julie hurried over to her and squinted at the spot of static in the upper left corner of the screen. She touched several keys that should have either cleared the reception or told her what the problem was, but the computer insisted all systems were in good working order. "Kara? Mandy? Are you having any problems?"

"Yeah," Mandy said. "I've got the same snow in the opposite corner."

"Mine's at the top," Kara added.

Julie went from one station to another, checking the monitors for each sector of space, then sat back down at her own place. Flickering spots were somewhere at the edge of every monitor.

It took nearly a full minute of intent staring at the screen before she realized the static was expanding and very slowly moving toward the center of the screen. She needed only a microsecond after that to guess what that meant. "Lord help us. Those are ships! There must be thousands of them closing in on the planet from all sides."

She ordered herself to be calm. Everyone else would react however she did. Taking a deep breath, she stood and faced everyone in the room. "All right. No one panic. Remember, they can't get through the barrier, they can only weaken it if they hit it. It's our job to notify our pilots of the hit locations so they can repair the spot before it gets hit again.

"Charlene, contact the flight center and get the rest of the pilots up in the air immediately, then sound the general alarm. The rest of you know what your jobs are. You did wonderful during the training exercises. Just think of this as more practice. Good luck."

Satisfied that her voice hadn't cracked through her prep speech, she sat back down, opened the channel to the ten pilots in her sector, and reported the situation.

"They're still some distance away, and definitely not using FTL at the moment. The computer is estimating that you should have a visual of them within an hour. We've already begun transmitting our request that they identify themselves on the universal frequency, but no response yet."

"Are you okay?" Logan asked, his voice filled with concern.

"I'd be better if you were here." She felt him smiling for her in spite of the deadly threat heading right for him.

"I'll be back before you have a chance to miss me."

"I love you."

"I love you too, angel."

"Hey, guys," Robin's voice chirped in. "None of that mushy stuff. I'm nervous enough."

"You, my dear, are never nervous," Geoffrey said

in a teasing tone. "You thrive on this kind of excitement and you know it."

A chorus of laughter filled Julie's ears. "Robin's right, everybody. No more chatter. This is the real thing."

Just as the computer had called it, the first visual sightings of vessels were reported an hour later. The giant wall screen that had shown nothing but empty space was now filled with the views from each of the hundred patrol ships. The massive fleet of approaching vessels was possibly the most terrifying thing Julie had ever seen, but she suppressed her fear to keep the rest of the women in the control room calm.

"They still haven't identified themselves or attempted to contact us in any other way," Julie said over the open channel. "We have to assume we will soon be under attack. Stand by."

She felt her heart pounding as she counted off the seconds to impact.

Suddenly the wall screen displayed a series of fiery bursts as the front line of invaders crashed into the barrier. The control room simultaneously reverberated with incoming reports and outgoing repair orders.

Like everyone else, Julie correlated locations of hits with pilot positions as quickly as she could. "Logan, 42.2 lat, 26 and 26.5 long. Robin, 44.1 lat, 25.2 and 25.3 long." For nearly fifteen minutes the explosions occurred at a faster rate than the barrier could be refortified. Then as abruptly as they had begun, they ceased.

When the smoke cleared, there was only a fraction of the original number of enemy ships left intact, but it was still a lot more than Heart had protecting it.

"They're going to try firing now," Logan declared. "Get ready for round two."

Julie held her breath and punched in the code that would reverse the polarity of the magnetic field in the barrier. This was the only part Geoffrey had been truly concerned about. Without knowledge of the enemies' weapons, they couldn't be entirely certain that the polarity reversal would do the trick.

The room was completely silent as the women watched every vessel on the screen fire what looked like torpedoes directly at them. Exactly as Geoffrey had intended, the torpedoes ricocheted off the field and went soaring back to their sources with lethal accuracy.

This time when the smoke cleared, there wasn't a single whole ship left in sight.

"Withdraw!" Commander Xytoc shouted as soon as he heard the dying screams come to an end. How could a planet of weak human females destroy nearly every ship in his fleet in a matter of minutes? They weren't supposed to have any defense system! He would see someone squashed for feeding him such misinformation!

There must have been something wrong with the ships themselves, he concluded a moment later. The scientists would be the first to pay for their error.

The invasion that he had thought would fulfill

astrologer Po's prediction had turned out to be a disaster. Thus there must still be another battle in his future. He considered the ten ships he had held back from the attack fleet. They didn't amount to much, but it was enough to begin building his army again.

Only next time he intended to know more about his enemy before striking.

Celebrations were carried on in every nation of Heart for weeks, despite the fact that the citizens learned that *men* had been primarily responsible for their salvation. It had been an overwhelming victory without a single weapon being fired by anyone on Heart. The earth crossovers were now heroes and heroines, and the media dubbed them "The Guardians."

Eventually, however, the excitement dwindled and the time came to discuss the future with Parisia. A meeting was set up with her, Iris, Brianne, and the original twenty members of the defense team.

"There is no question about your having more than fulfilled your part of our bargain," Parisia said. "But we would like to make you a new offer. We need you here on Heart. Surely you can understand that. If you would agree to remain here, in the positions of guardians, we would make sure your lives were rewarding and comfortable.

"We believe if we acted quickly, we could even find mates for each of your men. From the women I have spoken to, they would find it easier to live with one of Heart's heroes and adjust to his ways than learn how to be a heroine themselves."

"What about the other Earth men on the farm?" Logan asked.

Parisia was surprised by his question. "I suppose they could be brought over as well, but they have been taking the medication for many years. They may be capable only of servitude at this point."

Julie glanced at Logan and gave him a discreet wink, then said, "Your offer is very kind and we do see your need. We'll discuss it among ourselves and present it to the other men, but I seriously doubt if there will be more than a handful of people interested in staying. Going home is all anyone's talked about since the battle."

Parisia closed her eyes for a moment and appeared to be in some discomfort. Iris touched her hand and Parisia composed herself again. "I am very sorry that so many are looking forward to returning to Earth. I truly wish you could."

"What do you mean?" Julie asked warily. "Don't you intend to hold to your part of the bargain after everything we did for you?"

Parisia's expression was deeply troubled as she slowly shook her head. "It is not a matter of intention. We do not possess the technology to send you back."

"But you said you did!"

"I lied."

Iris quickly corrected her. "No lies were told. We merely promised to allow you to return. We never said we knew how to do it. You came to that conclusion on your own."

Before any of the Earth group could shake off their bewilderment, Parisia made another promise. "I will assign a team of our scientists to devote full time to the problem, commencing tomorrow."

"You offered to free the men," Julie reminded her.

"Yes, I will. Except for those involved in the attempted takeover."

"And you will permit them to choose mates?" Geoffrey asked.

"If they choose willing women," Iris amended. "Details will have to be worked out to everyone's satisfaction."

Logan still looked skeptical. "Freedom from the farm won't mean much if we have to behave as servants."

Parisia paused a moment before responding. "Earth men will be granted the special status of Guardians, and protection of our planet will be their responsibility. They will not be medicated in any way as long as they obey our laws."

They spent the rest of the day discussing ways to integrate the Earth men into Heart society with the least amount of disruption, but the problems facing them were too enormous to solve in a single day.

That evening, after Logan and Julie were finally alone, he asked, "Disappointed?"

"I don't know. I'm disappointed that Parisia tricked us, but I guess I can't blame her. And I'm disappointed that we can't go back and clear your name, but that's not really important to me. I only thought to do that for your sake. The truth is,

Heart or Earth, it doesn't matter which world I'm in." She wrapped her arms around his waist and cuddled close. "As long as you're there too."

Logan knew exactly what she meant. After all the lonely years, he'd finally found a place where he belonged—in Julie's arms.

Dear Reader:

Thank you for joining me on my maiden voyage to Heart. I have thoroughly enjoyed the challenge of writing about a parallel universe and an upside-down version of Earth, where the sky is green, grass is blue, and women have ultimate power. As with my Innerworld series, there were too many stories to all be told in one book. The second of The Gateway Tales, *A Perfect World*, will be out in June '95.

I love to hear from readers (self-addressed stamped envelope for reply, please): P.O. Box 7171, Lake Worth, Florida, 33466.

Dream On!

Marilyn Campbell

⬥ TOPAZ

ADVENTUROUS PASSIONS

☐ **REBEL WIND by Leanne Grayson.** When there is everything to lose and nothing to gain, when trust has vanished in the face of war, when a moment of passion might be the last, only love can melt a hardened heart and bring the hope of morning. (404122—$4.99)

☐ **BY LOVE UNVEILED by Deborah Martin.** Lady Marianne trusted no one—especially not Garett, the Earl of Falkham, the man who seemed to be her most dangerous enemy. Somehow, in a world of treachery and passion each would have to learn to trust one another, as a desire that could not be disguised turned into a passionate love that all the powers of the world could not defeat.

(403622—$4.99)

☐ **JADE DAWN by Susannah Leigh.** Rachel Todd was a missionary's daughter and . . . everyone suspected that Captain Matthew Barron was a rogue and an opium smuggler in the Far East. This suspicion and his impertinence made her forget her ladylike ways. . . . But the warmth of his laughter and his shocking proposal of marriage sparked a new sensation in her . . . a desire that went against all she'd ever known. (403983—$4.99)

☐ **HOMEWARD HEARTS by Alexis Harrington.** "A riveting, heartwarming love story . . . guaranteed to make you laugh, cry, and keep turning pages. It's intense, powerful, and wonderfully bittersweet. Alexis Harrington is bound for stardom. She has an extraordinary talent with words and a rare understanding of people and their emotions."—Catherine Anderson, bestselling author of *Indigo Blue*

(404971—$4.99)

*Prices slightly higher in Canada

Buy them at your local bookstore or use this convenient coupon for ordering.

PENGUIN USA
P.O. Box 999 — Dept. #17109
Bergenfield, New Jersey 07621

Please send me the books I have checked above.
I am enclosing $_____ (please add $2.00 to cover postage and handling). Send check or money order (no cash or C.O.D.'s) or charge by Mastercard or VISA (with a $15.00 minimum). Prices and numbers are subject to change without notice.

Card #_____ Exp. Date _____
Signature_____
Name_____
Address_____
City _____ State _____ Zip Code _____

For faster service when ordering by credit card call **1-800-253-6476**

Allow a minimum of 4-6 weeks for delivery. This offer is subject to change without notice.